West Sussex County Council Library

Please return/renew this item.
Books may also be renewed in person, by
phone and online.

www.westsussex.gov.uk

First published in Great Britain in 2025 by Boldwood Books Ltd.

Copyright © Judy Leigh, 2025

Cover Design by Rachel Lawston

Cover Images: Rachel Lawston

The moral right of Judy Leigh to be identified as the author of this work has been asserted in accordance with the Copyright, Designs and Patents Act 1988.

Every effort has been made to obtain the necessary permissions with reference to copyright material, both illustrative and quoted. We apologise for any omissions in this respect and will be pleased to make the appropriate acknowledgements in any future edition.

A CIP catalogue record for this book is available from the British Library.

Paperback ISBN 978-1-83751-479-3

Large Print ISBN 978-1-83751-478-6

Hardback ISBN 978-1-83751-477-9

Ebook ISBN 978-1-83751-480-9

Kindle ISBN 978-1-83751-481-6

Audio CD ISBN 978-1-83751-472-4

MP3 CD ISBN 978-1-83751-473-1

Digital audio download ISBN 978-1-83751-474-8

This book is printed on certified sustainable paper. Boldwood Books is dedicated to putting sustainability at the heart of our business. For more information please visit https://www.boldwoodbooks.com/about-us/sustainability/

Boldwood Books Ltd, 23 Bowerdean Street, London, SW6 3TN

www.boldwoodbooks.com

To all my Cornish friends.
Dew boz geno. Lowena tha whye!

GLOSSARY

Ansom, ansum – Nice, handsome, good.

Backalong – In previous times, a while ago.

Bleddy – Local pronunciation of 'bloody' as an emphasising adjective.

Dreckly – At some point in the future; soon, but not immediately.

Emmet – A tourist. It actually means an ant.

Giss on! – Stop talking rubbish!

Kernow Bys Vyken – Cornwall Forever.

Heller – Lively, troublesome child.

Jumping – Angry.

Maid – Any girl or woman, often used as a form of address.

My bewty – My beauty, a term of affection. Bewty can also be substituted with ansom.

Myttin da – Good Morning.

Oggy – Pasty (from Cornish language *hogen*).

Proper – Satisfactory, good.

Rufazrats – Not feeling great.

Teazy, teasy – Bad-tempered.

Tuss – An obnoxious person.

...my soul is full of longing
　　For the secret of the sea,
　　And the heart of the great ocean
　　Sends a thrilling pulse through me.

— HENRY WADSWORTH LONGFELLOW

1

Morwenna examined her reflection in the bedroom mirror and thought she looked fabulous. The costume design had been her own idea although her mum, Lamorna, still deft-fingered at eighty-three, had done the sewing. It was exactly what she needed for the Sea Shanty Festival today, Saturday 29 June. Everyone in Seal Bay had been preparing for weeks. And the dress code was so simple: *wear something to do with the sea.*

She posed in front of the mirror again. Fair play. Most people would be able to guess that she was a prawn. An almost-perfect prawn. Proper job.

Well, perhaps the colour wasn't quite right. Her leggings were purple rather than the translucent pink a prawn should be. The extra-large sweatshirt hung like a dress: it was tangoed orange, the sleeves cut off, the hood up to reveal googly felt eyes on the top and drooping antennae. Lamorna had sewn some extra yellow material across the front, ruched to suggest segments. Morwenna's legs protruded, and the whole look was topped – or bottomed – off with yellow trainers.

She tucked her long silver hair inside the hood and thought

that with the strings tied she looked fine, although she was no spring prawn. She would be sixty-three in August. Age didn't matter, of course, but she tugged a few wisps out for vanity's sake.

She made a pretty mean crustacean, even if she said so herself.

The plan was to go down to the Sea Shanty Festival after breakfast and blend in. The whole family was meeting at the Proper Ansom Tearoom. Lamorna would be dressed in her pirate's moll's costume: a flouncy dress and an oversized beauty spot. Morwenna had tried to persuade her mother to go as a feisty pirate woman such as Anne Bonny or Grace O' Malley, but Lamorna had said she wanted to be carried off as booty by some strapping pirate with an arm full of tattoos.

Then she'd cracked an archaic joke that had made everyone groan:

'What's a pirate's worst nightmare? A sunken chest with no booty.'

Morwenna's daughter, Tamsin, had said, 'That's not very PC, Grandma,' and even little Elowen had covered her ears.

'Well, I thought it was funny.' Lamorna had folded her arms as if everyone else lacked a sense of humour.

Elowen wanted to be Oggy, the invisible dog she'd invented when she was younger. She was sure that a dog suit would win the under-tens competition, although dogs had nothing to do with the sea. Tamsin had spent every evening for the past week making a fluffy purple costume out of faux-fur material. Lamorna suggested that Elowen could just stay at home – after all, Oggy was invisible. Elowen had put her nose in the air, clutched Oggy Two, her purple knitted toy dog, and whinged about wanting a real dog.

Ruan, Morwenna's ex, had agreed with her. Later on, when Elowen had gone to bed, he'd asked why she couldn't have one. Perhaps she was lonely, being an only child – that was why she'd made Oggy up in the first place. Three generations of Mutton women thought that he was a pushover. But that was Ruan; always kind, practical, thoughtful. Morwenna imagined him dressed as a pirate for the festival, lean and muscled in a stripy top and cut-off shorts.

She banished the thought and went back to being a prawn. It was best not to think about what might have been.

There was just time to stuff down a bowl of cereal, then it was off to the tearoom on her bike. Today would be really busy and, although Tamsin had help in the kitchen for the summer, they'd have customers marching non-stop through the door demanding tea and cake.

Morwenna took one more look at herself in the mirror.

Honestly? She looked nothing like a prawn.

She was blindingly tangerinely orange, googly eyes on the hood, dangling antennae, purple legs ending in yellow Crocs. She looked like a luminous worm. Or an alien.

But she'd do.

She munched muesli, the dry sort that stuck to her teeth. Too many oats, not enough fruit. In a rush, she gulped her tea. It was ten minutes to nine – Tamsin and Elowen would be in costume by now and the tearoom would be open.

Morwenna's phone rang. It was Louise, the full-time librarian.

'Morning. I wasn't expecting to hear from you. How's the life-guard costume?'

'It's just a swimsuit, a pair of shorts and a badge.' Louise's voice was flat. 'It's boring. But at least it's not disgusting, like Steve's costume. I've told him I'm avoiding him all day.' She sounded unimpressed. 'He's wearing a shark suit with an open mouth and his torso sticks out like he's been eaten. It's in really bad taste – he's even put ketchup all over his chest.'

Morwenna laughed. 'I'd pay to see that.' She paused. There was something in Louise's voice that wasn't right. 'What's up?'

Louise said, 'I'm at the library.'

'Are you busy?' Morwenna asked. 'It's the Sea Shanty today. There won't be many people in to borrow books.'

'I've got plenty to be getting on with but – have you got a minute?'

Morwenna was already running late for the tearoom. 'Yes. What do you need?'

Louise shivered audibly. 'Can you pop over, just for five seconds? Please?'

'Of course, no problem,' Morwenna replied. 'I'll text Tam and I'll be with you dreckly. Are you all right?'

'I think so,' Louise said nervously into the phone. 'I'll see you soon.'

Her voice trailed off and the call ended. It wasn't like Louise to be cryptic. Morwenna placed the bowl of muesli in the sink without thinking and set off towards the door.

She rode downhill from Harbour Cottages, the sea sparkling below, a shining saucer of glittering blue. The air was already warm despite the breeze, and the sun was blindingly bright: it was a perfect day for the Sea Shanty. On festival days, people were in carnival mood. There were processions of themed floats from rainbow mermaids to sea horses, surfers and bathing belles, although there had been complaints last year after some of the fishermen's costumes went a little too far.

Morwenna would be the only prawn riding a red electric bicycle.

On the beach, crowds were assembling, a few deckchairs, towels and parasols in place. Her costume was drawing attention: one or two people she didn't know whooped and waved. Emmets, probably – the tourists who arrived each week. The Proper Ansom Tearoom depended on their custom, so Morwenna waved back cheerily.

A juggler in a bright candy-striped costume was waiting to entertain children on the sand. A static float stood on the beach, playing sea shanties through crackling loudspeakers, a huge bright banner advertising Bay Radio. Morwenna waved to a young woman she knew, Irina, who sat on the float dressed as a mermaid talking to a few straggling visitors. She was holding her phone out, probably asking about their impressions of the festival.

Morwenna turned a sharp corner, negotiating a 'Road Closed' sign to weave her way to Seal Bay town centre. No one would notice if a prawn broke the rules of the road.

She rounded another bend and stopped outside a Victorian building with a wooden door. It was already unlocked. Hurriedly she wheeled the bike inside, leaning it against a wall – the faint scent of books was already in her nostrils. Morwenna breathed deeply and rushed into the library, where Louise was standing, hands on hips. She stared at Morwenna.

'Are you supposed to be ET?'

'I'm a prawn,' Morwenna said. She looked Louise up and down, the red hair and lipstick. 'That's a *Baywatch* costume beneath the raincoat.'

'Steve said I look like a flasher.' Louise sighed. 'But at least I don't look like something that's been washed up from the *Jaws* movie. I can just hear all those emmets singing as they walk past – "da-da, da-da, da-da, da-da..."'

Morwenna recognised the dramatic theme tune. She met Louise's eyes. 'So – why am I here? What's happened?'

'Well – look.' Louise waved a hand around the library, as if it were obvious. '*Look.*'

Morwenna looked. The library was just as she and Louise had left it on Friday evening, the books tidy, the trolley put away, the reception desk immaculate. Then she noticed. 'You've turned the laptop back on.'

'I haven't,' Louise insisted. 'It was like that when I came in.'

'I expect we left it on by mistake.'

'I *know* I turned it off,' Louise almost whispered.

'So – what caused it? A glitch? A restart?' Morwenna said.

'Look at the screen.'

Morwenna approached the laptop, her Crocs squeaking on the flagstone floor. 'It's a website.' She read aloud, '"Queen Elizabeth II of the United Kingdom (1926–2022) had links to the Grand Duchy of Lithuania, and among her ancestors were representatives of the Lithuanian Gediminid dynasty. Thus, Queen Elizabeth II also had Lithuanian blood." What's this about, Louise?'

'It's an article on the late Queen's Eastern European ancestry.'

'Are you planning to write a book about Vilnius?' Morwenna joked.

'No – but don't you see?' Louise said in exasperation. *'Elizabeth...'*

'The Queen?'

'The ghost.'

'I don't get it... ah, now I do,' Morwenna said. 'You think our library ghost has been up to her tricks again?'

'What else can it mean?' Louise lowered her voice dramatically. 'Lady Elizabeth Pengellen has made her presence known by turning on the laptop and bringing up a website about another Elizabeth.' She was serious. *'She's* called Elizabeth.'

Morwenna indicated the cupboard at the far end of the library and smirked. 'She left the storeroom door open too.'

'It's not a laughing matter,' Louise insisted. 'I tell you, she's back. Seal Bay Library is her spiritual home. Something must be troubling her – she's trying to tell us.'

'That we should tidy up after ourselves on Fridays?' Morwenna asked.

'I'm going to text Pawly Yelland,' Louise said firmly.

'Good idea. He might enjoy a bit of supernatural research.'

'I'm serious.' Louise was anxious. 'And can you smell something a little bit odd?'

Morwenna gazed around, inhaling deeply. She took in the old library with its arched roof, books stacked on shelves, that warm musty odour of old tomes and crisp fresh pages. She shook her head. 'I don't think so. Maybe a faint aroma, but that's just books.'

'It's an *old* smell – a scent of the past,' Louise said. 'Ancient lace dresses and fusty shawls, stale pomander, a tinge of lavender.'

'Your sense of smell is incredible.' Morwenna glanced at the high clock on the wall. 'I'm late. I should be at the tearoom.' She noticed Louise's disappointed face and gave her a hug. 'No, really – this is exciting – we'll do our own investigating. So, let's turn the laptop off, close the storeroom door and double-check everything. I'll see you for the swim on Sunday. Then on Monday, we'll see if Lady Liz has changed everything back.' She offered her most encouraging prawn smile. 'Pawly Yelland will have even more research to do for his book.'

Louise didn't seem sure if Morwenna was being serious.

Morwenna gave her friend a friendly nudge. 'You know I don't really believe in ghosts, but let's test your theory on Monday. I have to go – I'm needed in the tearoom. If you and Steve the shark's breakfast play your cards right, there's a pot of Cornish tea and a scone waiting, jam first, in the proper way.'

2

Morwenna turned heads as she cycled along the seafront. Crowds were gathering for the festivities, singing along with shanties, guzzling ice cream. Many were dressed as pirates: there were Jack Sparrows, others with eye patches and inked-on tattoos. There was even an Obby Oss: two people in a horse costume with huge nag's teeth and a pirate's hat. But Morwenna was the only prawn. She was greeted with whoops and applause. Someone with a Liverpool accent shouted out, 'Hey up – look – road krill!' Morwenna took it all in good humour.

Not far from the tearoom, she paused at the kerb. Irina, dressed in a silver mermaid costume, was surrounded by tourists in fancy dress. She was still holding out her phone, encouraging passers-by to comment.

'So,' Irina said to a family of pirates. 'What brings you to Seal Bay?'

'Oh, we're here for the weekend, me and the wife and kiddies. We're from Devon.' The father was keen to be interviewed. 'We love it here – the beaches and the food and that; we weren't expecting a festival though. We had to buy costumes at the last minute.'

'You all look fabulous,' Irina said effusively, turning to a little girl. 'And how old are you?'

'Eight,' the child piped up, too loud. 'I'm from Newton Abbot.'

'And what brings you to Seal Bay?'

'Mum was knackered and she needed the weekend off – Dad said it would be a quick drive down to Cornwall. He got that wrong – the roads were chocker. Mum says Dad's a numpty.'

'Well, you're in for some family fun – today is festival day.' Irina's laughter tinkled. She continued to speak into her phone. 'We're here with Bay Radio to celebrate the Sea Shanty. The crowds are gathering. The party will go on well into the evening, with live bands and dancing. So, get yourselves down to the seafront.' She raised a fist and the throng cheered, bang on cue.

Morwenna caught her eye and mimed drinking from a cup. Irina nodded back enthusiastically then returned to speak to the crowd.

'Well, let's meet a few more holidaymakers. Then I'm going to the Proper Ansom Tearoom for a cup of Cornish tea. There are some fabulous costumes here in Seal Bay. I've just had an invitation from a life-sized Nemo on a bicycle.'

'Prawn,' Morwenna called back and was on her way. She didn't want to be too late. She cycled on, braking outside the fresh blue and white cafe with a huge window that looked onto the beach. She chained her bicycle to a railing outside and rushed in.

'Ta-da! I'm here.'

The tearoom was packed. Lamorna, in flouncy moll costume, was clearing a tray from an empty table. She looked exhausted. 'I shouldn't be working at my age, what with my bad hip. Can you give Tam a hand and I can take the weight off...?'

Morwenna looked around. Every table but one was occupied. 'Where's Tam now?'

'She just took Elowen upstairs for breakfast.' Lamorna settled herself at the available table. 'It's been frantic in here since the second we opened.'

'It's good business – we'll be glad of it during the winter,' Morwenna said.

'Can you get me some toast and peanut butter?' Lamorna asked. 'The prawn costume's holding up, then?'

'I've had wolf whistles all the way here.' Morwenna tugged an apron around the orange hoodie and hurried behind the counter, pouring hot water on tea leaves and toasting bread. She had just plonked it all in front of Lamorna when Tamsin rushed down from the flat with Elowen. Tamsin was dressed as a pirate, with a high ponytail, cut-off shorts, an eye patch and a vest top that finished above her navel. Elowen was cute in a fluffy purple dog costume. She bounded over and woofed hello. Morwenna smiled. 'You both look nice.'

Elowen clutched a pasty. 'I was hungry, Grandma. I'm a growing girl. Mum got me something to eat while Zach's in the kitchen getting a wriggle on.'

Tamsin said, 'Zach's doing all right – it's just a bit of an eye-opener. He's never worked so hard.'

'I bet he hasn't.' Lamorna bit into the toast. 'Three weeks ago, he was sitting on his backside in a university studying – what is it?'

'Marine and Natural History Photography,' Elowen said, taking any opportunity to be a smart six-year-old.

'Now he's here cheffing for the next ten weeks, poor lad,' Tamsin said. 'He's hit the ground running.'

'We need the help.' Lamorna slurped her tea. 'Today's been frantic.'

'Mummy says Zach's slow – his favourite word is *dreckly*.' Elowen was showing off. 'He takes too long to butter the scones and when Mummy tells him to hurry up, all he can say is, "I'm on it dreckly."'

'You can sit down dreckly with your great-grandma,' Morwenna said. 'She'll help you with reading while your mum and I serve the customers.' She was already aware that someone at a nearby table was looking impatient.

Elowen sat next to Lamorna. 'All right, Grandma.' She offered a Little Orphan Annie pout. 'If I'm good, my grandad says I can have a—'

'Not now, Elowen,' Morwenna said quietly. 'And your grandad only said we'd think about it.'

'He said I could have a dog dreckly and that means nearly now,' Elowen countered, but Morwenna was already taking an order from a family.

The next four hours were busy; Morwenna lost count of how many customers she'd served. Elowen was a live wire, bounding around, holding up doggie paws and barking at everyone who came in. Lamorna was doing her best to calm her, but she'd had enough of listening to stories.

Tamsin was serving and glancing round to check on her daughter as Elowen clambered on a chair, demanding to be taken on a walk to meet other dogs. Morwenna heard Lamorna say desperately, 'One of my old boyfriends had a dog. He was called Harry Woon – the boyfriend, not the dog. Harry was the best snog in Seal Bay.'

Elowen threw herself into a chair, suddenly interested. 'What does snog mean, Great-Grandma?'

Morwenna thought it best to leave them to it – at least Elowen had stopped going on about a dog.

At two o'clock, Tamsin sat down for a break just as more customers came in. Morwenna headed to the kitchen where a young man in a white apron was piling toast on a plate.

Morwenna offered an encouraging smile. 'Only three more hours to go, Zach.'

'I'm not sure I'll last,' he joked as he pushed auburn hair back into his cap. 'This is the worst day of the season, right?'

'Festival day.' Morwenna winked. 'Fried eggs, toast and tea, for four people.'

'Right.' He hesitated, as if stunned. 'How many?'

'Four,' Morwenna reminded him gently.

'Got it,' Zach said, propelling himself forward. 'I'll have them done dreckly.'

Morwenna picked up a tray of scones and tea that Zach had already prepared and went back to the counter. Tamsin was up again, serving another family. Morwenna heard her say, 'Two coffees, two home-made lemonades? Coming up...'

She passed Morwenna and whispered, 'You take a break, Mum. I'm all over it from here.'

'Great – this is for table six.' Morwenna handed her the cream teas with a smile, helped herself to a bottle of water and a cheese sandwich, and plonked herself next to her mother and Elowen, just as they were standing up.

'Where are you off to?' Morwenna asked.

'I need a lie-down.' Lamorna yawned.

'Great-Grandma says I must be feeling tired,' Elowen complained. 'I'll play with my toys while she makes that snorty sound through her nose.'

'I do not snort,' Lamorna protested haughtily, then she grabbed Elowen's hand as the child bounded towards the door that led to the flat.

Morwenna took a bite of her sandwich and stared through the

window; the decorated floats had started to pass by. She watched the Seal Bay WI, half a dozen women dressed as fishermen in yellow oilskins, with long rods and paper fish on the end. She recognised Susan and Barb Grundy from the pop-up shop, wearing sou'westers, still knitting. The second float was a gymnastic group: multicoloured starfish youngsters did handstands and flips to The Beatles' 'Octopus's Garden'. A third float passed, the RNLI dressed as pirates, fighting with swords. Just looking at them made Morwenna feel tired.

Tonight there would be dancing in Seal Bay, but she wouldn't join in. An early night beckoned like a warm hug. She checked her phone; there were no messages. Ruan was on the fishermen's float. She hadn't seen him for a day or two, but she'd wait until his float passed by and wave. Jane, her friend and a local police constable, was on duty today, keeping an eye on the big crowds. Louise was with Steve on the beach.

And she hadn't heard from Barnaby Stone for a week or so. She wasn't surprised. He was probably having too much fun in the States at a conference, shadowing colleagues.

The bell clanged, interrupting Morwenna's thoughts, and Irina finally rushed in. Her clingy silver dress glittered as she moved. Morwenna was about to go back to clearing tables, but Tamsin called over, 'I've got this, Mum. Coffee, Irina?'

'Thanks. And cake – just a small piece.' Irina sat opposite Morwenna and flourished her phone. 'Bay Radio owes me overtime. I've been interviewing for hours.'

'How are you doing?' Morwenna asked.

Irina pushed back her long dark hair. A huge diamond ring glinted on her third finger. 'Let's say it's a good job I'm happy in my work.' She gratefully accepted the cup of coffee and slice of cake that Tamsin brought. 'I'm glad the Shanty Fest is only once a year.' She winked at Morwenna. 'You've been busy here.'

'Rushed off our feet,' Morwenna said as Tamsin cleared two tables, stacking plates. 'So, were you recording, Irina?'

'Yes – interviews for my afternoon show. I'm going straight over as soon as I've had a coffee. Then we're back on the seafront this evening recording the celebrations. Tom and I are off for a meal tonight – we're going to The Marine Room in St Mengleth. Have you ever been?'

Morwenna nodded. She'd had a date there a couple of months ago with Barnaby. 'It's nice.' She remembered taking selfies as the sun set over the ocean through huge glass windows. 'The portions aren't big.'

'That's good. I've got the perfect white dress.' Irina patted her stomach. 'We're getting married at Christmas. Can you believe it, me with someone like Tom? It'll be the most incredible wedding. The gown he's buying me is to die for. I daren't put on an ounce.' She sipped her coffee. 'So – what are you up to nowadays?'

Morwenna grimaced. 'Library, tearoom. Same old.'

'The summer's your busiest time?'

'It is,' Morwenna said. 'We make most of our money now – the winter can be a bit lean.'

'You see all the goings on in Seal Bay from here – you know most of the locals?'

'Yes, I suppose so.' Morwenna wondered what Irina was getting at.

'And I hear you're a bit of a sleuth,' Irina said. 'We mentioned it on Bay Radio – that business with Spriggan Theatre a couple of months back.'

'I'm learning on my feet. I helped Jane out a couple of times.' Morwenna remembered the scrapes she'd got into twice solving crimes, last autumn and again in the spring. 'Why do you ask?'

Irina narrowed her eyes. 'I might need your help.'

'Oh?' Morwenna was intrigued. 'In what way?'

She knew Irina fairly well; she listened to her show on Bay Radio, a small commercial, independent station. Occasionally, she'd served her coffee, lent her books. Irina had worked on the radio since last summer and was engaged to Tom, who virtually ran the station.

'I'm doing a lot of live work – interviewing people around the bay. It's all about local interest, the big build-up for the festival, but it's surprising what else you discover.'

Morwenna leaned closer. 'Such as?'

Irina pulled one of those 'I'm not sure yet' faces. 'I want to run something past you – what with you having your finger on the Seal Bay pulse.'

'Well, I'd hardly say that.'

Irina said, 'And since you're a sleuth, there's something I need to share.'

'Go on.'

'Not here.' Irina looked around as if she expected someone to be listening. 'It's big, though. Potentially explosive.'

'Oh?'

'It affects a lot of people – and it's illegal. You'll be at the swim tomorrow morning? The SWANs, right?'

'Bright and early,' Morwenna said. 'Are you coming?'

'Oh, I love a swim. I'll see you tomorrow.' Irina finished her coffee with a gulp. 'Who knows? I might have some concrete evidence by then – names, dates. I could make investigative journalist of the year with this.'

'Really?' Morwenna was interested. 'If it's illegal, shouldn't you tell Jane?'

'Yes, I will, soon as I can. But I'm not saying anything until I'm absolutely sure. Then I'll spill the beans. And if I'm right – wow! What a story it'll be! Heads will roll. Look – I know I can trust you.

But keep it under your hat, Morwenna – as soon as I've got facts, I'll tell the police everything. This could be huge.'

Morwenna remembered her costume: the hood, the googly prawn eyes, the drooping antenna. She checked it was all still there. 'I will,' she called as Irina rushed to the door, out towards the colourful passing procession of floats, disappearing into the crowd.

3

The following morning, Morwenna stood shivering on the beach in her red and green striped swimsuit, tucking her silver mane into a cap. 'Come on, Mum – everyone else is in the water.'

She pointed to where Louise was launching herself into the waves. Susan and Barb Grundy were scuttling towards the surf in sensible black swimsuits, and Donald Stewart, who worked the afternoon shift in the library, was lagging behind in baggy swim shorts.

Morwenna tried again. 'Mum – you'll get cold standing around.'

Lamorna, shivering in a rainbow swimsuit, hugged her towel tightly, her face red from the wind. She pointed to the groups of litter pickers a few yards away. 'Look, Morwenna – everyone's clearing away rubbish from the festival.' She was using delay tactics. 'Ruan said he'd be here, with the other fishermen – I can't see him.'

'He texted me to say he'd come later,' Morwenna said. 'Mum, let's dive in.'

Lamorna stared into the distance, watching the huge group of volunteers who scurried along the beach like ants, waving bin bags, stooping to collect litter. Seagulls pecked at scraps, discarding the wrappers. Her hand moved to her waist, rubbing just below it.

'My hip's sore.'

'Swimming will ease it.'

'The water's like ink. It looks cold.'

'You'll enjoy it.'

'What if my heart stops?'

'It won't, Mum. You'll feel the benefits, I promise.'

'It all reminds me of Daniel, how he died on stage backalong,' Lamorna said sadly. 'If he'd still been alive, we could have held hands and swum in the water together.'

Morwenna was full of sympathy. 'I'll hold your hand.'

'I'd have been happy with Daniel. We'd have enjoyed the sea, just like two dolphins, singing to each other.'

'Could he swim?'

Lamorna pulled a face. 'I've no idea, maid.'

'Let's go in, Mum.'

'Where's Jane?'

'She's on duty – patrolling in the car after the festival.' Morwenna wondered fleetingly what Irina's secret discovery was, and when she'd pass the details on to Jane.

Lamorna folded her arms. Her skin was mottled, blotched blue in places. 'I might stop here.'

'Well, I'm going in,' Morwenna said, adjusting her red swimming cap, then the straps on her costume. 'Follow me if you feel up to it.'

'I might, dreckly,' Lamorna mumbled, but she was already reaching for her cardigan.

Morwenna jogged steadily towards the sea. It was always the same with her mother. Every Sunday she said she wanted to swim with the SWANs but she'd never taken the plunge. Louise was in up to her neck, shrieking about the freezing cold. Susan, Barb and Donald were splashing around; Morwenna could hear Barb talking about the young woman who'd been crowned Miss Seal Bay yesterday. Apparently, she said, rumour had it that she was of dubious moral character where Seal Bay boys were concerned.

The icy water bit at her ankles, then her knees and thighs. Morwenna caught her breath with the intense cold, but she felt the whoosh of exhilaration. A voice shouted beside her, 'Sorry I'm late.'

Morwenna turned to see Irina Bacheva making strong strokes.

Irina gasped, her mouth full of water. 'I love being cold sometimes. It's so hot in my office. I always leave the windows open, but it's still unbearable.'

Morwenna was pleased to see her. 'How was the festival last night?'

'Didn't you hear me on the radio? It was a riot.' Irina laughed. 'The party was still going strong when Tom and I left for The Marine Room.'

'What did you think of it?'

'Great. I'd definitely go again. The sunset through those huge windows was to die for.' Irina was treading water. 'Tom was a bit moody. We left without having pudding and I came back here to join in the fun.'

'Didn't Tom come?'

'No, he went home.' Irina laughed it off. 'Men, eh?' She met Morwenna's eyes. 'Are you still dating the plastic surgeon from London?'

Morwenna was amazed. 'Does everyone in Seal Bay know everything?'

'I think so. And as a journalist, I make it my business to know what goes on.'

'Oh?'

Irina grinned. 'Such as – your plastic surgeon's back in the UK. I heard he's staying with his sister.'

Morwenna shrugged: Barnaby hadn't messaged her. Perhaps their romance was stone cold, just like the sea. She kicked her legs; pins and needles pricked her flesh. She asked, 'Do you know Barnaby?'

'I do.' Irina pressed her chin, indicating the dimple. 'He did this for me.'

Morwenna didn't understand. 'What did he do?'

Irina threw back her head, droplets spraying from dark hair. 'Gave me a pretty chin. I had a face for radio before that, but I'm more presentable now. I might get some Botox next.'

'Botox? You can't be thirty.'

'Thirty-two,' Irina said with a light laugh. 'I'm thinking about those wedding photos.'

'You're fine as you are.' Morwenna swam through the surging water, keeping her head up, out of the cold. 'Let's move around a bit – I can feel my feet numbing.' She glanced to where Louise was swimming in shallower water. Susan, Barb and Donald were already standing on the sand. Donald was talking to Lamorna, who was dressed and wearing a jacket and a woollen hat. She propelled herself further out to sea. Irina was beside her.

'You're a strong swimmer,' Morwenna observed.

'I used to swim all the time, up until I met Tom. When we lived in Bulgaria, my family home was by the sea. My father insisted we settled near the coast when we moved to England. I was twelve years old.'

'So where did you live before Seal Bay?' Morwenna plunged deeper into the cold water.

'On the south coast, Sussex. Then I went to university in Plymouth to do journalism. I met Pawly there.'

'Pawly Yelland, the writer who's in our library?'

Irina closed her eyes for a moment, remembering. 'He was a visiting lecturer. We got to know each other. We were close – of course, he was a lot older than me, and still married then. That was the problem.'

Morwenna was surprised. 'Is he why you came to Seal Bay?'

'No, not at all.' Irina shook water from her face. 'I got the job at the radio station. Tom promised me I could do some investigative work here and expand my show.' She caught her breath, teeth chattering. 'Of course, I usually talk to locals, have fun. But I've found things out – I've got a theory about something that's going on in Seal Bay.'

'Shall we swim back now?' Morwenna was shivering. 'We can talk on the beach.'

'There are too many people around.' Irina was already swimming powerfully towards the shore. 'Can I meet you tonight, somewhere private?'

'I suppose so, yes.' Morwenna glanced towards the sand where hordes of people were picking up litter. 'Where?'

'The Smugglers. At eight,' Irina said. 'I'll tell Tom I'm popping out for a drink with a friend.'

'Who's the suspect? What are they up to?' Morwenna asked. 'Doesn't Tom know about it?'

'I can't mention it to anyone yet – I've got some final details to check. I want to run it past you first. And if I'm right, heads will roll.' Irina was ahead of Morwenna now. Her voice drifted back.

They hurried across the beach, skin all gooseflesh, and Morwenna accepted the towel Lamorna handed her.

'Thanks, Mum.'

'You look freezing – I'm glad I didn't come in.' Lamorna shook her head. 'That's the problem with these health kicks – they do more harm than good.' She took a step forward and groaned. 'Oh, I must see the doctor about this hip – it's getting worse.'

Irina dried herself quickly and pulled a hoodie over her swimsuit. She shook her car keys as she hugged Morwenna. 'Thanks for letting me join the SWANs. I think I'll come every week – I loved it. I have to dash though.' She put her lips close to her ear. 'Eight o'clock sharp, at The Smugglers. And say nothing. I trust you, Morwenna.' She waved once and was gone.

'It was nice to see Irina.' Louise was by Morwenna's side. 'Did you hear her radio show yesterday? She's a real personality.'

'She is,' Morwenna agreed. 'It's a shame she couldn't stay on for a hot chocolate. I'm glad the tearoom's open on Sunday mornings. Let's go and warm up.'

Susan and Barb each hooked an arm through Donald's. Susan said, 'I'll have hot chocolate. If you're buying.'

'And one of those squidgy brownies too,' Barb decided.

Donald turned to Morwenna and Louise. 'I hear the ghost of Lady Elizabeth has made a reappearance.' His eyes shone, as if with affection. 'It'll be good to meet her again.'

'It will. And I've invited Pawly Yelland,' Louise added. 'He'll come on Tuesday morning – he's writing a book about her, you know...'

'Hurry up, Morwenna.' Lamorna grabbed her arm. 'You're lagging behind.'

'Oh... sorry.' Morwenna was still thinking about Irina, and what she might have discovered.

Something big in Seal Bay. What had she said? *Heads will roll...*

* * *

At ten minutes to eight, Morwenna wandered into The Smugglers Inn wearing a grey raincoat with the collar turned up and a black beret. Apart from the fact that the Cornish weather had taken a turn for the worse and it was bucketing down, she wanted to be as anonymous as possible. She would have worn sunglasses, but it would have looked ridiculous in the downpour.

The Smugglers was busy. It was a local fishermen's haunt; the usual crowd were leaning against the bar. Damien Woon, who owned the boatyard, was there, along with Milan Buvač, who fished with Ruan. Morwenna recognised other fishermen as she bought herself half a pint of Doom Bar. One or two raised a hand in greeting and she waved back. Clearly, she was not completely incognito.

When she and Ruan had been together, she'd spent more time there with the fishermen, their wives and families. Now she saw a few of them in town, in the library or the tearoom, and they chatted amicably. But since the split, despite her friendship with her ex, her social life with the fishing community wasn't what it had been.

She gazed around for Ruan; he'd be at a table, sharing a pint, telling a yarn. She knew he'd taken Elowen to Hippity Hoppers earlier; they'd spent the afternoon on the beach. He'd messaged to ask if she wanted to come along, but she'd had lunch with Lamorna, who'd been complaining about her aching hip. They'd watched TV all afternoon, drinking tea and eating biscuits.

Morwenna took her beer to a table near the window and stared out across the dark road towards the beach. Street lights illuminated the drifting rain, making the drops dance like sparklers. A car glided past on the shining tarmac. Tyres squelched audibly. She hoped the weather would perk up tomorrow; whether it did or not, there would be streams of holidaymakers in the tearoom. Emmets always seemed eager for Cornish cream teas, whatever the time of day. If it was raining, they'd be arriving in droves, dripping water, sand and mud all over the floor.

It was eight o'clock. Morwenna slurped the creamy top of her Doom Bar and glanced towards the door, but there was no sign of Irina. A police car idled outside the inn and Morwenna recognised young PC Jane Choy at the wheel. She thought about waving, but Jane drove away into the rain and Morwenna went back to her beer, staring into the glass.

She glanced across to where two men were buying pints. Damien Woon was laughing, talking to Ruan. Her ex, Tamsin's father. She felt her heart lurch in that familiar, uncomfortable way. She reminded herself sharply that she and Ruan were good friends, nothing more. Ruan looked up from his pint of shandy and their eyes met. Morwenna noticed the smile linger on his lips and she took out her phone to check for calls.

There was a message from Lamorna, complaining that it was too quiet in the house now she'd gone. Tamsin had texted with a photo of Elowen and Ruan on the beach that afternoon. Elowen was on her grandfather's shoulders, clutching her knitted dog, Oggy Two. Ruan was in swim shorts, knee-deep in the sea. Morwenna wished she'd been there.

There was no message from Barnaby. They'd dated twice before he headed off to the US on business and she wondered if Irina was right, if he was in Seal Bay, at Pam's house. Morwenna felt a twinge of disappointment.

It was eight fifteen now and there was still no sign of Irina. Morwenna didn't have her phone number – she should have asked for it. She hoped she'd be here soon. Perhaps the rain had put her off. But Irina had a car. Morwenna would have to walk up the steep hill back to Harbour Cottages. She'd be drenched to the skin by the time she got home. She was already planning a steaming shower, a mug of hot chocolate and an early night.

Monday morning always came round too soon.

Morwenna sipped the Doom Bar, checked her phone, staring

out of the window as time dragged by. By the time it was nine o'clock Irina still hadn't arrived. Morwenna finished the dregs of her beer, feeling less like a detective in an espionage movie and more like a tired woman who'd have to walk half a mile uphill in a downpour.

She stood up, tugged her collar vertical, tucked her hair into the beret and made her way out into the cold, teeming rain.

4

Head down, Morwenna struggled into the heavy rain that soaked into the back and shoulders of her raincoat. Her beret was drenched. She slogged on uphill, past the neat houses behind privet hedges, cars parked in their drives, lights on at the windows. People were snug and dry inside. Irina must have stayed at home because of the weather.

As she forged onwards, a vehicle drew level, the engine idling with a low purr. Morwenna wondered if Irina had finally turned up or if it was Jane Choy in her patrol car; it wouldn't be the first time that the twenty-something constable had given Morwenna a lift home, making jokes about community service and senior citizens needing a ride. She blinked rainwater, and, from the corner of her eye, Morwenna was aware of a white van and a window rolling down.

Ruan called cheerily, 'Jump in – I'm going in your direction.'

Morwenna smiled at the joke – he lived across the road, at number nine. She protested weakly, 'I'm soaked to the skin, Ruan.'

The passenger door had already been pushed open. 'Then you'd better get in – we don't want you catching a cold.'

Morwenna clambered in gratefully, leaving the rain outside. She was conscious that she must look a state.

'It's properly mizzling,' Ruan said, referring to the weather.

'It is,' Morwenna agreed.

'Not nice to walk home in.'

'It isn't,' Morwenna said. She and Ruan were making small talk again. So much had passed between them over the years, and now they were discussing the weather.

'I saw you in The Smugglers. I'd have come over but you looked like you were waiting for someone.' Ruan's eyes were on the road. 'Damien told me the plastic surgeon from London was back – Pam mentioned it when she was down at the boatyard. She's spending a lot of time on the *Pammy* now summer's here.'

So that was it, Ruan thought she'd been stood up by Barnaby Stone. She'd put a stop to that immediately.

'I was waiting for Irina Bacheva.'

'The Bay Radio DJ?' Ruan asked. 'Are you going to be on the radio?'

'Why ever would I go on the radio?'

'Something to do with the library? Sleuthing, perhaps? You've made a name for yourself, solving mysteries.'

Morwenna shook her head. 'Irina had something she wanted to tell me. A big story.'

'And she didn't turn up?'

'You're quick to catch on, Ruan.'

'I'm really on the ball today. It's been good. We were playing football on the beach this afternoon, me and Elowen. You should have been there,' Ruan said.

'And you've been out for a drink tonight.' Morwenna smiled affectionately. 'You get about.'

'I had a shandy with Damien. He wanted to tell me – he and Beverley are engaged.'

'The artist from Half Moon Cottage?'

'She sold the place a couple of months ago to a family from Surrey. It's a holiday home now.'

'Is it empty, then?'

'No, their daughter's just finished exams and they're spending the summer here.'

'Is there anything you fishermen don't gossip about?' Morwenna said. The van turned the corner; they were almost home. Ruan slowed down outside Morwenna's house, number four, the engine idling.

In the distance, the harbour lights twinkled in velvet darkness. Morwenna met his eyes. 'I suppose you could do with a nightcap.' She tried again. 'Hot chocolate? Brandy?'

'I wouldn't say no,' Ruan said. 'We need a catch-up.'

'Do we?'

'Tam's working too hard and Elowen's being a little heller in school again. She winds her teacher up. I feel sorry for Imelda Parker, having to teach Elowen. She asked her how to spell SOS the other day. And during a lesson on Shakespeare, she wanted to know if 1564–1616 was his mobile number.'

'Mutton women have enquiring minds,' Morwenna said with a smile.

'Tam thinks she likes to make the other children laugh.'

'I'll have a word with her,' Morwenna said firmly. 'She'll be in a different class in September – she can make a fresh start.'

'She's just a kid,' Ruan said and Morwenna shot him a look that told him he was a soft touch. She opened the car door. 'So – are you coming in?'

'Just a quick one,' Ruan said.

Morwenna took a deep breath and replied, 'Right.'

It was always difficult with Ruan, trying not to remember what had been, what they had lost. But what was done was done.

They'd have a quick family chat over a cuppa and a biscuit and she'd send him on his way. They both needed to be up early the following day.

* * *

The next morning, bright sunshine flooded through the bedroom window and melted on the duvet like lemon curd. The cat, Brenda, stretched on her back as Morwenna opened her eyes, reached down a hand and felt the exposed tummy, a moment of mutual trust, then Brenda was in her face, all fur and itchy whiskers, pestering her for breakfast.

Morwenna pulled on rainbow leopard print leggings – it was the first of July, after all, the height of the holiday season, so she needed to dazzle – and a black T-shirt with butterflies on it and a logo that said 'Peace, Love, Summer'. No one ever grumbled in the library or the tearoom that she wore bright clothes – in fact the opposite was true. If she were ever to turn up in a beige frock, the Seal Bay community would wonder what was wrong.

She fed Brenda from a china dish with her name on; the cat wolfed it down and demanded more. Morwenna relented with a handful of dried biscuits and Brenda purred like a motor.

She checked the time. It was just after eight. She didn't need to be at the library until nine. Enjoying the sun's warmth on her skin, she steered her bicycle outside, locked her door and clambered onto the saddle. She was off downhill, pedalling energetically. It warmed her heart to see the shining harbour down below, the trawlers static against the skyline. She imagined Ruan, already out at sea in yellow oilskins, hauling in the nets, his muscles working hard.

Instead of heading straight for the library, she turned into a small side street, pausing outside a neon sign that said Bay Radio, with the logo of a palm tree with green leaves that resembled the top of a pineapple. She locked her bicycle to a railing, pressed the buzzer and a distant female voice came back to her.

'Hello – do you have an appointment?'

Morwenna wasn't going to say no. Instead, she said, 'Eight o'clock with Irina Bacheva.' It was true – just the wrong time and day.

'Who is it, please?' the voice asked curtly.

'Morwenna Mutton.'

There was a pause, a click. The door opened and Morwenna stepped inside. A woman with a clipboard was waiting, her expression inscrutable. 'Mrs Mutton?'

'Ms Mutton... or just Morwenna,' Morwenna said.

'I'm afraid there's nothing in the book about an appointment with Irina.'

'Oh, just ask her – she'll tell you,' Morwenna said breezily.

'She's not here at the moment.'

'What time's she due in?'

The young woman fluttered her false eyelashes. 'I have no idea. Her show's in the afternoon – I suppose she might come in around one. But she'd be too busy to see you then.'

'Can you ring her?' Morwenna asked, as if it was a no-brainer.

'That's not possible.' The young woman replied tonelessly. Morwenna glanced at her silver lanyard, which said her name was Trudi.

'Well, I need to talk to her, Trudi. How can we resolve this?'

'I'm afraid I can't help.' Trudi smoothed the yellow hair that led to her ponytail. It was already straight as silk.

'Who's on air right now?' Morwenna wasn't going to be put off. She'd get hold of Irina one way or another.

'Mike.' Trudi shrugged as if that were all Morwenna needed to know.

Morwenna thought quickly. Mike Sheridan was one of the DJs who had a morning show. He always sounded friendly and pleasant, although Morwenna had never met him.

'Mike Sheridan. Oh, that's great – I'll talk to him. He'll know where Irina is.'

'Mike can't talk to you – he's doing his show.'

'I'll wait.'

Trudi frowned, dark eyebrows coming together in a knot, unsure what to do. She lifted the clipboard as if it were a magic wand. 'All right – I'll check. Follow me, please.'

Trudi slipped a card into a lock and another door sprang open. She indicated a seat in a row of five, green plastic, all vacant.

'Wait here, please.' She waved her clipboard, hurrying on high heels into another glass-fronted room where several people sat at laptops. Mike Sheridan's voice came from speakers on the wall.

'So, the big question today is, are festivals a thing of the past or do we need to hang on to tradition? Yesterday, tons of litter was left on the beach, causing an environmental hazard. Bottles were thrown in the sea. Yet Seal Bay needs tourism as its life blood, to keep its heart pumping. What do you think? Give us a call, the Mike Sheridan Show at Bay Radio on...'

Morwenna picked up a newspaper. It was a local weekly, dated 24 June. She put it down again and selected a magazine. There was an article at the back about preparing your skin for summer. Morwenna glanced at a model, her face dewy as an apricot. Beneath the picture was a bottle of golden serum called Botanium Liquid Lift. Morwenna scrutinised the small print. It retailed at £89 a bottle. She took a quick breath and put the magazine down.

Mike's voice was crackling in the speakers again. 'Listeners have been ringing in their dozens. It's no surprise most people want to keep the festival, but they want the format changed, and a greater police presence. In a few moments, we'll be talking to DI

Rick Tremayne of the Seal Bay Police. But before that, it's The Kinks and "Sunny Afternoon".'

Morwenna approached the glass door and pushed it. To her surprise, it opened easily. No one was aware that she was there, which she thought was a miracle, given her rainbow leggings. Several young people continued to work at laptops, their faces down, earpieces in. Morwenna glanced around, taking in the moss-green carpet, the two doors at the far end, leading to offices. Trudi was waiting outside one of the studios, clipboard aloft. Mike Sheridan could be seen inside wearing headphones.

Morwenna wandered in the other direction towards the offices; the far doors were closed but she peered through the glass. Identical spaces, desks with laptops, one in disarray, one tidy. Both offices had windows left slightly open; both had small handbasins, a mirror, posters on the wall.

Morwenna glanced over her shoulder. Trudi was talking to the DJ at his desk in the studio. Mike Sheridan was a lean man in his late thirties or early forties, with longish curly hair and tinted glasses, a tight black shirt open at the neck. Morwenna sidled over.

Trudi said, 'There's a woman outside, Mike, looking for Irina.'

Morwenna stood behind Trudi's shoulder, not making a sound. Mike said, 'I've no idea where Irina is and frankly – why would I care?'

Morwenna surged forward, past Trudi, into the small studio. 'Mike, so pleased to meet you at last. I'm Morwenna Mutton.'

'You can't go in, Mike's on air,' Trudi said. The Kinks were still singing.

Morwenna extended a hand. 'I've heard so much about you. I wonder if you can help – I'm supposed to meet Irina and I can't seem to find her.'

Mike raised both hands in front of him, pushing an imaginary Morwenna back through the door. 'I'm doing a show.'

'When did you last see her?'

Mike seemed flustered. 'I don't know. Saturday? I can't remember.' He took a breath. 'I don't keep track of that woman. She does as she likes here.'

'Can you give me her mobile number?'

'That's not allowed,' Trudi said quickly.

'Do you know her well?' Mike asked, his face betraying sudden awkwardness. He hadn't had a good word to say about Irina.

'She's a member of the Seal Bay swimming group – we were going to discuss the next swim. She's a very good swimmer...' She paused; as an afterthought she said, 'We're the Seal Bay Wild Aquatic Natation. SWANs. Irina wants to do an interview with us – tomorrow, first thing.'

'Oh, give the woman her number, Trudes,' Mike said quickly, fiddling with his earphones. 'It doesn't matter – she knows her.' He waved frantically to indicate that he needed the door closed, then his voice was suddenly silky. 'That was Ray Davies and The Kinks. Now we go to the phone line to talk to the most important man in Seal Bay, DI Rick Tremayne. Rick, good to have you on the show.'

Morwenna heard Rick's familiar gruff tone. He sounded awkward. 'Oh, I wouldn't say that I was important, Mike. But thanks for having me on your show.'

Trudi closed the door. 'I'll get you the number.' She picked up her own phone and began to scribble. Morwenna was listening to Mike's interview through the speakers on the wall.

'So, Rick, what are your views on the Sea Shanty Festival?'

'Well, Mike, it brings in tourism, and that's important. But it comes at a cost to the taxpayer. We have to draft in more manpower throughout the summer months.'

'And what is the biggest threat to our residents, Rick? Is the crime rate increased during the summer?'

'Oh, it is, Mike, and all the responsibility falls to me, with inadequate resources, I have to say. It's not just petty pilfering and a bit of drunken antisocial behaviour that causes me the most grief, oh, no.'

'What do you think is the biggest threat to Seal Bay, Rick?'

'Recreational drugs,' Rick said. 'There's an increased use of Category C drugs such as marijuana amongst young people, and it needs stamping out.'

'Indeed? And how do the police deal with this?'

Rick cleared his throat. Morwenna recognised the sign – he was winding up for a monologue. 'Well, Mike, while we cannot condone the use of any drugs, rather than prosecute, we have introduced awareness and education programmes for offenders. We bring in those who've been caught and explain to them the side-effects of drugs misuse, including criminality. Participants in the programme don't receive a criminal conviction, despite my personal view that short, sharp shocks are most effective.'

Morwenna had stopped listening. She took the piece of paper that Trudi was holding out with Irina's mobile number on it. 'Thanks, I'll ring her – you've been very helpful.'

Before Trudi could say anything else, Morwenna made for the door. It was ten to nine. She'd get to the library on time, just. As soon as she arrived, she'd give Irina a call.

Trudi was next to her, opening the electronic door, and Morwenna hurried through, almost colliding with a tall, casually dressed man in a jacket, T-shirt and jeans. Morwenna recognised him at once; he was clean-shaven, early thirties, handsome, with neatly styled dark hair.

She said, 'Tom, hello. It's Morwenna...' and thrust out a hand.

Tom Fox clearly didn't recognise her. He had that expression on his face; half snarl, half smile, as if he wasn't sure which one to use yet. She let out a peal of laughter as if he was being silly not remembering who she was.

'Morwenna Mutton – of the library, the tearoom.' He was still confused, so she said, 'I'm the Seal Bay Sleuth.'

His face relaxed with recognition. 'Oh, yes – we met, didn't we? My fiancée interviewed you after the unfortunate business with – Daniel something, the actor?'

'From The Spriggan Theatre, yes.' Morwenna was all smiles now. 'I've just come to see Irina, but she's not here. I have an appointment with her.'

Tom's handsome face suddenly changed from a smile to alarm. 'With Irina?'

'I promised her that I'd be here – at eight.' Morwenna tried again. 'We were supposed to meet.'

'Irina?' Tom said again. 'She's not turned up, then?' He shook his head. 'I thought she'd be here – that's why I came in early.'

'What do you mean?' Morwenna asked. He was making no sense. 'Don't you live in the same house?'

'She went out last night – about six – to meet a friend. I assumed they'd made a night of it, but I've messaged her several times this morning.' He glanced around to see if anyone was listening. 'She often comes into the office to work late. Sometimes, she's here into the early hours.'

Morwenna shook her head. 'So where is she now?'

Tom was staring in disbelief, his face all concern.

'I've no idea – I haven't heard from her.' He took a deep breath. 'She didn't come home.'

5

Morwenna was still wondering where Irina could be as she wheeled her bicycle along the library corridor and secured the padlock. She'd ring the mobile number as soon as she could find a few free minutes. The scent of books filled her nose, thick dust in the air, despite the fact that Louise was fastidious about keeping the library tidy and was a huge fan of the plug-ins that filled everywhere with floral scent. Morwenna approached the reception desk. Louise waved a mug in greeting.

'I've got you a cuppa. And guess what? She's been here again.'

Morwenna was still thinking about Irina. 'Who has?'

'Lady Elizabeth Pengellen.' Louise lowered her voice. 'Come and see.' She placed her mug down and grabbed Morwenna's hand. 'I noticed it as soon as I came in.' She dragged her over to the reference section where heavy volumes stood on shelves, and pointed to the middle shelf. 'Look.'

Morwenna saw. Several books were missing. On closer inspection, a dictionary and two encyclopaedias had gone. She scratched her head. 'That's funny.'

'It is.' Louise gave her one of those 'you know what this means' looks.

'Who'd steal big books? They're heavy. I mean – someone would look pretty obvious leaving the library with huge volumes stuffed up their jumpers.'

'Exactly.'

'Has someone left them out on a desk?'

'No. I checked.'

'People don't use reference books now – information's accessed online.' Morwenna said.

Louise folded her arms. 'I know.'

'So where are they?'

'They've disappeared,' Louise said emphatically. 'Into thin air – just like our ghost.' She met Morwenna's eyes. 'You know what this means?'

'No.' Morwenna knew Louise had a theory. 'But you're going to tell me, right?'

'Books spirited away? It's a sign.' Louise took her arm, leading her back to the reception desk, and thrust a cup of tea into her hands. Morwenna sipped from her favourite mug with the slogan 'Kernow Bys Vyken'. She swallowed a glug.

'Lady Elizabeth's left a message. She's telling us something big and important is about to disappear from our lives – just like the books.' Louise's eyes shone with excitement.

Morwenna wasn't sure. 'Such as?'

'We might be about to lose money – or a friend, or a beloved relative or... someone might not love us any more.' Louise gasped dramatically – a thought had come to her. 'Have you heard from Barnaby?'

Morwenna shook her silver hair. 'No – I hear he's back in the UK though.'

'You don't think the romance might be – over?' Louise asked, all concern.

'It never really got started,' Morwenna said. 'We only dated a couple of times.'

'Lady Elizabeth's definitely saying that something important has disappeared.'

'Or somebody,' Morwenna muttered. She ought to give Irina a ring.

The library door swung open with a bang and a teenage girl sauntered in. She had long hair, thickly braided at both sides, ending in a light-coloured ponytail. She was wearing a pristine white crop top and shorts. Green fingernails clutched the latest mobile phone. She slouched against the reception desk.

'Have you got any French books?'

'Do you mean phrase books or literature? We have lots of books in French and some with English translations.' Louise took charge. 'But you'll need to have a local address. Are you on holiday?'

'I live here.' The girl sniffed. 'I'm here for the whole summer, worse luck.' She inspected her phone. 'They have to be in French. The more sophisticated, the better.'

Louise glanced hopelessly at Morwenna, whose spoken French was better than hers.

Morwenna offered a smile. 'What about *Cher Connard* by Virginie Despentes? Or if you want a classic, there's *Les Liaisons Dangereuses* by Choderlos de Laclos.'

'What's that one about – the dangerous one?' the girl asked.

'Sex, lies and deceit,' Morwenna said easily and Louise shot her a nervous look.

The girl looked interested for the first time. 'Sounds cool – have you read it?'

'Yes – and there's a film of it with Glenn Close and John Malkovich.'

'Who?' The girl wrinkled her nose. 'Never mind. I'll take that one – The Dangerous – whatever it was.'

'Do you speak French?' Louise wanted to know.

'No – I'm rubbish at languages.'

'Why do you want to borrow it, then?' Louise glanced at Morwenna, her face suspicious.

'So I can pretend to read it on the beach. All the fit surfers'll think I'm French and they'll chat me up.' She gave a yawn. 'I spend most days on the beach. There's nothing to do in Seal Bay. I like it better in Reigate – all my friends are there.'

'Reigate in Surrey?' Morwenna remembered Ruan's words about Beverley Okoro's cottage being sold and put two and two together. 'Do you live in Half Moon Cottage?'

'My mum and dad bought it as a bolthole, but it's too far from the beach.' The girl smoothed her hair with her emerald nails. Louise hurried to the shelves and returned with a copy of the book, showing her the cover, a man leaning in to kiss a coy woman, both in eighteenth-century costume. The teenager took it and glanced at the design.

'You say there's sex in this?'

'Lots of it,' Morwenna said cheerily.

'Can I take it?' the girl asked.

'You'll have to fill in a form online,' Louise said. 'Your name, date of birth, address.'

'No problem.'

'And if you're under sixteen, you will need to ask a parent, guardian or adult family member to register on your behalf,' Louise said professionally.

'I'm already sixteen,' the girl said, disgusted that Louise should think she was younger.

'That's good to know.' Morwenna held out a hand. 'I'm Morwenna. Welcome to Seal Bay.'

The girl made a face as if Morwenna were practising an ancient custom. She held out soft fingers and made a slack attempt at a handshake. 'Phoenix. I'll fill the form in. When do I need to bring it back?'

'You can borrow it for three weeks,' Louise advised. 'Or – if you're not actually reading it – you can come in any time and swap it for another.'

'You could try *Madame Bovary* by Gustave Flaubert next time – that's full of drama and passion,' Morwenna said. She waved her phone towards Louise, who was busy filling out a form. 'I need to make a call.'

Louise glanced at her and mouthed, 'Barnaby?'

Morwenna shook her head and moved away, pressing a button, her mobile against her ear. She listened for a ringtone but heard nothing. Then a voicemail came through, saying that the number was not available.

Morwenna was puzzled. Why would Irina's phone go straight through to voicemail? She wondered where she could be. She moved her fingers quickly, sending a text to Jane Choy, to ask her opinion.

MORWENNA

Hi Jane – can we catch up for a chat? I need to
know about what happens when a person goes
missing.

A reply came almost immediately.

JANE

I'm at the nick. I'll pop into the tearoom later. Is it
serious?

Morwenna replied.

She added a thumbs up, shoved her phone in her pocket and turned back to the desk as Phoenix strode out through the doorway, swinging her bag.

There was work to be done in the library but Louise wanted to talk about ghosts. Morwenna pushed Irina out of her mind for now – no doubt her absence was easily explained. She'd gone to a friend's house, drunk too much wine, forgotten about her meeting with Morwenna. Irina was probably on the beach now, interviewing tourists, talking about what a great place Seal Bay was. Morwenna decided she wouldn't think about it until she met Jane later.

But her thoughts wriggled like a persistent worm. Something wasn't right...

* * *

Donald arrived early for the afternoon shift. As Morwenna left, he and Louise were still talking about the mystery of Lady Elizabeth and the disappearing volumes. She was glad of the electric bicycle as she cycled through town and along the seafront towards the Proper Ansom Tearoom – it was so much better than the old sit up and beg she'd used a year ago.

The swim yesterday had made her legs tired – Irina was a strong swimmer and they'd gone out quite far. Fleetingly, she wondered about Barnaby, Pam's brother, the handsome plastic surgeon. Was he in London or Seal Bay? If he was at Pam's house, would he ask her to dinner on the boat again? She'd enjoyed it last time; he was pleasant company, but she wasn't so sure she and Barnaby were a match made in heaven.

Her mind moved to Ruan again, but she forced him out of her thoughts – he'd been in her head a lot recently, and she wasn't sure why. She put it down to being tired – or lacking a project. Perhaps she needed a good crime to solve, some clues to get her teeth into. The thought made her laugh. In truth, the last two times she'd found herself being a sleuth had been a steep learning curve – she'd landed in enough hot water to last her a lifetime. She ought to get used to quiet and routine, but it wasn't in her nature.

She passed the pop-up shop and waved to Susan and Barb Grundy, who were busy knitting in aid of the Lifeboats, staring out to watch the world go by. The beach was packed with holidaymakers, but there was no sign of Irina. Morwenna cycled on towards the tearoom and secured her bicycle, hurrying in, tugging on her apron. Tamsin was rushing around with trays of food and young Zach was probably in the kitchen preparing sandwiches and scones for all he was worth.

A young man at a nearby table caught her eye, grinning cheekily, his feet up on a spare chair. He was dressed in a black top hat, a long cape, red waistcoat and grubby white trousers. He waved a menu in her direction. Morwenna smiled back and he called out in a soft northern accent, 'Morwenna. Good to see you. I'm gagging for a coffee. And have you got any of those heavy cakes I had last time?'

'Hevva cakes?' Morwenna said. 'I'll get you one.'

'I'm starving and they fill me up proper good,' the magician said. 'And they're cheap.'

'They're made from flour, lard, butter, milk, sugar and raisins, so you'll get a complete meal,' Morwenna said kindly.

'Belting.' He licked his lips at the thought.

'How's business, Sheppy?' Morwenna asked.

The magician took off his top hat, revealing flossy brown curls. 'I've been entertaining kids all morning, but they're a tough crowd. The parents are even tougher – they don't put their hands in their pockets. Ah, no, it's my fault. I'm too disorganised. I should advertise properly, sell tickets upfront. But I do the show live and pass my hat round, then no one sticks any money in.'

'How much have you made this morning?' Morwenna asked sympathetically.

Sheppy shrugged as if it didn't matter much. 'Seven pounds fifty. I usually make more as a juggler but I do that Tuesdays, Thursdays and Saturdays. It's Magic Sheppy today. I've got food and accommodation to pay for. I mean, you'd think after four weeks in Seal Bay, I'd have got it together but...' He grinned. 'My dad always said I wouldn't make much of myself. Perhaps he was right.'

Morwenna felt sorry for him. He couldn't be much older than his early twenties. He had an earthy, woody smell around him, as if he hadn't had a shower for a while. He stretched his legs on the chair.

'Ah, I'll be all right. Life's good. I'm staying over at Woodpecker caravan site. It's cheap there and no one bothers me.'

'I'm sure you'll make your fortune one day, Sheppy. I'll get you that hevva cake.'

'Thanks, Morwenna.' Sheppy tipped his top hat and pushed it back over his curls. For a moment, he looked like the Artful Dodger. 'Hey, but it's banging here. I don't care if I don't go back to Levenshulme until Christmas. I think I'll be Cornish from now on.'

Morwenna walked away with a wave; the tearoom was heaving and she was too busy to chat for long.

Sheppy called after her in a ridiculous accent, 'Bleddy ansom – that's what you lot say down here, isn't it? And thassit, me luvver, geddon, ooo arrr.' He burst into a peal of laughter, amused at his own mimicry.

Morwenna called over her shoulder, 'Right. I'll be back with your hevva cake and a nice cuppa, my ansom. Dreckly. In two shakes of a lamb's tail.'

She'd see if she could find a pasty for him too. The poor kid looked hungry.

6

Morwenna flopped onto a chair and placed her elbows on the table. She'd hardly stopped all afternoon – she'd eaten a pasty on the go, and that wasn't good for digestion. Jane Choy sat opposite her in uniform, her hat on the table, sipping hot coffee. Her dark hair spilled from its tight bun. They looked at each other and spoke together.

'I'm proper bushed,' from Morwenna.

'I'm shattered,' from Jane.

They both laughed and Morwenna asked, 'Tough day at the nick?'

'I'll say.' Jane looked as though she'd just run a marathon.

Morwenna gazed around. It was almost six o'clock. Tamsin had closed the tearoom; the rest of the tables were cleared and the floor swept. A weary Zach had gone home to his mother, who lived on the edge of town. Elowen was upstairs, doing her homework, and Tamsin was making something for them both to eat. As usual, Morwenna had been invited to stay, but she wanted to go home, feed Brenda and do some thinking. She caught Jane looking at her as if trying to work something out.

Jane said, 'So tell me what's bothering you.'

'You first.' Morwenna raised an eyebrow. 'Is life tough with Rick?'

'He's a nightmare, to be honest.' Jane gave a dry laugh. 'He was on Bay Radio this morning talking about drugs and since then, he hasn't shut up about it. He thinks he's a pioneer.'

'Like Nancy Reagan?' Morwenna suggested.

'Who?' Jane asked. Morwenna sometimes forgot that Jane was in her late twenties.

'First lady, USA. Ronald's wife. She did the Just Say No campaign against drugs in the eighties.'

'Oh, before my time.' Jane pushed back a stray lock of hair. 'Well, in that case Rick thinks he's Seal Bay's answer to Nancy. He's on about us being more visible to young people. He's sticking posters up everywhere in the nick saying "From Harm to Hope".'

'That's good though, isn't it?' Morwenna said.

'We're already rushed off our feet. And Rick wants us all to make an impression on the new chief inspector who's coming from London.'

'Oh?'

'A new broom. The old chief inspector, John Beatty, was a nice man but he's retired. This new one sounds like a stickler – young, ambitious.'

'They might be really efficient, bring some energy into the place and help Rick out.'

'Or they might make my life a misery,' Jane said. 'Chief Inspector Barnarde from the Met. Starting tomorrow.' She groaned. 'I just get this bad feeling. I suppose it's because I missed my swim yesterday.'

'It was fun, too.' Morwenna thought of Irina again. 'We should go tomorrow morning before work – bright and early.'

'Great idea,' Jane enthused. 'I'll meet you on the beach at seven.'

'Ansom,' Morwenna said. 'So – I wanted to ask...'

'Ask away.'

'What's the police policy on missing persons?'

'You mentioned that in your text.' Jane frowned. 'So – who's missing?'

'I'm not sure yet. I just wanted to check what happens.'

'It's a myth that you have to wait twenty-four hours – you can make a report to the police as soon as you think a person is missing. You'd ring us at the station. Or if you were concerned about the person's welfare, you'd dial 999 and ask for the police.' Jane leaned forward. 'I know you too well, Morwenna – what's going on?'

Morwenna took a sip of tea. 'Do you know Irina Bacheva from Bay Radio?'

'Yes, of course,' Jane said. 'She's engaged to Tom Fox who runs the station. He's very much the smooth operator.'

'Oh?'

'He was driving too fast one night. I pulled him over. It was late. I did a PBT on him as a matter of procedure.'

'What's a PBT?'

'A preliminary breath test – it's routine. But I didn't like his attitude.'

'Why?'

'He was full of himself.' Jane pulled a face. 'You know how some men are with women. He actually called me "love".'

'Patronising,' Morwenna said. 'I can't see Irina standing for that.' She was thoughtful for a moment, remembering her conversation with Irina during the swim. 'I was supposed to meet her for a drink last night. She didn't show up.'

'It was tipping down – I was out in the car,' Jane muttered. 'Perhaps she thought you'd stay home. So have you texted her to ask her what happened?'

'No, but I tried ringing, and her phone goes straight to voicemail.'

'There must be a simple explanation.'

'I saw Tom at the radio station earlier and he said she hadn't come home.'

'Maybe she had a better offer,' Jane said glibly. 'I wouldn't blame her.'

'I don't know.' Morwenna stared into her empty cup. 'It doesn't feel right.'

'I trust your instinct,' Jane said, her voice low.

'The thing is—' Morwenna rubbed a bit of spilled tea across the tabletop with her finger '—Irina said she'd discovered something important.'

'Such as?'

'She wanted to tell me in The Smugglers. She said that heads would roll if it came to light. Her work in the bay talking to people had made her suspicious about something.'

'Have you any idea what it was?'

'No, she was on the verge of talking to you lot about it. She just had a few facts to check.'

'And she didn't turn up last night?'

'Or this morning.' Morwenna said as an afterthought, 'Tom didn't seem too worried though.'

'Oh?'

'He assumed she'd stayed with a friend – he said she often worked in her office until late.'

Jane pushed a hand across her forehead. 'Well, we can't do anything until Tom or someone else reports it.'

'Mmm.' Morwenna was thinking. 'Perhaps he needs a little nudge?'

'How do you mean?'

'If she's missing, Jane – isn't it important to start a search straight away?'

'Of course.'

'Maybe I should start looking?' Morwenna said.

Jane tapped her hand. 'You know the rules – don't get involved in anything illegal or dangerous. You leave those things to the police.'

'Of course,' Morwenna said sweetly. 'When have I ever overstepped the thin blue line?'

'Don't tempt me,' Jane said. 'But seriously, Morwenna, I mean it.'

Morwenna was on her feet. 'Right. I'd better get off home. I've got a cat to feed.'

'I'll give you a lift,' Jane offered. 'My daily good deed for an OAP.'

Morwenna shook her head. 'I have an electric bike, I'll be ansom. Mind you, it's still murder up that hill. We'll catch up early tomorrow for the swim.' She was already at the door, turning back and winking. 'I might have some news for you then. Wait and see...'

* * *

Morwenna wasn't sure what time would be best to go out and search. It was dark already; nine-thirty. She'd shared a pasta salad with Brenda, who loved begging for fusilli from her plate, especially if it was smothered with cheese. Brenda was utterly spoiled.

Morwenna was still thinking about her plan – Seal Bay was busy until midnight, or even later at this time of year. Perhaps she'd be wiser to go out in the early hours. She wasn't sure – she didn't want to be seen. There would be security cameras around the front of the building she intended to visit, but the back street would be deserted, she was positive. She wouldn't be recognised if she wore all black, a hood up.

Brenda was curled on her knee, purring; it would be so easy to settle down for the evening, read, go to bed and forget her silly plan. And – honestly – it *was* silly. Foolhardy. Plain wrong.

But her instinct argued back – she had a strong feeling she'd find something important about Irina. Morwenna made up her mind: she'd set her alarm for half past four. Her plan was to creep out, do a spot of detective work in the half-light and come back in time for Brenda's breakfast and the wild swim with Jane. Maybe she'd have something to tell her.

There was this gut feeling she couldn't ignore.

* * *

The alarm went off at four-thirty. Morwenna opened her eyes. The sun rose at 4:47 a.m. She'd checked. Brenda was asleep on the duvet, paws in the air, grunting – dreaming of cheesy treats, no doubt. Morwenna sidled out of the bed and tugged on the clothes she'd organised: a dark hoodie with plastic bags stuffed in the pockets, black leggings, gloves. She grabbed her phone and a banana – Lamorna had always said you shouldn't go to work on an empty stomach and this was work, of sorts. Full of apprehension, she pushed her bike outside into the cold air.

There was a light in the bedroom window over at number nine – Ruan was up. He'd be out on the trawlers soon. She wondered momentarily if she should ask him for a lift into town but dismissed the idea. It wasn't light yet and although the bike had lights, she didn't want to be seen. Morwenna tugged up her hood and clambered onto the saddle, checking that her phone was in her pocket – she'd need it. She hoped she was right about the layout of the building she was going to visit – but she knew the back streets of Seal Bay well enough to know where an access might be.

The ride into town was all downhill. Tiny lamps glimmered from the harbour, but everywhere was quiet. There was no traffic around as she deliberately took the narrow streets, avoiding the town centre in case there were security cameras. She rode through a maze of back streets and eventually came to a halt in a narrow alley of high brick walls. There were dustbins every-where but no place to lock her bicycle. She hoped it'd be all right to leave it. If everything went to plan, she'd only be a few minutes.

Using the torch on her phone and the dim dawn light, Morwenna glanced up at the office window of Bay Radio. The top one had been ajar and it looked as if it still was. She hoped it would wriggle open wide enough for her to find a way in. She had no idea what she was looking for, but if her hunch was right, she'd find something useful in Irina's office. The best possible scenario was that Irina would be in there, working early at her desk. Perhaps she'd come home safely on Monday night.

Morwenna wasn't tall, and it took a great effort to reach the top window. Her knee hurt as she balanced on a narrow sill, stretching an arm to jiggle the window wide open. She levered herself upright and pushed a sleeve through, reaching out to grab a handle. She forced it down with a grunt and the main window opened outwards. She slid down again, her feet on solid ground, and eased it wide. Then she hoisted herself up and wriggled inside. She sat on the sill and surveyed the dimly lit room: a desk, a chair, strewn photos on the table, a basin, a mirror. It was an office, the untidy one. The poster on the wall was of Irina, a dimple in her chin, smiling, wearing headphones. Beneath were the words 'The Rina B Show, Bay Radio'.

Morwenna had forgotten that Irina's show came out under that name.

She tugged the plastic bags from her pocket and pushed her trainer-clad feet inside them. She didn't want to leave grime or a footprint. Standing up, she pulled out her phone and began to take photos. It was important to be quick, in and out – her heart was beating too fast and Jane's stern voice was already grumbling in her head, telling her that she was doing something illegal.

Morwenna imagined herself in the local newspaper: Sexagenarian Seal Bay woman arrested for breaking and entering.

She took a deep breath to steady herself. She was being foolish, but her instincts were screaming to keep going.

First, she photographed the table. There were toppled photos of Irina and Tom, smiling into a camera. She hoped it was her office, not Tom's. She photographed the table, a few books, an upturned pot of pens, a laptop, switched off. In places, the table veneer was a different colour, patches of lighter wood. She snapped away again.

Morwenna gazed around. There was a lot of water beneath the basin; a small pool of it that had soaked into the green carpet, making it darker. She pointed her camera and pressed the button; it might be important.

On the back of the door there was a woman's light raincoat. Morwenna wondered if Irina had worn it on Sunday evening during the downpour. She felt in the pockets but they were empty apart from a crumpled tissue. Morwenna moved back to the desk and photographed the top again. There was Sellotape, a pair of reading glasses, notecards, all in a haphazard pile, as if they'd been flung to one side. She opened the top drawer. There was a magazine inside, *Perfect Wedding*, with a photo of a woman on the front wearing a delicate veil decorated with translucent pearls.

The bride was looking down coyly. This was definitely Irina's office.

Morwenna lifted the edge of the magazine and her fingers touched a small book beneath it. She pulled it out. It was an A5 diary. She shoved it up her hoodie without another thought. After all, she could always return it to Irina with an apology, explain how she'd been concerned about her, so she'd broken in to the building. Right now, standing in an empty office in the half-light, Morwenna imagined explaining herself to Rick Tremayne or the new Chief Inspector Barnarde from the Met. She had a feeling that somehow it wouldn't wash.

Morwenna tugged open the second drawer, shining her phone torch inside. There was a bag of crisps, the nice ones with sea salt, unopened. An assortment of pens. Some notebooks; Morwenna flicked through but they were all empty. Below was a stiff piece of card, jammed against the sides. She frowned: the drawer was much deeper. This was a false bottom of sorts.

She lifted the card out gently and pushed her fingers beneath. There was something there, cardboard. She wriggled a file out, a simple black loose-leaf folder. A quick peek told her there were sheets of paper inside, a thick wad of them covered with writing in black pen. She was about to take the top sheet out and examine it when a noise on the other side of the door made her heart lurch.

Someone was pushing a key in the door; she could hear the sound of the lock being turned. Morwenna held her breath. Her first thought was – who was coming into the office at five-thirty in the morning? It had to be Irina. She could stay where she was, make her excuses. But something propelled her to close the drawer; she tucked the loose-leaf folder beneath her hoodie with the diary, crouched down on her knees and crawled beneath the desk, almost too afraid to breathe.

Someone was in the room, just a few inches away.

Morwenna held her breath. She peered out at large black trainers, probably a man's feet. It definitely wasn't Irina. She closed her eyes, trying to calm her thudding heart. The man walked around the office quietly, as if searching for something. His legs were clad in black joggers in a fleecy material. She heard something move on the desktop above her, a scratchy sound as if items were being rearranged. Then he was pacing around again, standing near the sink. She wondered if he was looking at himself in the mirror. There was silence for a moment; she saw him bend over – she could see the curve of his arm as he wiped the carpet with some sort of cloth in an attempt to soak up the water. His hands worked quickly – he was wearing a watch, a metal one. Her breathing was so ragged she was sure he'd hear her.

He stood up and made a low sound, a sort of grunt. She was grateful he hadn't turned on the light – he'd have definitely spotted her if she hadn't been concealed beneath the shadow of a large desk.

He was inches away again, fiddling with something on top of the desk. Morwenna wished he'd hurry up and go.

He cleared his throat, a sound of determination or finality perhaps. Then he strode towards the door, which closed behind him with a click. He was gone. Morwenna waited a little longer, in case he'd forgotten something and came back. Finally, holding her breath, she crept out.

This had definitely been one of her worst ideas. She stood in the office, trembling like a leaf in a stiff breeze. The laptop had gone. The top of the desk had been rearranged; everything was tidy now. There was a paper towel in the bin where the carpet had been wiped. Morwenna took more photos quickly – the tidied room, the desk, the bin – and moved on wobbly legs to the window. She eased herself out into the cold air and left the window open.

She stood in the alley amongst the bins and breathed in deeply, still trembling. The loose-leaf folder was still stuffed beneath her hoodie with the A5 diary, her phone in her pocket. It was almost light now. At least her bike was still where she'd left it. She threw a leg over it gratefully and set off down the alley at a pace, doing her best to avoid a pile of broken bottles. As quickly as her shaking legs would allow, she weaved through the narrow backstreets towards Harbour Cottages. It had been a crazy plan, Morwenna told herself, but once she was home, she'd check the photos on her phone and pray that Irina would be back at work today and there would be a logical excuse for her absence. That would be the best scenario. She'd call into Bay Radio and say hi, offer to take her for a drink in the evening, return her folder and diary. They'd have a laugh about how silly and suspicious she'd been.

But, Morwenna asked herself, who had crept into the office? Why did he have a key? And why had he taken Irina's laptop?

* * *

An hour later, Morwenna ate another banana for energy before clambering into her swimming costume, tugging clothes on top, ready for her swim with Jane. She wished she could be honest about what she'd done, sneaking into Irina's office, looking for clues. But she couldn't, not yet; she'd broken the law and Jane would be furious. Morwenna wheeled her bike outside into the cool morning air. There must be another way to explain her concerns to Jane. But first of all, she needed to check if Irina had come home. If she was back with Tom or at work, there was no need to worry. Morwenna resolved to call into Bay Radio later. She'd be a little late for the library – Pawly Yelland was due in at ten, so she'd have to be quick.

Jane was parked at the seafront in her car, wearing a huge coat over her wetsuit and trainers. She grinned as soon as she saw Morwenna.

'I don't start until half ten this morning. I might treat myself to breakfast. Tamsin does breakfasts now, doesn't she?'

'Eggs, pastries, rolls, beans on toast,' Morwenna explained. 'Just stuff she and Zach can easily knock up between them.'

'How's young Zach doing?' Jane asked.

Morwenna was already tugging off her layers. 'Fine. Tam says he's a natural chef – he'll get paid well for the summer. His parents are both cooks so he knows what he's up to. He's got another year to do at uni. Marine photography, apparently.'

Jane pulled a face. 'I think he'd stand a better chance of a job as a chef.' She wriggled from her coat, took Morwenna's clothes and bag and stuffed them all inside her car. They stood together on the sand, watching the surf roll in. There were some surfers further down the beach, catching the morning waves.

Jane rubbed her hands together. 'I'm looking forward to this. It'll set me up for the day.'

'Me too.' Morwenna tucked her hair into a swimming cap. 'I'll race you.'

Jane was always up for a challenge, taking off at a sprint, leaving Morwenna behind her, puffing and laughing. They reached the ocean and dived in with a splash. Morwenna yelled with the shock of the cold.

Jane swam out to sea strongly, and Morwenna followed, the icy water biting her flesh like invisible crabs. They paused for a moment to bob in the water, Jane's teeth chattering. 'Swimming always makes me feel so much better. I've been really tense this week.'

Morwenna wondered what Jane had to be tense about. 'Rick?'

'He's the worst boss in the world. Do you know, he told me the other day that all I was fit for was filling in forms.'

'Cheeky tuss,' Morwenna said, and immediately thought that she sounded just like Lamorna.

'I ought to look for promotion somewhere else – I'm ambitious,' Jane said. 'I've been on all the courses and thought about progression. My last boss told me that if I embrace the work, I'll have a really rewarding career. I've thought about applying for MCIT, firearms, child protection, even dog handling. But I want to stay in Seal Bay.'

'That's understandable.' Morwenna moved her arms, splashing water in her face, kicking her legs to stay warm.

'But we have this chief inspector arriving. I have no idea what to expect. I just hope they are sympathetic and good to work with, not like—'

'Rick?' Morwenna laughed.

'He's so arrogant. He takes credit for everything and he's lazy. I don't know how his wife puts up with him.'

'I don't think she sees much of him,' Morwenna said. 'Sally's nice. The boys too.'

'How old are they now?'

'Jonathan's sixteen and Ben's a couple of years younger.' Morwenna snorted. 'I wonder if they'll join the force like their dad?'

'Can you imagine having a dad like Rick for a boss? He's no role model,' Jane said. 'Your mum's a great role model though. I envy the way you Mutton women are so close.'

'We're lucky,' Morwenna agreed. 'Are you from a big family?'

'Not really.' Jane looked sad. 'There was just me and my father. My mother left when I was a teenager. And my dad was very ambitious for me – that was the background he came from: discipline, hard work. He disapproved of just about everything I did as an adolescent. I joined the police force and we drifted apart.'

'That's a shame,' Morwenna said. She was starting to shiver. 'Shall we swim around for a bit?'

'Isn't this the best exercise?' Jane rolled over, moving her arms in a backstroke. Morwenna plunged below the surface and bobbed up again.

'It keeps me sane,' Morwenna said. 'It helps me put everything into perspective.'

'I meant to ask.' Jane pressed her lips together. 'What happened to your missing person? Irina from the radio?'

'I don't know. I'll pop in the studio this morning and ask Tom. I expect she's home now and everything's fine.'

'Do you want me to do it?' Jane offered. 'I have some leaflets Rick is anxious to put everywhere – the "From Harm to Hope" ones aimed at stopping kids taking drugs. I can pop in on the pretext that Rick has sent them.'

'Oh – right.' Morwenna was disappointed. She'd wanted to see for herself if Irina was back. For a moment she almost offered to help carry the leaflets. She ought to tell Jane what she'd done. But

Jane would have no sympathy – she'd say Morwenna had gone rogue again, acted impetuously.

Jane gave a violent shudder. 'I'm getting cold.'

'Let's have one more minute, shall we, just for ourselves?' Morwenna said. She wasn't ready to move on yet. 'It'll be ghosts all morning and cakes all afternoon. I love the summer, but it's always full-on. We'll be flat out at the tearoom. And Elowen breaks up from school in a couple of weeks. Then we'll be really frantic.'

'How will Tamsin manage?'

'Mum will take Elowen out, and Ruan'll step up. He's pretty good. We all muck in, the Muttons and the Pascoes.'

'I envy you, having such a close-knit family. And even though you and Ruan aren't together, you're so supportive. I'm in my little square box all alone.' Jane pretended to make a joke of it. 'All work and no play make Jane a dull copper.'

'You're always welcome at Harbour Cottages,' Morwenna said. She plunged beneath the water one more time and when she reached the surface, she glanced towards the azure line of the horizon. A fishing boat was in the distance and another, a pleasure craft. The sun's rays dazzled on the dark surface, making the waves sparkle like diamonds.

'I'll race you back,' Morwenna said. Jane was already ahead, lithe arms, strong legs. Morwenna struggled behind her, but she wasn't deterred. Jane was thirty-five years younger and Morwenna was able to keep up, almost. Her feet touched the seabed and she stood shivering, shaking pearl drops from her face.

Jane asked, 'Do you have time for a hot drink? I'm buying.'

'Or we could pop up to my house?' Morwenna offered. 'I'll put the kettle on...' Her voice trailed off as her eyes moved from Jane's car to something several yards to one side that had been abandoned by the sea wall. It looked like a bundle of rags, or a wet bag. There was something smaller lying next to it.

'What's that?' Morwenna pointed.

Jane narrowed her eyes. Then she was running, Morwenna hard on her heels. The closer she came to the heaped bundle, the more Morwenna's heart sank. She knew what it was. Not rubbish, not rags, not a damp sleeping bag left by one of the tourists who'd decided to camp on the beach overnight.

It was a person, slumped, dark hair soaked, arms flopped in an unnatural position. A few feet away, there was a handbag, abandoned. Everything was drenched with seawater.

Morwenna reached the body seconds behind Jane and they stood together, gooseflesh limbs, shivering, not just from the cold of the sea breeze. The woman lay crumpled, as if she had been washed up by the sea. Her skin was blueish grey, yet somehow without colour. Her clothes were torn. A bare arm was visible, and Morwenna noticed dark marks above the elbow. She caught her breath and fear made her move backwards.

Jane tugged out her phone, stepping in front of Morwenna professionally, blocking her view.

'I'm calling this in,' she said rapidly. She knelt next to the body. 'Victim found deceased, female, accident or possible homicide, forensics – the area will need to be cordoned off.'

Jane was in full efficient police mode now, calling for the CSI. Morwenna took another step back, then another. She was in shock.

Irina's body lay washed up on the sand, twisted, bloated, her skin marbled. Morwenna put a hand to her mouth and felt her stomach heave. She might be sick.

She turned away and felt her legs give. She flopped down on the sand, staring out to sea, terrifying thoughts filling her mind.

What had happened to Irina? And why didn't it feel like an accident?

8

Morwenna sat in Jane's car, teeth chattering, wrapped in a blanket a kind paramedic had given her. Forensic police officers in white suits had arrived; the area was already cordoned off. Jane placed a cardboard cup of coffee in her hands and it felt good just to hold something warm and comforting. Morwenna's lips were numb as she said, 'That was Irina.'

'Leave it to the CSI.'

'CSI?'

'Crime scene investigators.' Jane dried herself roughly with her towel, tugging on her coat. 'We have to go through procedure now. It's got to be done by the book, Morwenna, so let's just think about getting you home. I can organise for someone to call round.'

'I'll probably go to the library.' Morwenna stared ahead at the sea, at the waves rolling in. There was a swarm of busy forensic investigators being watched by a few straggling surfers and a man in a flat cap who had strayed towards the police cordon, not far from where Irina was being carried to an ambulance. A police officer ushered them away.

Morwenna blinked to try to refocus her thoughts. 'What do you think happened to her, Jane?'

'Who knows? An unfortunate accident?' Jane's eyes flicked back to the activity around Irina.

'But she was a strong swimmer.'

'The pathologist will work out the cause of death,' Jane soothed. 'Do you want me to get you home? Or we could go to the tearoom, get you something to eat? It might be good for you to spend time with Tamsin.'

'What about Tom Fox?' Morwenna's mind was racing.

'We'll send someone round. Of course, he'll have to give a statement. So will you, I'm afraid.'

'Me?' Morwenna looked up, alarmed. 'Why?'

'Because of what you told me, about the meeting you had with Irina and that she didn't show. It might tie in with the time of death and we can retrace her movements.'

Morwenna was glad she hadn't told Jane about breaking into Irina's office and hiding under the desk, watching the legs walking around the room. She shouldn't have been there. What she'd seen might be important, but she couldn't tell Jane, not yet. She was keen to look at the photos on her phone, the diary and the folder, in case there was a clue. She thought again about Irina swimming with her on Sunday, how positive and hopeful she had been, excited about the secret she wanted to share with Morwenna. Now Irina was dead. Morwenna felt tears come, warm on her cold cheeks.

'She was a strong swimmer,' she said again.

Jane placed a gentle hand on her shoulder. 'I'll get Jim Hobbs to run you and your bike up to Harbour Cottages. Get a shower and see how you feel. I'll text you.'

Morwenna nodded. 'Right.'

'I'll have to rush home and get changed. Work's started for me already.' Jane smiled grimly. 'And I'll have to wait a few hours for my breakfast.'

Morwenna watched, still stunned, as Jane turned to talk to a colleague. She saw PC Jim Hobbs throw her a glance and his mouth moved but the words were taken by the wind. Morwenna shivered and hugged the blanket. Her thoughts wouldn't clear.

She just felt sad.

* * *

It was eleven o'clock when she secured her bike in the corridor outside Seal Bay library and stood, in yellow T-shirt and sun and moon leggings, wondering what to do next. She wasn't ready to go in and face the barrage of questions.

Someone rushed past her, a young man with blonde hair, in a flash of bright T-shirt, colourful shorts. She heard him say, 'Hi, Morwenna.'

She replied with a mumbled, 'Hi,' but she had no idea who she'd just spoken to. Her mind was jumbled. In truth, she was still standing beneath the scalding-hot shower at home, steam all around her, thinking about the last time she saw Irina, wondering what had happened. She still couldn't believe it.

She hesitated outside the door to the library, listening. She knew the minute she went inside, all eyes would be on her. News travelled fast around Seal Bay. There were three low voices. She recognised Louise's tone, fascinated and inquisitive. She'd be leaning forward on the reception desk with a smile on her face. The serious voice of Donald Stewart came next. She heard the words 'supernatural' and 'respect for the dead'. She shuddered, not able to clear her mind of the image she'd seen on the beach. She'd hardly recognised Irina. There had been no trace of the vibrant young woman with so much ahead of her: a career, a marriage, a great life.

She listened to the third voice: of course, it was Pawly Yelland, whose recent book *Hidden Secrets of Seal Bay* was so popular. Morwenna had read it: he was informative and knowledgeable. She took a deep breath, plastered a smile on her face and sauntered inside.

Three figures were huddled around the desk. Louise, with her bright red hair and lipstick, turned a compassionate smile towards Morwenna. Donald was hunched in a blue anorak, scratching his goatee beard. Pawly Yelland had his back to her: he was in his fifties, with a thick thatch of hair, muscular in a Save the Earth T-shirt and khaki shorts. They were drinking tea and there was a spare mug on the desk, half empty. Morwenna noticed it had been made with lots of milk. Louise plonked her mug down and rushed across to Morwenna, arms wide.

'You're here? We didn't expect you. How are you? We heard about what happened at the beach – it's all over the news.'

Morwenna knew who they were talking about. 'Irina.'

'It must have been an awful shock, seeing her like that.' Louise's eyes were wide. 'Oh, you poor thing.'

Morwenna nodded slowly. 'It was, yes.'

'I'll make you a hot drink. Tea, in your favourite mug. The kettle's just boiled.' Louise busied herself with the kettle.

Donald shot her a look of pure sympathy. 'You look like you need a dram in your tea. It must have been terrible.'

'I don't want to be drunk in charge of a bicycle,' Morwenna quipped, shrugging off how miserable she felt.

Pawly Yelland turned to her. He seemed upset. 'I heard from Louise a moment ago – a reporter was found.'

'Irina.' Morwenna met his eyes, expecting more of a reaction – he'd known her well. Instead, he shook his head.

'We never met. I heard she was popular in Seal Bay.'

'But...' Morwenna remembered Irina's words. Why was Pawly suggesting they didn't know each other? Something made her say no more, but why had he claimed not to know someone he'd had a fling with? Perhaps it was their age gap. Perhaps he was embarrassed. She was determined to find out more, but now wasn't the time.

She took a breath. 'Poor Irina. The police want to interview me.' That was playing on her mind.

'Why? You didn't do anything,' Louise said quickly.

'Procedure,' Morwenna muttered. She accepted the mug of tea gratefully. 'I was due to meet Irina for a – a friendly drink – on Sunday night. She didn't show.'

'Oh?' Louise paused, eyes wide. 'She *disappeared*?'

'I suppose so.' Morwenna knew straight away where the conversation was going. And Louise didn't disappoint her.

'It's exactly what I was saying. Lady Elizabeth warned us yesterday morning that this would happen. Books disappeared from the shelves. Irina disappeared from Seal Bay.'

Morwenna was unconvinced. 'That's a bit tenuous.'

'Not at all,' Donald said. 'Louise has a point. How else is Lady Elizabeth going to contact us about what happened to that poor woman?'

'Does her fiancé know yet?' Louise asked.

Pawly took over. 'Do the police know how she died? Was it an accident or did she take her own life?'

Morwenna had no idea. 'I suppose Forensics will come up with something, or the pathologist. Jane will text me later.'

'I think you're brave, coming into work today,' Louise said. 'We were having a meeting about Pawly's latest book. Are you up to it?'

'I suppose it will take my mind off things,' Morwenna said weakly.

'Pawly's new book will be about the Victorian Pengellens and their influence on Seal Bay,' Donald said.

'He wants to find out about Lady Elizabeth. Her refuge was in our library, her ghost is here. So Pawly will be spending time with us, investigating,' Louise said excitedly.

'But she died in Pengellen Manor,' Pawly added. 'It's good to have the Pengellen family on board with my research.'

'Oh? Have you spoken to them?' Morwenna asked.

'The son was here a few minutes ago for a brief meeting,' Donald explained.

'Tristan Pengellen. He works in London, in hedge funds,' Louise said 'But he takes a lot of time off in the summer to come home and surf. He's a playboy, apparently. He's always on the beach with some girlfriend or other.' Louise was keen to tell more. 'I saw Pippa in the supermarket recently. She loves having Tristan home. Apparently, he's just finished with a woman from Mexico who was a model – she was called Fernanda. Pippa said that it didn't last long. The poor girl was obsessed but Tristan has moved on, it seems. I think his father was just the same – Julian didn't settle until his thirties. He still owns the big house in London.'

Pawly took a breath. 'Tristan's invited me to meet his parents. The Pengellens are delighted I'm going to write about their family. I'll get the full tour of their manor house.'

'But the library is where you need to be, Pawly. The Pengellens built it in 1842 for the people of Seal Bay and Lady Elizabeth loved coming here. It was her refuge,' Louise insisted.

'Elizabeth's dates were 1828–1859. She'd have been fourteen when the library was built.' Pawly rubbed his chin. 'Imagine a young woman here, reading to herself alone in a chair, transported to a different world through literature.'

'She'd have been reading the Brontë sisters,' Louise said. '*Wuthering Heights*, all passion and romance.'

'That was published in 1847. She'd have been nineteen when she read that,' Morwenna murmured.

'Hardy,' Louise persisted. '*Far from the Madding Crowd.*'

'Nope. Published after she died,' Morwenna said. '1874.'

'Jane Austen?' Louise tried.

'Definitely. She was published between 1811 and 1817. The library might have had them in stock by 1842. It takes time even now for things to reach Cornwall.' Morwenna tried a weak grin. 'Austen's novels are perfect for a refined young woman like Elizabeth.'

Pawly was staring at her. 'You have incredible knowledge, Morwenna.'

'Our Morwenna's brilliant.' Louise wrapped an affectionate arm around her. 'That's why she's such a good sleuth.'

Morwenna shrugged modestly. 'Oh, I'm just me.'

'I hope you're not thinking of sleuthing now?' Pawly asked. He looked a bit concerned.

'Now?' Morwenna met his eyes. 'What do you mean?'

'The poor reporter who was found this morning.' Pawly still wouldn't mention Irina by name.

Louise asked, 'Do the police think she was murdered?'

'Murdered?' Donald repeated. 'I wonder what our resident ghost will say. Do you think Lady Elizabeth will leave us a message about it?'

'I want to find out about Elizabeth Pengellen's connection to the library,' Pawly said, changing the subject. 'I'll spend as much time here as I can within my schedule. Readers love to hear about ghosts and her presence will bring in visitors.' He seemed pleased with himself. 'That will be good for the library.'

'I wonder if she'll talk to us again, now that...' Louise glanced at Morwenna '...now that poor Irina has died? I mean...' She was trying hard not to be insensitive. 'Perhaps she can tell us what happened?'

'We ought to leave it to the police.' Morwenna was feeling tired. It had been a long day and it wasn't lunchtime yet.

'Do you believe in ghosts, Morwenna?' Pawly asked.

'I believe in things I can see with my own eyes,' Morwenna said simply. She turned to Louise. 'Do you know, I might go home and get my head down for an hour. I'm feeling a bit under the weather.'

'Oh, you must.' Louise soothed. 'You've had such a shock. But will you be all right on your own? Can Lamorna come round, or Ruan perhaps?'

'I'll be fine.' Morwenna looked away. 'I'll get some sleep. Brenda will keep me company.'

'Brenda?' Pawly queried.

'Her cat. We found her in the library, a stray. She was so thin,' Louise explained.

'She's not thin now,' Morwenna said. 'I'll text you, Louise.' She turned to Pawly and Donald. 'I'll be seeing you – we'll have another meeting?'

'Of course,' Pawly said suavely, glancing at the shiny watch on his wrist. 'Many of them, I hope.'

'It's almost time for my shift,' Donald said kindly. 'You go home, Morwenna. And take good care of yourself.'

'I will, thanks.' Morwenna waved a hand and walked towards the door. Moments later, her cycling helmet firmly on her head, she pushed her bike outside. The light was blinding, the sun high. She wasn't looking forward to the long ride back, all uphill. Her thighs ached and her heart ached more.

She cocked a leg over the bicycle, watching traffic stream by. She was almost in a dream, waiting for the moment to join the flow. She closed her eyes and listened to the chug of engines, the light spluttering of a small motorbike, the heavy thunder of a lorry. She opened her eyes and saw a Korrik Clay truck shudder past. Behind it was a gleaming E-type Jaguar, the top down. The driver was a tanned, handsome silver-haired man in his sixties, and his sister, blonde, wearing sunglasses. Morwenna watched as they glided past, oblivious.

So, Barnaby Stone *was* back in Seal Bay, but he hadn't contacted her. Morwenna gave a deep sigh. That was it, then: the end of a brief romance. She ignored the sinking feeling and told herself it probably didn't matter. She had more urgent business to worry about.

She took off from the kerb into the traffic and began the long cycle home with a heavy heart.

9

Morwenna had only travelled for a quarter of a mile. At the roundabout, she took the turning to the seafront, ignoring the hill that led to Harbour Cottages. She bicycled past the beach, where tourists and locals sat beneath parasols, swimmers dived in the sea and children paddled, oblivious of what had happened further down the road.

Morwenna cycled on, past shops and B & Bs, past The Smugglers, towards the area where the beach was cordoned off. She slowed down. A police car was parked by the side of the road, a uniformed officer talking to a member of the public. Morwenna recognised PC Jim Hobbs, but he was too engrossed to notice her wave. Beyond the police tape, forensic experts in white suits still loitered. Morwenna wondered what they had found.

She paused outside the Proper Ansom Tearoom, secured her bicycle and checked her phone. There were missed calls, countless messages. Tamsin had sent various texts, telling her not to come into the teashop today, to stay home. They could catch up tomorrow. Lamorna had messaged; Morwenna wasn't to worry – she'd help out at the teashop today and collect Elowen from school.

Morwenna was suddenly more anxious than ever – her mother wanted to do too much. There was a sweet message from Jane, saying things were frantic at the nick so she wouldn't have time to call round tonight, but Morwenna should take care of herself. Morwenna closed her eyes; she imagined how she'd feel next time she swam in the ocean. All sorts of things would prey on her mind, not least the idea of Irina's body floating past on a rolling wave. She took a breath, steeled herself and hurried inside. The tearoom was packed, with every table crowded. Tamsin looked up from placing a tray.

'Mum. How are you? I said not to come in today! I heard what happened at the beach this morning. Everybody's heard.'

Morwenna fell into the hug, relieved to be in her daughter's arms, smelling the sweet almond of her hair conditioner. When she looked up, she saw every face staring at her. Susan and Barb Grundy were sitting with Carole Taylor who owned The Blue Dolphin Guesthouse. They had joined Lamorna, their heads together, a pot of tea and four cups between them – Morwenna knew straight away that they'd turned up just to hear the latest gossip.

Sheppy was slumped at a table. He was in his juggler suit today, a stripy shirt, braces, baggy trousers, chomping on a hevva cake. There were so many faces she had never seen before – families, visiting emmets, but they all seemed to know that she was the woman who wore the loud leggings and worked in the tearoom, the one who found the body on the beach that morning.

'Are you sure you're up to an afternoon shift, Mum?' Tamsin asked. 'You really don't have to. We'll cope.'

'I'll be right as rain – it will be good to take my mind off things.'

'You're sure?'

'I'm fine, Tam.'

Lamorna called over. 'Come and join us, maid. Tell us what happened.'

Susan Grundy called out, 'Did you really see the body floating in the water?'

'Have you worked out who dunnit?' Barb asked.

'Tell us all the news,' Carole said, beckoning her over. 'Sit down, take the weight off.'

Morwenna was struggling into her apron. 'I'll just clear a few tables first. I'll be over when I get a minute.'

She launched herself into her work, a forced grin on her face, chatting to the tourists, asking people how they were enjoying their holiday in sunny Seal Bay, the friendliest resort in Cornwall.

* * *

It was almost six o'clock when she biked back up the steep hill, feeling exhausted. Despite the electric power, every revolution of the pedals was hard. Tamsin had begged her to stay for something to eat, but she was almost asleep on her feet. Elowen had hugged her and told her that Billy Crocker had told everyone in the class that her grandmother had found a 'horrible drownded woman' on the beach and Elowen had retorted that Billy was the reason God created the middle finger. The conversation had occurred during a lesson on religion and about how blessed the peacemakers were, so Miss Parker had not been best pleased.

Morwenna decided to have a sandwich and go straight to bed. It had been a horrible day. She didn't even want to look at the pictures she'd taken of Irina's office on her phone. Right now, she wanted to sleep and to forget about what had happened today.

She dragged her bike into the hall, fed Brenda and made herself a cup of chamomile tea, the stuff that was supposed to relax you but smelled to her like cat's pee. She collapsed on the sofa with a steaming mug and a packet of chocolate biscuits and closed her eyes. There was a familiar bump as something landed on her lap: two paws padded on her chest, kneading too firmly. Morwenna pushed out a palm and rubbed Brenda's ears, exhaling, relaxing slowly. The cat settled down and began to purr.

Immediately, the image of Irina popped into her mind, the one she never wanted to see again. One minute, the bright young woman had been chatting to people on the beach about holidays and festivals, the next she'd been happily swimming in the sea with Morwenna, telling her about the wedding she was planning. And now...

Morwenna felt instinctively that perhaps all hadn't been as well in Irina's life as her smile had suggested. She thought back to some of the things Irina had said about Tom being bad-tempered. And there were the comments others had made about Irina: Mike Sheridan, Pawly Yelland.

What was going on?

There was a sharp knock on the door and Morwenna reluctantly opened her eyes. She assumed it was Ruan. He'd be back from the trawler by now; the men would have all been talking about the incident on the beach. He'd be checking she was all right. She eased Brenda from her knee and shuffled towards the door, opening it to find a tall, fierce woman in police uniform. Morwenna took a step back, a little surprised. 'Hello.'

'Morwenna Mutton?'

Morwenna nodded. The policewoman was almost six feet tall, broad-shouldered, certainly not much older than thirty. She removed her hat to reveal short hair, cut close to her head. She didn't smile as she took out a warrant card with her identification and photo. 'I'm Chief Inspector Blessed Barnarde.'

Morwenna closed her eyes and opened them, trying to think

where she'd heard the name before. Her limbs were tired and her head had started to pound. 'How can I help you?'

'Can I come in?'

'I'm really tired.'

'I need to ask you a few questions.'

'Right.' Morwenna knew it was futile to protest. She led the way into the living room and faced the chief inspector. 'You're new.'

'First day,' Blessed Barnarde said bluntly. 'I'm hitting the ground running.'

'Would you like a cup of tea?' Morwenna was Cornish – it was always the first thing you said to a visitor.

'No.' Blessed wasted no time on niceties. 'Do you want to sit down?'

Morwenna flopped down on the sofa and picked up her cup of smelly tea. She took a mouthful. Yes, it definitely tasted like cat's pee – or how she supposed it would taste. The chief inspector plonked herself on the armchair opposite and watched as Brenda leaped onto Morwenna's knee, a feline gesture of moral support.

'Ms Mutton. What was your relationship to Irina Bacheva?'

'I knew her quite well,' Morwenna said simply, adding, 'Most people did. She was a radio presenter.'

'Was she well liked?'

'She worked for the radio. So – yes, she was popular.' Morwenna didn't mean to sound sassy – she was just being honest.

'Did you get on with her?'

'Yes.' Morwenna frowned. 'She was warm, easy to talk to. Most people liked Irina, as far as I could tell.'

'Someone didn't, clearly.' Blessed's face was serious, bordering on irritable.

'You'll have to ask them all.' Morwenna was feeling dizzy now. She'd hardly eaten. And today had been a shocker.

'Tell me about the deceased.'

The word hit Morwenna like a thunderbolt. She'd known Irina was dead – it had been clear on the beach – but the word *deceased* was so final. She decided to settle for something simple. 'She came in the library and the teashop.' She paused, thinking. 'We went swimming on Sunday morning.'

'Oh?' Blessed leaned forward, her eyes glistening like hard diamonds. 'Tell me about that.'

'Some of us go sea swimming every Sunday.' Morwenna stifled a yawn. 'A regular group. It's good for you.' She met the chief inspector's eye. 'Do you swim?'

'Not often enough. I'm from London,' Blessed replied as if that answered the question. 'Was Irina a good swimmer?'

'Very.'

'But she drowned.'

'Did she?'

'So it seems.'

Morwenna was about to ask if it was an accident but she thought she'd better not show too much interest at this stage. Instead, she said, 'Poor Irina, poor Tom.'

'Do you know her fiancé?'

'A little. Just to say hello to.'

'And the last time you saw Irina was on Sunday morning when you were both swimming?'

'Yes.'

'Who else was there?'

'Louise Piper, Susan and Barb Grundy, Donald Stewart.' Morwenna thought it might be wise to omit the fact that her mother was there too. She hadn't gone in the water so perhaps it didn't count.

The chief inspector was taking notes. 'And you haven't seen Irina since then?'

'No.' Morwenna wondered whether to mention that Irina hadn't turned up to The Smugglers. She was about to say something when Blessed narrowed her eyes.

'Who might have had a grudge against Irina?'

Morwenna was quiet for a moment. That was an interesting question. Blessed suspected that Irina's death wasn't simply accidental drowning.

'I've no idea.' Morwenna shuddered. 'It was awful seeing her lying on the beach today. I just assumed something unfortunate had happened.'

'Such as?' Blessed asked.

'I don't know. Maybe she fell into the water?'

'You said she was a strong swimmer,' Blessed said.

Morwenna was impressed. This officer was a smart one. For a moment she thought about the inevitable clash of personalities with DI Tremayne at the station. Sparks would fly.

Morwenna said, 'I don't know how to help you.'

'You can keep your ear to the ground,' Blessed suggested.

'Pardon?'

'I hear you're something of an amateur sleuth, Ms Mutton I've been checking up on you. It seems that you've been in the centre of a couple of nefarious mishaps of justice that have occurred in Seal Bay.'

'I've been in the wrong place at the wrong time.' Morwenna met the sharp gaze.

Blessed said, 'What do you think happened to Irina?'

'I'm not sure.' Morwenna was thoughtful. 'She told me she was on the verge of discovering something important.'

'Such as?'

'I've no idea – but she said it would definitely be of interest to the police. She was about to tell you.'

'Really?' Blessed's gaze was piercing. 'Tell us what?'

'I don't know. Irina had found out about something illegal but she didn't say what it was. She thought she had a scoop, which she said would be "explosive" when it came out.'

'In what way?'

'She was about to tell me but she didn't turn up, the last time we arranged to meet. She went missing. I trusted Irina. She had a good instinct.'

'I believe you do too,' Blessed said quickly.

'Are you asking for my help, Officer?'

'Just keep your eyes open. I think I'll get a couple of MCIT down for a day or two, just to check things out,' Blessed said.

'MCIT?'

'Major Crime Investigation Team. Irina goes missing just as she discovers something important and is about to tell us what it is. If you hear anything, come straight to me,' Blessed said firmly. She stood up. 'But you're not to meddle, do you hear? I'm new to the area, but we have this covered – I won't stand for any interference. Got it?'

'Mmm.' Morwenna gave a placatory nod. She wanted to say it was too late for that – she was already involved.

Blessed Barnarde had arrived in Seal Bay with her London ideas and her efficient practices. Morwenna wondered how she'd get on in Cornwall. She certainly seemed like the new broom that Jane had spoken about, that would sweep cleanly through the tired, dusty little seaside town. Seal Bay people were set in their ways, unwilling to change, not always keen to accept new people. But, she thought, if Irina had been murdered, if the new chief inspector could find out who'd killed her, she'd be only too pleased.

Blessed Barnarde stood up. 'I'll see myself out, Ms Mutton.'

'You're most welcome, and call me Morwenna.' Morwenna replied. 'Just let me know if you need anything else.'

'You can be sure I will,' Blessed said and closed the door crisply behind her.

Morwenna stroked Brenda, feeling half asleep. A knot of hunger gnawed at her stomach, but her legs were too numb to move. Brenda settled into a rhythmic purr, a rolling motor, and Morwenna breathed deeply. It had been an awful day.

Tomorrow she'd have more energy, she'd feel better. For now, she needed to rest. A new day would come and she'd set about finding out who had killed poor Irina.

10

Morwenna woke on Wednesday morning, her head heavy with sleep. She could hear someone moving around downstairs. It wasn't Brenda; the cat was stretched on the duvet like a flat rug. She sat up and listened harder. There was definitely someone bumping about. She slithered out of bed and looked for something to whack the intruder with. There wasn't much in the room she could use as a weapon – a coat hanger might give someone a nasty poke in the eye, but it wouldn't offer much protection. In the end she settled for the alarm clock, an old-fashioned metal thing she'd had for years that woke her every morning without fail. If she remembered to set it, which of course she hadn't last night. It kept the time well though – it told her that it was ten to seven.

She tugged on her dressing gown, her fountain of hair dishevelled, her pyjamas crumpled, her eyes stuck together, not yet properly open. She thought with a smile that her appearance might well frighten any burglar away. The alarm clock clutched in her fist, she padded downstairs.

The burglar was in the kitchen cooking something that

smelled delicious. A pan was sizzling away. Morwenna could hear soft singing too. She recognised the song – it was Bob Marley's 'No Woman, No Cry'.

Ruan loved Bob Marley. She recalled him telling her not long after they met that he'd hitchhiked with a schoolfriend to London in 1976 to see The Wailers in concert. He'd been sixteen, and his father had taken a dim view of his son taking off to a foreign country beyond the Tamar Bridge. Ruan said the trouble he'd got into was well worth it just to watch The Wailers. And now he was in her kitchen, cooking something delicious and singing. She wondered if he was singing the song for her, if he knew how awful yesterday had been. Morwenna loved the timbre of his voice; it had a plaintive quality, as though he understood all the pain in the world.

Perhaps he did.

She put the alarm clock down and called, 'Ruan?'

Ruan emerged, a pot of coffee in his hand. 'I let myself in with the spare keys,' he said. 'I thought you'd be hungry. After what happened yesterday, I guessed you didn't eat.'

He knew her so well. 'Thanks, Ruan. That's good of you.'

'And I've made ricotta hotcakes.'

Morwenna's stomach growled. 'What are they?'

'Coconut pancakes with bananas and Italian cream cheese.' He popped back in the kitchen and emerged with a pile of pillowy pancakes, topped with runny honey. Brenda sprang on an empty chair, ready for her helping. The table had already been set for two.

Morwenna met his eyes. 'Is this for us to share?'

'I can stay for about fifteen minutes.' Ruan indicated the oilskins he'd deposited in the corner. 'I can't be late.'

'Right.' Morwenna accepted the chair he pulled out for her,

plonking herself down gratefully next to Brenda. 'I'm really hungry.'

'Dig in.' Ruan sat opposite, poured coffee and placed a pancake on each plate.

'This is nice.' Morwenna lifted a forkful of pancake and Brenda stuck out a claw. Morwenna took a small piece, blew on it and placed it by the cat's foot. Brenda snaffled it in a mouthful.

'So.' Ruan took a breath. 'I hear you were in the thick of it again yesterday.' For a moment Morwenna thought he might reach out across the table and take her hand. Instead, he sipped his coffee. 'Do you want to talk about it?'

'Not yet. Soon.' Morwenna shuddered. 'The thing is, Irina was murdered, I think. I've been looking into it a bit.'

'How do you mean, looking into it?'

'Oh, I've got a lot of things to tell someone. I can't go straight to the police because I've probably done things I shouldn't by way of investigating. But something is going on, Ruan. What happened to Irina isn't right. And I mean to find out.'

Ruan paused, fork in the air. 'Do you need my help?'

'I don't know anyone else I can tell,' Morwenna said and immediately regretted it. 'I mean – give it a couple of days for the dust to settle. The police might think her death was an accident or they might suspect something else.'

'Such as?' Ruan tried.

'I just know something awful happened. Irina was about to tell me a big secret – she said heads would roll.'

'I wonder what that means,' Ruan said thoughtfully.

'I'm going to find out, for Irina's sake,' Morwenna said.

'You're some maid,' Ruan muttered and their eyes met.

Morwenna was the first to look away. She forked a second pancake. 'These are really delicious.' She gave him a look of gratitude. 'Thanks for being kind – for knowing how I'd feel.'

'I always know...' Ruan's voice trailed off.

'Right,' Morwenna said.

'Right.'

She took a breath. 'Come round for your dinner tonight. By then I'll know what I'll know. I want to tell you all about what Irina said to me and what I've been up to.'

'I'd like that.'

Brenda reached out a claw and hooked a piece of pancake from Morwenna's plate, but she hardly noticed. 'I have to tell someone to get my thoughts in order. I think I'd better talk to Jane soon to find out what the police think happened. They have a new chief inspector – she's from London and very smart. Maybe they'll put her in charge of the case and Jane won't be told anything.'

'Phone Jane now,' Ruan said. 'You could take the morning off from the library and meet her – everyone will understand after what happened yesterday.'

'It would put my mind at rest to talk to her. I'll give her a call, see if I can squeeze something in between the library and the tearoom.'

Ruan stood up. 'Don't take too much on.'

'I won't – you know me,' Morwenna said.

'I know you won't leave it alone.' Ruan reached for his oilskins. 'I'd better be off. Fish to haul.'

'Right.' Morwenna met his eyes and a moment passed between them. She couldn't put a name to it: affection, desire, understanding, empathy? Perhaps it was just easy friendship nowadays. She wasn't sure.

'This evening, then? Dinner?' Ruan turned to go.

'Six-thirty.' Morwenna looked at the pile of ricotta hotcakes. 'I don't know what I'll cook.'

'I'd be happy with a pasty.' Ruan smiled and was gone.

Morwenna sat back in her seat and sighed. Tears filled her eyes. Her emotions were all over the place.

She reached out for her phone to call Jane. There was a lot she needed to say. And she needed to talk to someone who'd understand.

As it turned out, Jane wasn't available until half past four so Morwenna spent the morning in the library, listening to Louise's excited chatter. It seemed that half of Seal Bay wanted to borrow a book, simply to cast their eyes over Morwenna, to ask if she had any nuggets of information about the body on the beach. Morwenna had nothing to say, not even when Susan and Barb Grundy came in to quiz her.

Louise could tell she wasn't herself and looked anxious when she took herself off to sit in the store cupboard for half an hour with a cup of tea. It was remarkably comfortable in there, with a little window open letting in fresh air, an old armchair, a transistor radio. She was amazed to find the lost reference books piled on the floor there too – Louise must have placed them in the cupboard in a senior moment. Morwenna closed her eyes for a while and listened to Mike Sheridan on Bay Radio playing jolly songs from the seventies. He didn't mention Irina. She assumed his attitude was that the show must go on. Tom Fox's too.

She worked the afternoon shift in the tearoom with hardly a moment to break for a chat. Tamsin was busy as ever, helping poor Zach out the back who had run out of scones, with the demand for cream teas so high. Morwenna promised to babysit Elowen on Friday night. Her granddaughter could come to Harbour Cottages for a sleepover. Tamsin was planning a night out with Becca Hawkins, her friend who ran The Celtic Knot gift shop next door.

She needed some fun in her life, Morwenna thought, and she was glad to help out.

At four-thirty, the bell tinkled and Jane Choy stood in the doorway, looking round. A silence fell immediately among the customers, teacups in the air, forks pausing near mouths. Everyone assumed that Jane had come on official business to arrest someone. Morwenna stood, tray in hand.

'Hi, Jane.'

'Can we have a word?'

'Of course.' Morwenna was aware that heads were turning from Jane to her and back again, as if the customers were watching Wimbledon. 'Do you want a cuppa?'

'Let's take a walk,' Jane said enigmatically.

Morwenna offered her broadest grin; it was normal for her and Jane to spend time together. It wasn't at all what the punters thought: that she was being taken to a patrol vehicle and asked to come to the station. She turned to Tamsin, who was standing at a table, holding out a card machine. 'Is it all right if I pop out for a bit?'

'Of course,' Tamsin said. 'We're not too busy. Grandma will be back from school with Elowen at any moment – they'll have stopped for ice cream. We'll be fine – you go on.'

'I'll leave the bike.' Morwenna tugged off her apron, reached for a jacket and she and Jane stepped into the open air.

The beach was busy, seagulls swooping, the tide rolling in, holidaymakers relaxing. In the distance she could see a man dressed as a magician, surrounded by a group of children. He took off his hat and produced a toy rabbit and the children cheered.

Morwenna said, 'How are things going?'

She and Jane walked towards the sea wall, keeping pace. Jane spoke quietly. 'They think Irina drowned, but it wasn't an accident.'

'Oh?' Morwenna was intrigued. 'Are you allowed to tell me this?'

'It will come out anyway. Irina had bruise marks on the back of her neck, as if someone had grabbed her and she'd struggled.'

'So it was force?'

'Possibly. And there were other marks.'

'Bruises on her arms – I saw them,' Morwenna muttered. 'So – what do your colleagues think?'

'There are ructions already at the nick.' Jane forced a smile. 'Rick's trying to prove he's the best cop in the world to impress the new chief inspector. Have you met her?'

'I have,' Morwenna said. 'She seems on the ball.'

'That's one way of putting it. I'm keeping my head down. She and Rick clearly aren't a marriage made in heaven.'

'Oh?'

'He got Tom Fox in today. The poor man's lost his fiancée, he was grief-stricken. He had to identify the body.'

'That's awful.'

'But Rick thinks he's the star in a TV crime drama. He keeps saying things like "you have to start with the victim's partner" and "we have to dig deep beneath the surface". He thinks he's Inspector Morse,' Jane said.

'Who does the new chief inspector suspect?'

'She has a wider perspective. She's asking everyone to search for possible suspects in Seal Bay, people who knew Irina, who may have had a grudge, who she socialised with. Your name came up.'

'Did it?' Morwenna lifted her chin. 'Does she think I did it?'

'No – but she knows you're smart. She mentioned the other two crimes you helped solve and she told me directly that you were useful to the police because of your inside knowledge. She said you were perfectly placed in the library and the tearoom to keep your ear to the ground.'

'That's good.' Morwenna brightened. 'So, I'm almost part of the team.'

'It seems it's OK for you and me to talk from time to time,' Jane said. 'Of course, Rick's all for arresting Tom Fox, so that he's seen to have dealt with it. If he's said "short, sharp shock", "swift swoop" and "that man will get his collar felt" once today, he's said it ten times. You can tell Blessed thinks he's a numpty.'

'Perhaps he is,' Morwenna observed.

'She's certainly efficient – and straight-talking,' Jane said. They had reached the sea wall and they leaned against the railings. The sea lifted Morwenna's hair. Jane's was neat, a smooth bun beneath her hat.

Morwenna stared into the distance, where a trawler seemed to stand at the edge of the sea. There were several pleasure craft, white sails in the breeze. 'So – who's chief suspect?'

Jane shook her head. 'We have several names on the whiteboard – not so much suspects as avenues of investigation and persons of interest. Irina had a father, who lives in Sussex. He's been informed. He couldn't really help – he said she lived her own life. And she was known to so many people in Seal Bay because of her high profile.'

'I think she might have been on to something interesting,' Morwenna murmured.

'I remember you telling me her radio work in the bay had made her suspicious about something.' Jane narrowed her eyes. 'Where had she been on Sunday night? Why didn't she turn up at The Smugglers?'

'If we knew that, we'd know who killed her,' Morwenna said, her eyes on a seagull who was pecking at an empty carton on the sand.

Jane took a sharp breath – she had noticed something else. 'Well, will you look at that?' she exclaimed, pointing into the distance. 'Over there – those two kids. Are they doing what I think they're doing?'

'What? Where?' Morwenna asked, but Jane had taken off at a brisk pace, tearing down the stone steps onto the beach, marching across the sand. Morwenna hurried after her. She had no idea what was going on.

11

Morwenna scurried behind Jane, catching her up just as she paused in front of two teenagers who were sitting on a mat, huddled against the sea wall, sharing a handmade cigarette. One was a girl with long hair, braided at the sides, wearing a bikini top and shorts, who was inhaling deeply, closing her eyes. A book lay open in front of her, *Les Liaisons Dangereuses*, the pages dusted with sand. The other was a boy of the same age, wearing red swim shorts, his hair just starting to curl at the nape of his neck. The girl noticed that she was being watched and quickly passed the cigarette to the boy.

'We weren't doing anything.'

Morwenna recognised them both. Phoenix had borrowed the book from the library with the intention of appearing sophisticatedly French. Jonathan Tremayne was a handsome young man with his father's brown eyes, although they were currently wide with shock. Everything else about him resembled his mother, his light hair colour, his small frame.

Jane took a position facing the youngsters, folding her arms. 'Are you smoking what I think you're smoking?'

'No,' Phoenix said sulkily.

'Yes,' Jon Tremayne muttered. 'But we've never done it before. We've only been here for half an hour. We haven't done anything bad. Lots of people do it.' His voice trailed off. 'You won't tell my dad, will you? He'll go mental.'

'Where did you get the weed from?' Jane wanted to know.

Jon looked helplessly at Phoenix. He clearly had no idea.

'Some dude on the beach gave it to me. I don't know him.' Phoenix shrugged elaborately. 'A surfer. He was chatting me up. He gave it to me when I asked for a cigarette. I had no idea what was in it.'

Jane said, 'I'll have to follow procedure.'

'Oh, please,' Jon stammered, his face flushing. 'Can't we just say sorry?'

'You can't tell my parents,' Phoenix said histrionically. 'They'll kill me and you'll be responsible.'

Jane gave them an inscrutable look. 'Jon, how old are you?'

'Sixteen,' Jon said, as if it made all the difference.

'Under eighteen, then. Juveniles. And who are you?' Jane asked Phoenix. 'Do you live locally?'

'I'm Phoenix Rice. My parents have a holiday cottage. They are friends with Rick and Sally. Rick's had dinner round our house loads of times.' Phoenix's face took on a sulky expression. 'It's rubbish here. I hate it.'

Morwenna felt that she should be elsewhere. She touched Jane's arm lightly. 'I'll head back. Text me – there's a lot we need to talk about.'

'I will.' Jane turned her attention back to the teenagers. 'Now listen to me. You've both been foolish. I'm going to issue you with a warning.'

As Morwenna walked away, Jane was explaining gently to the youngsters what was going to happen next. She pressed her lips together in a smile as she approached the tearoom. Rick Tremayne's eldest son, smoking weed! And what had Rick always said to anyone who'd listen? Zero tolerance. He'd been on the radio, talking about the recreational drugs problem in Seal Bay. Morwenna recalled that he believed in short, sharp shocks.

She imagined the scene, Jon hanging his head as he was told not to do it again, Phoenix gazing around, not caring less, and immediately her sympathy was for Rick's son. He was only a kid. Morwenna wondered briefly if he was with Phoenix because their parents socialised, and if she was a bad influence. No, it was too easy to blame her. Jane would sort it out and they'd catch up later. Morwenna had other things on her mind. She turned her thoughts to what she was going to cook for dinner, since Ruan was coming round. She'd need to call in a supermarket on the way home and buy something tasty. Perhaps together they'd plan her next move.

She was determined to find Irina's murderer. She owed it to her. But most of all, Morwenna wanted some justice for Irina, who had trusted her, who had almost told her the whole explosive story. Before someone had stopped her forever.

* * *

That evening, much to her surprise, Morwenna somehow cooked a passable risotto. After they had eaten, she stood at the sink, her hands immersed in water, Ruan next to her holding a tea towel. The domesticity made her feel strangely nervous.

Ruan said, 'I can't imagine Rick being happy with his son smoking weed. It won't do his reputation any good.'

'I expect he'll blame Phoenix,' Morwenna muttered. 'She doesn't seem to be settling well in Seal Bay.'

'I'd heard Rick and Sally were friends with the couple who bought Half Moon Cottage.'

'Oh?'

'I was down the boathouse, talking to Damien. Rick and Sally have been to dinner with them. They're a professional couple, from Surrey, taking the summer off. It's all right for some.' Ruan wiped suds from a plate. 'He said Beverley got a good price for the cottage. She and Damien will use the money to get married, have a honeymoon and plough the rest into the boatyard.'

'How's business at Woon's?' Morwenna asked; Seal Bay gossip always came from a warm interest in others' well-being.

'Good – it's the summer. People want their boats in top condition.' Ruan avoided her eyes. 'The *Pammy*'s been out a lot: Pam Truscott and her brother love sailing.'

'I know Barnaby's back in Seal Bay.' Morwenna decided she'd get the awkward bit out of the way. 'I haven't seen him though.'

'Oh?' Ruan did his best not to look pleased. 'Right.'

'All the talk is of Irina.' Morwenna changed the subject as she handed him a wet plate.

'Everyone thinks it was murder,' Ruan said. 'The police don't appear to have any suspects. The word down The Smugglers is that Rick thinks it's Tom Fox.'

'Jane said the same – he was closest to her.' Morwenna held a wet fork over the sink, watching the water drip. 'I might pay Bay Radio another visit.'

'Another one? How many times have you been?' Ruan asked. Morwenna was impressed: he was quick. She took a breath.

'I broke in.'

'When?'

'The night after Irina didn't turn up at The Smugglers.'

Ruan held up a dripping dish. 'What did you do that for?'

Morwenna couldn't help but smile – he looked so astonished.

'I just had to. There was a window open around the back – I couldn't resist having a look around Irina's office.'

'Rick won't be impressed.' Ruan was trying not to laugh. 'You weren't seen?'

'It was half-five in the morning,' Morwenna said. 'I climbed in and took some photos, but someone came in and I hid under the table.'

'Someone came into the office at half-five?'

Morwenna nodded. 'I saw legs – I'm sure it was a man. He cleaned up the carpet, which was a bit weird.'

'Blood?' Ruan asked.

'Water, I think, or some other liquid.' She was cross with herself. 'I should have taken a sample.'

'You're in Forensics now?' Ruan teased.

'The man tidied the room, then he was gone and I climbed out of the window and came straight home – I had to get to the beach. Jane and I were going swimming.' Morwenna indicated her phone on the table. 'I haven't seen the photos yet – I haven't had a minute.'

Ruan dried the last fork. 'So – shall we have a look now?'

Morwenna met his eyes. 'You're as bad as I am, Ruan.'

They leaned over the table, shoulders touching, and Morwenna pressed buttons, bringing up pictures. The office was dimly lit, the corners grainy. Ruan pointed. 'That patch on the carpet is dark – you can see it's been soaked.'

'And look.' Morwenna indicated the desk. 'The desk is a mess. Do you think there was a struggle or was someone looking for something? The books and photos are all over the place.'

'Someone came back to tidy up?' Ruan said slowly.

Morwenna enlarged a photo of Irina's desk. 'Can you see the light patches? It's as if the sunlight through the window has affected the wood in some places and not others.' She met Ruan's eyes. 'That's where the photos of Irina and Tom would have been placed.'

'And her laptop,' Ruan added.

'The man took it away,' Morwenna remembered. 'When I crawled out from where I was hiding – look.' She showed him the photo of the desk surface, tidy now, photos in place, but the laptop had gone.

'What if he'd seen you?' Ruan was concerned. 'I wonder who came into the office, and at that time too.'

'They had keys – that narrows it down,' Morwenna said grimly. 'Unless someone stole a set.'

'Or had some cut,' Ruan said.

'The question isn't just who, but why? What were they looking for? The laptop? And why were they cleaning up? Were they the person who untidied the room in the first place?' Morwenna had an idea. 'I wonder if the diary and the file will throw any light on it.'

'What diary and file?' Ruan asked.

Morwenna produced the A5 diary and Irina's black loose-leafed folder that she'd hidden on top of books on her bookshelf.

'Did you take these from the office?'

'The file was in her drawer – beneath a piece of cardboard, as if she was hiding it,' Morwenna said.

She handed Ruan the diary and he began to leaf through. He said, 'She didn't use this much. Birthdays, that's all. It's virtually empty.'

'Where did she record things? Her laptop?' With deft fingers, Morwenna opened the folder and lifted out single sheets of paper. 'Right, what's this?'

'Dates.' Ruan looked over her shoulder, interested.

Morwenna traced the numbers with her finger. 'Mon J 24, Tues J 25, Wed J 26. 04:07. 10:35. 16:33. 23:10.'

'Definitely dates and times... appointments, perhaps,' Ruan said. 'Go on.'

Morwenna glanced through the notes.

H 4 m, L 1.7 m.

She wasn't sure what that meant, so she turned over the next page. There was more handwriting: Irina's?

Friday 28 June, 20 degrees... Sunshine, overcast, showers.

'It's a weather forecast for Seal Bay.' She was thoughtful. 'Irina need to know about the weather for when she was on location around the bay, I suppose, but why write it down?' She turned a page. 'Look, there are lots of locations in Seal Bay. She's written, "Scatterbee Fruit Farm, 12:00, Thursday. Woodpecker camping, 9:30 Friday." And more.'

'Local places she's visiting to interview people?' Ruan was puzzled.

'It could be.' Morwenna was thinking hard. 'I know Scatterbee Fruit Farm. A man called Pen delivers strawberries to the tearoom in the summer and veggies in the winter.'

'I know it too. It's quite a big place. They grow all sorts – daffodils, fruit. It's just outside Seal Bay,' Ruan said. 'I don't know where Woodpecker camping is – there are lots of sites around Seal Bay, full of campers this time of year.'

'We'll find out.' Morwenna turned the page. There were more notes, just scribbles on a page. 'I need to give all this some thought. I'll pay Tom Fox a visit tomorrow...'

'I can help,' Ruan offered. 'I'm worried about you, hiding under desks, taking risks. If you need a lift or someone to come with you, I'll tag along. Just so you're safe.'

Ruan was quiet for a moment and Morwenna knew what was going through his mind; she was too independent to ask for help, but he'd always felt a need to take care of her. He grinned. 'A great sleuth needs an assistant – I'm offering to be your Dr Watson. So, what have we got?'

'Times, places, weather forecasts?'

'Are we looking for a fisherman?' Ruan asked.

'It's certainly a recording of data,' Morwenna said.

'You should show it to Jane.'

'I will. Let's just have a think about it first.'

'Maybe we should go to some of the places, the fruit farm or the camp site. Maybe that would throw up some clues.'

'We should.' Morwenna looked at Ruan. There he was, as he'd always been, trustworthy, smiling, handsome, casual in jeans and T-shirt. His face was filled with that familiar affection. She said, 'Thanks, Ruan – I'll need to do some investigating. You're the first person I'll ask to come along.'

They stood opposite each other, silent, their gazes tangled. Ruan said, 'It was nice sharing a meal.'

'It was.' Morwenna wanted to say that they should do it more often, but something stopped her. Instead she said, 'It was just a meal.'

'I thought – if you're not seeing Pam's brother now...' Ruan began.

'I'm not,' Morwenna replied, wondering if he'd take it as a sign that she was available. He was looking at her in the old way, his eyes filled with warmth, and she felt the tug of affection, of something stronger. In a desperate effort to send out a different signal, she added, 'I'm happy by myself.'

'I'm always here though,' Ruan said softly. 'You know that, don't you?'

'I do, yes.' Morwenna wondered if he was going to kiss her. It worried her, all those tender feelings she'd had for as long as she could remember, now bottled up and confused. It was difficult to deny that they'd never really gone away. Morwenna asked herself what she'd do if he did kiss her – would she pull away? She ought to.

She felt her muscles stiffen in anticipation. He was still staring and she was staring back. Time ticked.

Finally, Ruan said, 'I suppose we had our chance years ago.'

'What do you mean?'

'We were good together. We still are. But you're happier now.'

'I am,' Morwenna said, without being sure if she was or not.

'Maybe one day?' Ruan murmured hopefully.

'Who knows?' Morwenna looked down at her hands. 'I suppose you'd like a cup of tea before you go back to number nine?'

'No – no, thanks, I won't.' Ruan took a step back, reaching for his jacket. 'I'll get off. The risotto was good though. Next time you can come across the road and I'll cook something.'

'Right,' Morwenna agreed. 'That might be nice.'

'It would.' Ruan threw his jacket over his shoulder. 'Well, I'll be getting on.'

'Of course. Night, Ruan.'

'Night.'

He didn't move immediately. Again, Morwenna wondered if he'd peck her cheek. Instead, Ruan turned towards the door and called back, 'I'll see you over the weekend. I'm taking Elowen out on Saturday morning – we'll meet up in the afternoon, when you finish at the tearoom, shall we?'

'OK,' Morwenna called after him. The door clicked as he left and the room was silent.

She plonked herself on the sofa. Where Ruan was concerned, she just didn't know how she felt. Her emotions were a yo-yo, and she certainly couldn't deny the past. They had been good together for years, but then there had been arguments, silences, too much distance. They had split up and it had hurt Morwenna more than anything had ever hurt in her life. The sadness and loneliness had been so difficult that she hadn't breathed properly for months. She couldn't let that happen again. And she wouldn't hurt Ruan. Besides, they were fine as they were, parents, grandparents, neighbours.

Exes.

Morwenna picked up Irina's folder and stared at it. She shuffled through the contents again; there were pieces of paper with random names, scribbled notes. She wondered what it all meant. She texted Louise quickly and said she might be half an hour late to the library tomorrow as she had something urgent to do first thing. Louise replied immediately that it was fine and she couldn't wait to find out if the ghost had left any more signs.

Morwenna sent a scream emoji, and leaned back into the sofa, closing her eyes, taking a deep breath. She had to get access to Bay Radio and talk to Tom Fox. There were things she needed to find out about Irina.

12

___

Morwenna was brushing her teeth in the bathroom the next morning when she heard a sharp knock at the front door. It was eight o'clock. The radio was on in the bedroom. Morwenna had set the dial to Bay Radio in the hope of picking up a random clue. Mike Sheridan's breakfast show crackled through the little speaker, music playing, Mike telling everyone that Thursday 4 July was going to be sunny all over the bay. Then he started making jokes. 'Why do Americans celebrate Independence Day on 4 July? Because it's the day Will Smith saved the Earth from aliens.' He followed it up with an exaggerated hooting sound, as if he were the funniest man in the world.

Morwenna didn't understand the joke. It puzzled her that Mike was playing cheery music, trying to make listeners laugh. She thought it might have been more appropriate to say something kind about Irina, that she'd been loved by the people of Seal Bay, she was bright and vivacious. She was badly missed. But Mike was chuntering away regardless, as if she'd never even existed. It didn't feel right.

There were questions she needed to ask.

The abrupt knock pounded from downstairs again and Morwenna hoped it was the postwoman, or at least someone who wouldn't take up her valuable time – she was dressed, breakfasted and raring to go. She bounded down the stairs, missing each alternate one, and flung open the door.

A smart man in expensive jacket and designer jeans was holding out the most beautiful bouquet of flowers. She gaped with surprise and immediately inhaled a waft of floral scent.

'Barnaby.'

'Morwenna.'

She'd forgotten that engaging smile, the twinkling eyes. She saw the bouquet and wondered what on earth he wanted. But it was obvious. Her heart sank: she hadn't planned for this, and she had no idea what to say, so she blurted, 'How are you?'

He moved, as if to take a step forward. 'Can I come in?'

Morwenna glanced over his shoulder at the sleek Jaguar parked beyond the gate. She shook her head. 'I'm on my way out.'

'Oh.' He looked disappointed. 'Are you off to work? Can I give you a lift to the library?'

'I have a call to make on the way there so no, thanks. But...' Morwenna felt she was being too negative. She tried again. 'How are you? How was the USA?'

'Oh, it was tremendous. I learned so much from the other surgeons. And the sailing was fantastic in San Francisco Bay. I came back last Thursday – I'm up at Mirador with Pam.'

'That's nice.' Morwenna wasn't sure what else to say.

'My son, Dom, and his family stayed with us for a few days. We've been showing them round Cornwall, going out on the *Pammy*. But now they've gone and I'm not due back in London for a while.' Barnaby held out the flowers again. 'I wanted to come round and say hi.'

'Hi,' Morwenna said. So he hadn't forgotten about her after all;

he'd called at the very moment that she'd decided to forget about him. She took the bouquet. 'These are lovely – thank you.'

He was smiling in a way that she found unnerving. His grin was too big, too hopeful. 'I wondered if we could – see each other. Maybe carry on where we left off?'

Morwenna wasn't sure whether to say yes or no. She had no idea if she wanted to date him again. It had been months; she'd just come to terms with the fact that their relationship was off and now it might be back on. But he was a nice man, good company, easy-going.

'We might.' She peered at him over the flowers. 'Can I message you?'

'Of course.' Barnaby's hands were free again. He waved them about a bit to show he was happy for her to message him whenever it was convenient. 'I can see I've caught you at a bad time.'

'I'm so busy,' Morwenna said behind the flowers.

'I heard about the murder – they found a woman's body on the beach.'

'Did you know her?' Morwenna asked.

'She was a reporter, wasn't she?' Barnaby said. 'No, our paths didn't ever cross.'

'Ah.' Morwenna remembered Irina saying something about Barnaby operating on her chin. 'I knew her well.'

'It's such a tragedy,' Barnaby said quickly. 'Pam says she was always interviewing people in the bay. Apparently, she had a magnetic personality... and a really sweet way with the people she spoke to.'

'She was nice all round,' Morwenna said sadly.

'Such a shame,' Barnaby repeated. 'I hope they find out who did it.'

'They will.' Morwenna was determined.

'Oh?' Barnaby seemed surprised. 'Are you working with the police?'

'Not exactly. But I liked Irina. It would be good to see the person who killed her behind bars.' Morwenna noticed his raised eyebrow. 'I'm just saying.'

'Well, do ring me soon – it would be good to catch up,' Barnaby said smoothly, glancing at his expensive watch. 'We can have dinner on the *Pammy*, or at the Marine Room. Or I could take you somewhere new.'

'I'd like that,' Morwenna said, and wished she hadn't been so effusive. Complying with men's requests without considering them first had never been the way of Mutton women. 'I'll give you a call. And – thanks again for the flowers. I'll see you soon, Barnaby.'

She turned and rushed into the house, the delicate, musky scent in her nose. Her head was too crammed with thoughts of Irina to think clearly about anything else. But ironically, the bouquet was what she needed – and she was sure Barnaby wouldn't mind it being put to good use on Irina's behalf.

* * *

Morwenna arrived at Bay Radio, the front entrance this time, with the bouquet stuffed in the basket of her bicycle. She swung a purple Lycra-clad leg over the red frame, whisked the flowers under her arm and rang the bell. A female voice crackled. 'Hello – do you have an appointment?'

'Trudi – it's Morwenna. I'm here to see Mike.' Morwenna knew the DJ would be in his studio.

'Morwenna?' Trudi clearly didn't remember her.

'Yes – I'm due here for eight-thirty,' Morwenna said, hoping she sounded believable.

Morwenna waited and after a while there was a click and the

door sprang open. Morwenna went inside. Trudi was waiting, the lanyard around her neck, her blonde hair loose, a look of disappointment on her face. 'Oh, it's you.'

Morwenna offered a huge placatory grin and waved the flowers. She was suddenly sombre. 'I've brought these.'

'Why?'

Morwenna lowered her voice. 'In memory of Irina. She and I were close.' She sniffed. 'I can't believe she's gone. Poor Tom.'

'He's in his office,' Trudi began.

'I have to give him the flowers. Lead on,' Morwenna said, already on the move.

Trudi looked dubious, but she opened the door with a swish of her card. 'Please can you wait?'

Morwenna waited in the room with the empty seats, listening to Mike's chirpy voice. 'And now it's the infectious surfing summer sound of The Beach Boys with their "Good Vibrations"...'

The main door was ajar and Morwenna had no intention of waiting. She pushed through onto the carpeted room where several people sat working on laptops. She paused. Trudi had reached the door to Mike Sheridan's studio. Mike was inside, seated at his turntables, talking to a tall, casually dressed man who was clean-shaven, his handsome face unhappy.

Trudi said, 'Tom, there's a woman outside who knew Irina.'

'Please, Mike, don't ask me this again.' Tom groaned, his voice clearly strained. 'The answer's still no.'

'But there's no one doing the community work. I'd be ideal for it, out in the town, talking to punters. Before you arrived, people said I was the voice of the bay.'

Tom said, 'That's the problem, Mike. You *were*. You've been on this radio station for ten years.'

'And you've been here for ten minutes, Tom. I get that this is your project, but I *know* the people of Seal Bay. I understand what they want.'

'You think they want you?' Tom said. 'You're hardly Irina.'

'She was all teeth and tittle-tattle – I'm sorry, Tom, but I could bring a gritty investigative line to our radio show. I could do a topic a week on the air, like Irina's stuff but no punches pulled. I could talk about the police, what a waste of space they are, about the emmets and the trouble they cause. It would be hard-hitting and muscular.'

'Believe me, Mike, you don't want to be doing that,' Tom said.

'Tom, there's a woman outside,' Trudi tried again.

The Beach Boys had finished their happy song and Mike was speaking to listeners again, his voice smooth and professional. 'And now let's keep the happy summer vibe going. Let's all get out there and have some fun in the sun with Martha and the Vandellas, "Dancing in the Street".'

'I've brought flowers,' Morwenna said, poking her head into the studio, holding up the bouquet. 'For Irina. To say how sorry I am.' She glanced at Mike. 'Perhaps you should play Eric Clapton's "Tears in Heaven"?'

Mike frowned. 'What's she doing here again?'

Morwenna ignored him and put on her saddest face. It wasn't difficult: she felt genuinely sorrowful. 'I brought these flowers, Tom. For Irina.'

'It's Maria Mutton, isn't it?' Tom marched out of the studio and closed the door behind him. 'Would you like to come to her office? Thank you for bringing flowers. Trudi, two teas – do you drink tea, Maria?'

'Morwenna, and yes, please, no sugar, just a dash of milk.' Morwenna was secretly delighted she'd found a way in. She thrust the flowers into Tom's hands and followed him as he led the way to one of the offices. He pushed open the door and they stepped inside. She recognised it immediately as Irina's.

'I'd like to put the flowers here. It was her workspace,' Tom said.

'Of course.' Morwenna glanced around. The carpet was dry now. The desk was tidy. The window was still ajar. The poster of Rina B in headphones had been taken down. She said quietly, 'Is this where Irina did her work?'

Tom slumped down at her desk, the chair revolving slightly as he did so. Morwenna glanced at the space beneath, remembering when she'd hidden there in semi-darkness and watched a pair of male legs walk around the office in expensive jogging bottoms. She noticed Tom was wearing jeans and black trainers. The photos of Tom and Irina were still on the desk; they hadn't been moved. Tom noticed Morwenna looking at them and sighed. 'We were getting married at Christmas.'

Morwenna knew. 'I'm surprised you allow Mike to play cheerful music. I mean – it's only been a few days...'

'We discussed it,' Tom said. 'Bay Radio is popular with locals and tourists. It's the sound of summer, the backdrop to the holiday season. We felt that Irina would expect us to give the punters what they wanted.'

'Who'll do her radio show?' Morwenna asked. 'The local flavour was what she excelled at.'

'I know.' Tom put his hands over his face. When he took them away, his eyes were filled with tears. 'I'm doing The Rina B Show for now, in her memory. But I'll advertise – get a new DJ. The show won't be a replacement for Irina's work though, going out into the community. We'll change the format completely.'

'Oh?' Morwenna raised an eyebrow.

'That was Irina's thing. We'll do something different now.'

'That's a shame,' Morwenna said. 'I loved what she did – she told me so much about it. And – did I hear right? Mike Sheridan wants to take on her investigative stuff?'

'Mike's a hack. He's just a lonely has-been, a divorced saddo who drinks alone most nights and feels bitter. I'd let him go if I could,' Tom said flatly.

Morwenna asked, 'Why do you keep him on?'

'I think he'd fall apart if he lost his job. It's all he has.'

'And Irina?'

Tom shook his head, half listening. 'The police still have no idea what happened.'

'Who have you spoken to?' Morwenna looked around for a seat. She noticed a winged armchair in the corner and settled down, offering her most interested expression.

'DI Tremayne.' Tom seemed distracted and troubled. It was hardly surprising. 'He just kept asking the same questions. He has no idea.'

'What about Jane Choy or Blessed Barnarde?' Morwenna deliberately used first names to imply that the police officers were her friends. Tom looked up sharply.

'I remember – you've helped the police out a couple of times.'

'I know them well. They trust me because of my... local knowledge.' Morwenna narrowed her eyes, gauging his reaction. He rubbed a hand over his face: he looked tired.

'You'll know the pathologist's report is out,' Tom said. 'And that Irina's death wasn't accidental or misadventure. Someone's responsible.'

'I'd heard as much. Poor Irina.' Morwenna wanted to encourage Tom to talk. 'She was special, so bright. Everybody loved her.'

'I loved her.' Tears brimmed in Tom's eyes.

'So who'd want to harm her?'

'People were jealous, I suppose. She was charming and smart.'

'But that's no reason to hate her.'

'Oh, hate keeps some people going,' Tom said sadly. 'And you're right – she was talented, beautiful. That's why someone killed her.'

'What do you mean?' Morwenna was interested.

'I don't mean anything really.' Tom shook his head. 'Except that it's too late now – she's gone. Nothing can bring her back.' He ruffled his hair, sat back in his seat and exhaled. 'Well, thanks for the flowers. It was very kind of you. I've no idea when they're going to release the—' He closed his eyes briefly, stood up and pushed a hand across his brow. 'I've a radio station to run. Trudi will show you out.'

'Of course. Thanks, Tom,' Morwenna said. 'I appreciate you letting me bring the flowers round. I know how hard it must be.'

'You have no idea,' Tom said. 'I'm sorry, Morwenna – I have things to do. Please excuse me.'

'Of course.'

Tom's face was etched with misery as he strode across the carpeted floor towards the studio just as Trudi appeared with a tray and two cups. She said, 'Oh – you won't be needing tea now.'

'Thanks – no. I ought to go. Tom's a busy man,' Morwenna said. She gazed around the office, her mind filled with jumbled thoughts.

Tom was clearly devastated by his fiancée's death. But instinctively she felt that there was something he wasn't telling her.

13

When Morwenna arrived at the library at ten to eleven, Louise had hardly noticed that she was late. She was far too excited about the ghost. Lady Elizabeth Pengellen had visited overnight, and Louise was phoning Pawly Yelland, Donald Stewart and someone at the Pengellen home to say that the phantom had left another message for the living.

Apparently, Lady Lizzie had been browsing through the poetry section and selected a book by a famous British poet, leaving it open on the reception desk at a significant page: Stevie Smith's poem 'Not Waving but Drowning'. It was a message from beyond the grave, Louise insisted. Lady Elizabeth wanted the world to know that poor Irina had been fighting for her life, waving an arm before she drowned. The pathologist was completely wrong. It must have been misadventure, not murder.

Morwenna explained that the poem was in fact an extended metaphor, the act of drowning being the death of the relationship between society and the individual. And the book had probably been left out by a customer. But Louise wasn't convinced.

Later, Morwenna arrived at the Proper Ansom Tearoom to see

a van parked outside with the doors open. The name on the side was Scatterbee Fruit Farm, surrounded by a design of bees, fruit, vegetables and flowers. The driver was an older man with a cap pulled down over large ears, a ready smile with a few teeth missing and a hairy chin. He clambered from the driver's seat, greeting Morwenna, his eyes sparkling. 'Ow be, my bewty?'

'Hello, Pen – *Myttin da*,' Morwenna said with a grin as she secured her bicycle. 'How are you feeling today?'

Denzel Penberth, called Pen by everybody in the bay, took off his cap, scratched his scalp, and replaced his hat with a flourish. 'I'm rufazrats. I'm a silly old tuss – I had a drop too much to drink last night. But I'll mend. How's your ansom mother? I haven't seen Lamorna for a while.'

'She's fine, Pen.' Morwenna recalled that he always flirted with Lamorna and Lamorna was never very flattered. Truth be told, she couldn't stand him. Morwenna thought him a little too familiar too. 'How long have you been working for Scatterbee Farm?'

Pen shrugged. 'Fifty-seven years, man and boy. I ought to retire. I'm pushing seventy.' He chuckled. 'I've seen some owners come and go. Years ago, Scatterbee was Cornish owned. For twenty years we had old John Trebullet, that teazy old fool from Penzance. Now we got these new people come from up country. You never see them, one day to the next. I suppose it's better that way. I like the quiet life now. Mind, I got some beans left in me – if your mum's got nothing to do one night, she should come round to my cottage. I'll show her a good time, tell her that from me.' Pen began to laugh, his shoulders shaking. Morwenna wouldn't say anything; Lamorna would let him know what she thought of that in two short syllables.

The tearoom door clanged open and Zach came out, holding his phone, texting, multitasking. 'Pen – I've come to get the strawberries...' He hurried round to the back of the van, trying to unload the fruit, phone in hand, and turned awkwardly to Morwenna. 'Can you hold this a minute, please?'

Morwenna took his mobile. It was open on the home page; a swish phone, not like her own basic one.

'I brought some blueberries and all,' Pen muttered. 'Tamsin asked me for some berries for her muffins.' He winked at Morwenna. 'Ansom maid, Tamsin, just like all the Mutton women.'

Morwenna watched him and Zach rush inside, each clutching a tray of fruit. She glanced at Zach's phone. It gleamed as she turned it over. She pressed the button that said 'Photos': after all, Zach studied photography – he wouldn't mind if she looked at a few pretty pictures of seals swimming around the bay.

The first photos that came up were of a young woman in a bikini, striking a model pose. His girlfriend, perhaps? Morwenna knew she shouldn't, but she continued to flick. There were photos of various women, not posing, oblivious that they were being photographed. Some were on the beach, others in various locations around Seal Bay, talking to friends, apparently unaware of the photography student who was snapping away. The one thing they all had in common was that they were young women. Morwenna caught her breath.

Irina.

Zach had taken so many photos of her, as she interviewed people, smiling, talking into her recorder. In one photo, she was surrounded by a crowd of people, asking questions. She had a wide smile, shining eyes: she'd loved her job. There was one of her sitting at a table in the tearoom, drinking coffee. Morwenna continued to look through the photos. There were three pictures of Tamsin, carrying a tray, talking to customers. Morwenna heard a noise. She flicked her thumb, quickly hiding the pictures.

Zach was at her side. 'Have you got my phone?'

Morwenna gave him a searching look. 'Fruit all packed in the kitchen, is it?'

'All done and dusted,' a voice came from behind her.

Pen made to slap her backside and Morwenna twisted away. 'That's off-limits, Pen, and you know it.'

'You can't blame a young man for trying.' Pen chuckled as he clambered into the van.

'Oh, I can.' Morwenna said. 'Some people need to know what boundaries are.' She handed the phone back to Zach meaningfully, and he scurried back to the kitchen. Morwenna stood outside for a moment, thinking. She'd talk to Zach later.

She went inside, wrapping her apron around her waist, scanning the tearoom. Lamorna was sitting with Susan and Barb Grundy, a cup of tea and a pasty in front of each of them. Lamorna waved. 'Pop over here. We're having a chat and we need your point of view.'

Morwenna looked around. Tamsin was serving a table with a large family, eight people. Sheppy, in his juggler suit, was drinking coffee, slumped comfortably on his chair. Several tourists were eating and drinking, chatting loudly. She'd be all right for a moment. She walked over to Lamorna's table and Tamsin followed her.

'What's going on, Mum?'

'We were talking about Irina.' Lamorna lowered her voice. 'It's on the radio. They think it's murder.'

Susan made a face. 'I always liked The Rina B Show. She wasn't afraid to speak her mind, that one.'

'Now she's drowned,' Barb added sadly. 'Bleddy shame.'

'But somebody drowned her – it wasn't an accident.' Lamorna's brow puckered. 'Tell me – how do they know that, Morwenna? I mean, when you're drowned, you're drowned.'

'Perhaps she was stabbed as well?' Susan said.

'Or maybe the body had been – you know...' Barb lowered her voice '...dismembered.'

'No, the pathologist does an examination,' Morwenna said gently. 'It's an official part of police work, that they check the cause of death.'

'Oh, that's gruesome. I wouldn't like anyone poking at my dead body,' Lamorna said.

'It's their job to determine what happened from the clues,' Morwenna explained. 'There were pressure marks on the back of the neck, I think.'

'Like someone had grabbed her?' Barb said.

'And held her under the water till she drowned?' Susan was shocked. 'Poor Rina B.'

'I expect her lungs were full of water too,' Lamorna said. 'I hope you don't mind us asking,' she added. 'We couldn't quite work it out, how the poor girl was drowned yet a killer was responsible.'

'We knew you'd know, being a sleuth.' Susan patted Morwenna's arm.

'You tell us if you need our assistance again,' Barb whispered. 'I proper enjoy finding new stuff out about people.'

Morwenna wasn't listening. Something that her mother had said was preying on her mind. She walked away, drifting towards Sheppy's table. He met her eye, his a little guilty. She offered a grin. 'All right?'

Sheppy took his feet from the chair. 'How do, Morwenna?'

'Good. How's business?'

'Fair to middling,' Sheppy said. 'A lot of the parents on the beach want me to entertain the kids for free. And Farmer Rodgers at Woodpecker is talking about the rent going up. He collects the money for someone else who owns the caravans. It's not as if those caravans are even clean – there are as many rats as residents.'

'What's the name of the site again?'

'Woodpecker.'

'Where is it?' Morwenna asked. She'd heard the name before.

'On Polkerris Hill, overlooking the bay. It's a lovely site for the view, but it's become well run-down.' Sheppy grinned. 'It's like the Ritz for paupers. You can't get a caravan up there for love nor money. It's full up.'

'Do the emmets rent there?'

'Oh, the residents tend not to mix much – they're all out in the daytime. It's summer. And the place is cheap and dog rough.' Sheppy laughed. 'Stay away, that's my advice.'

Morwenna glanced around. 'Do you want a cup of anything?'

'Tea?'

'And hevva cake?'

'If you're offering.'

Morwenna glanced down at Sheppy's feet, where he'd placed a plastic bag of shopping. Sheppy tried to cover it with his jacket quickly, his expression suddenly too innocent. Morwenna sat down and put her face close to his. Her voice was a whisper. 'Is that a Proper Ansom Tearoom mustard squidger in there? And a tomato sauce bottle? I see they're missing from the table.'

Sheppy closed his eyes for a moment. 'I didn't mean to rob them.'

'They fell into your bag by accident, then?' Morwenna offered him a half-smile.

Sheppy's mouth twisted in embarrassment. 'I like a bit of sauce with a pasty. The ones I eat in the caravan are dry and cold.'

'Heat them up, then.'

'The microwave doesn't work.'

Morwenna stared at him. His cheeks were gaunt. His eyes were ringed with dark shadows. 'What did you have for breakfast?'

Sheppy shrugged. 'Cornflakes.'

'With milk?'

'No, just out of the box. I needed to go to the supermarket – the cupboard was bare back at the caravan and the fridge is broken. I just bought milk and bread and beans – that's all I could afford.'

'How much money did you make this morning?'

'A tenner – and twenty-seven pence,' Sheppy said.

Morwenna said, 'Do you want some food?'

'Oh, I couldn't ask again.'

'If you come here when we're closing, I'll give you what's left over, a pasty, a bit of cake, scones, some fruit, a bottle of milk.'

Sheppy was surprised. 'Why would you do that?'

'Because you're hungry.'

'But I nicked your sauces.'

'Put them back, then,' Morwenna said simply. 'And next time, ask.' She patted his cheek. 'That's your first lesson in understanding Cornish hospitality.'

'Thanks, Morwenna,' Sheppy said gratefully, but she was on her way, clearing a table of cups and saucers, calling cheerily to Tamsin that table three wanted more tea. But as she worked, her mind was racing. This lunchtime had given her a lot of things to think about. Two things, certainly. Once she was home, and had some time to herself, she'd work it all out.

* * *

At five-thirty, Sheppy called back from his juggling session on the beach. He'd made another fifteen pounds. Morwenna sent him off as promised with a few food items she'd collected. Lamorna was sitting with Elowen in the corner, arguing over a mathematical problem. Elowen said that her great-grandma was doing the homework all wrong. Morwenna was just settling down with Tamsin for a chat over a glass of lemonade when the bell chimed and Jane Choy stood in the doorway, removing her hat, looking tired.

Tamsin jumped up. 'I'll get you a pot of tea, Jane. No doubt you've got things to talk about.'

'Developments?' Morwenna asked, raising an eyebrow.

'I'll say.' Jane sat down, disgruntled. 'It's mayhem at the police station.'

'Oh?' Morwenna leaned forward. 'What's happened?'

'Rick is like a man with ants in his pants since his son was given a warning about smoking weed. He thinks there's a drugs ring in the bay and he wants arrests made. He's been shouting all day that we should step up a police presence, to pull in the people responsible for supplying drugs to his son, who's a minor and therefore vulnerable. He's made friends with the couple who have the holiday cottage over at Pennance Hill and he wants to impress them. Their daughter's quite precocious – Phoenix Rice.' Jane took a breath. 'She was the one with Jon. Phoenix claimed to have got the weed from someone on the beach. I wasn't really going to make a fuss about it, but the way Rick is talking, unless we step things up, Jon will be a crack addict by the end of the week.'

'What does Blessed say?'

'She agrees we should keep our finger on the pulse, but she's more concerned about The Cream Tea Killer.'

'The what?' Morwenna tried to stifle a smile.

'Haven't you heard Mike Sheridan's latest radio show?'

Morwenna shook her head. 'What's he said?'

'The last hour of his show today was dedicated to Rina B.'

'Irina? I thought they weren't going to mention her on Bay Radio. Tom Fox said this morning that he wanted to keep things upbeat.'

'Don't you think that's strange?' Jane asked, offering Tamsin a smile as she placed a tray of tea and biscuits in front of her. 'Tom's just lost his fiancée, but he doesn't appear to be grieving.'

'I spoke to him in Irina's office this morning and he was in tears,' Morwenna remembered. 'Mind you, someone had taken the Rina B Show poster down.'

'I bet it was Mike. He's started playing sad songs in her memory and he said several times on the show that he intends to find out who killed her. Blessed has been round to the studio to advise him not to talk about it on air.' Jane took a breath. 'He's nicknamed Irina's murderer The Cream Tea Killer.'

'Why?'

'Because it happened in Cornwall. Because it's catchy. Because Mike Sheridan fancies himself as the new Seal Bay Sleuth – he even called himself that – and promised to bring whoever killed Irina to justice.'

'That's strange. He didn't even like her – he was jealous of her.' Morwenna poured tea into two cups. 'When I went in to ask him and Tom if they'd seen Irina on Monday morning, Mike said something along the lines of "I've no idea where she is and frankly – why would I care?" So he clearly wasn't a fan.'

Jane met her eyes. 'Who's in the frame for this, Morwenna?'

'You're asking me?'

'I trust you – you're intuitive.'

'I'm giving it some thought,' Morwenna said enigmatically. 'Ask me in a day or two – I'm working on it.'

'There are a couple of MCIT hanging around the bay, keeping their ears open, since Irina was discovered. Blessed wants to find out who's guilty of the foul play – she's keeping Tom on her radar. The pathologist's report says the body was bruised, as you know.'

'And was there water in the lungs?' Morwenna asked.

'I'm fairly sure.'

'Sea water?'

'As opposed to...?'

'Can you check, let me know?' Morwenna was thinking the same thought she'd had earlier. 'What if poor Irina was dead before she hit the sea? We need to be thinking about who might want her dead and why. She was about to tell me something important last Sunday night. I have a few leads I'm working on – but things don't add up. Blessed's right – there's been foul play – but we're missing a crucial clue somewhere. We have to work out what it is. Something's not quite right here, Jane.'

14

'You should go out with him, even if it's only to find out how you feel,' Louise said, folding her arms. 'I mean, you might fall in love with him – he's very handsome and his sister has a lovely boat.'

'Maybe.' Morwenna looked around. The library was neat and tidy. Lady Elizabeth Pengellen's ghost hadn't visited last night, so Louise needed something interesting to discuss and Morwenna's love life had come up.

'I suppose I could see him one more time,' Morwenna said, wrinkling her nose. 'He's a nice man, good company. I just don't know where it's going.'

'It could become the real thing,' Louise coaxed.

'I don't think so. I'm too long in the tooth.'

'And I think you still aren't over Ruan.' Louise looked pleased with herself.

Morwenna sighed, leaning against the reception desk. 'Ruan and I know each other. We've settled to being friends.'

'You care for each other.'

'As friends.'

'I don't know so much.'

Morwenna rubbed a hand across her brow. She felt tired. 'To be honest, Louise, I'm more concerned about who killed Irina at the moment.'

'The Cream Tea Killer?' Louise said. She'd heard Mike's show too. 'Do you think it might have been an emmet? Someone who was visiting the bay and got on the wrong side of her, maybe pushed her in the water?'

'I'm not sure. My instincts tell me it was someone she knew.'

'She knew half of Seal Bay – and those she didn't know personally knew her from The Rina B Show. Steve says he used to listen to it when he was driving his lorry. He says she was very good. Of course, I told him I don't get time to listen to the radio, working all day in the library.'

'I think she'd stumbled on something,' Morwenna said.

'Could it be something illegal? I hear Rick Tremayne's son was caught selling drugs on the beach.'

'He wasn't selling drugs; he was smoking a bit of weed with Phoenix Rice.'

'Who?'

'The girl who borrowed *Dangerous Liaisons*.'

'She's an uppity little madam, if you ask me. I bet Rick's furious.' Louise's thoughts returned to love. 'So – are you going to go out with Barnaby?'

'I don't know.'

'Please ring him, Morwenna. You said he gave you beautiful flowers – you ought to at least talk to him.'

'I will.'

'When?'

'Later?'

'No – there's no time like the present. I'll make us a fresh brew and you can ring him.'

'All right.' Morwenna recalled her conversation with Barnaby outside her house as he'd handed her the flowers. What had he said about Irina? That their paths hadn't ever crossed. But that wasn't what Irina had said.

Yes, she'd see him again, even if it was only to find out why he was lying.

She picked up her phone and paused. She wanted to see him on neutral territory. Inviting him round for a meal might be risky. Taking him to The Smugglers wasn't ideal – too many people knew her there, and Ruan would be at the bar, drinking with the other fishermen. She wasn't sure she wanted her ex to be in the background if she was buying Barnaby a pint and a pie.

The perfect place came to her, and she pressed a button. The phone rang for a while until a gravelly voice said, 'Morwenna, good to hear from you.'

'Hello,' Morwenna said cheerily. 'I wanted to say thanks again for the flowers.'

'I'm at Woon's boatyard – I'm about to go out with Pam on her boat,' Barnaby replied. 'I wish you were coming.'

'Well, I wanted to invite you somewhere.'

'Oh?'

'Are you doing anything tomorrow night?'

'Not if I can be with you,' he said.

'Right, then – I'll take you to Seal Bay funfair.'

'A funfair?' Barnaby was quiet.

Morwenna knew that wasn't the sort of date he'd had in mind. She tried to sell it to him. 'And I'll buy you chips.'

'All right.' He laughed lightly. 'I'll look forward to it. What time shall I pick you up?'

'Seven?' Morwenna suggested.

'Perfect. I'll see you tomorrow evening.' He sounded delighted now. 'It's been a long time since I've been to the funfair. I'll try and win you a prize at the shooting gallery.'

'We'll have a great time.' Morwenna grinned into the phone. 'I'm looking forward to it.'

'Me too,' Barnaby said and the phone crackled. Morwenna wondered if she'd been too encouraging. She'd intended it to be a very casual meeting in which she explained that they were friends, nothing more. At least that was what she thought right now; with Barnaby next to her, suave and persuasive, she had no idea what she'd feel tomorrow.

Morwenna put her phone down and looked up into the bright blue eyes of a blonde-haired young man. She wondered how long he'd been there, listening. She recognised him immediately; the last time she'd seen him, they'd almost bumped into each other in the library corridor.

'Tristan,' she said with a smile. 'What can I do for you?'

He gave her the sort of complicit grin that suggested he knew that she'd just been arranging a date on the phone. 'Have you got Pawly Yelland's book?'

'*Hidden Secrets of Seal Bay*? I think it's out on loan.'

'Oh, OK,' Tristan Pengellen said. 'I just thought I ought to read it, since he's going to be working with my parents on this Victorian project.'

'How are Julian and Pippa?'

'Dad's in London and Mum's busy with food banks and charities. Dad laughs at her and calls her Lady Bountiful, but I think she's doing great work. She heard somewhere that one in five people in Cornwall live in poverty, and the unemployment rate is nearly double the national average. Dad's a bit focused on his work, although Mum's winning him round to donating a bit more.' Tristan smiled and Morwenna was reminded how handsome he was. 'I'm in London most of the year, but while I'm in Seal Bay for the summer, I help my mother. It's what the Pengellens have always done, and it's as important now as ever.'

Morwenna thought what a nice young man he was, although she'd only met him a few times. She had to ask. 'Did you know Irina Bacheva?'

'I heard her show once or twice. Rina B. Mum knew her – they worked together on a few local projects to help single-parent families and mums on low incomes. It's a real shame.'

'What does Pippa think happened?'

'In all honesty?' Tristan met her eyes. 'Mum thinks that Irina wasn't afraid to stand up for the underdog and that she had waded into something a bit deep.' His expression was sad. 'No pun intended.'

'Pippa thinks she'd found something out?'

'Irina was an investigative journalist,' Tristan said simply. 'Mum told me that she was a smart woman, and that she wouldn't be surprised if she got into trouble because she was so outspoken.'

'Right.' Morwenna let the thought sink in. 'Shall I let you know when Pawly's book is back in the library? I ought to buy in an extra copy.'

'I'll buy my own – and get Pawly to sign it,' Tristan said. 'Thanks, Morwenna. I'll be seeing you.'

Morwenna watched him go as Louise returned with two mugs of tea. She gave Morwenna a friendly nudge with her elbow. 'Did you arrange a date?'

'Date?' Morwenna had forgotten already. Her mind had been on Irina. 'Oh, with Barnaby. Yes – I'm taking him out tomorrow.'

'Where to?'

'The funfair.' She offered Louise an enigmatic Mona Lisa smile. That was enough information for now.

* * *

The afternoon in the tearoom whizzed by, one tray of cream teas following another, then the empties had to be cleared away. Zach was busy in the kitchen; Morwenna had no time to talk to him, although she kept her eyes peeled for a convenient moment to pounce. Tamsin was in a good mood; she and Becca were going out on the town.

Visitors to the tearoom came and went; Elowen arrived with Lamorna, each carrying a pink ice cream, and went upstairs to pack an overnight bag. Elowen declared she needed toys and clothes for her sleepover, despite Lamorna saying that in her day all she'd take to a friend's was a pair of pyjamas and a toothbrush and if it was a male friend, she wouldn't take the pyjamas. Tamsin shot her grandmother a look; Elowen didn't need leading astray – she was already a handful.

By five Morwenna was wiping tables and Tamsin was vacuuming the floor. They were both exhausted. Tamsin had put the kettle on for a much-needed cuppa when the kitchen door opened and Zach came out wearing a jacket, carrying his phone. He avoided Morwenna's eyes and turned to Tamsin. 'I'll see you tomorrow.'

Morwenna straightened, cloth in hand. 'Are you leaving early, Zach?'

'I arranged it with Tamsin,' he said hurriedly. 'Mum has a doctor's appointment. I have to take her.'

'Oh?' Morwenna raised an eyebrow and Tamsin sent her a 'don't say any more, I'll explain later' look.

'Have a nice time tonight, Tam. I'll see you tomorrow, Morwenna.'

'Yes – we need to catch up,' Morwenna said and Tamsin shot her another look. They watched him leave. Tamsin poured two teas, bringing them over just as Lamorna opened the door that led to the flat upstairs.

'Make that a third cup – that little heller's driving me mad.'

'Elowen?' Tamsin looked concerned.

'She's got all her clothes out of the drawer and she's trying them on to take to Harbour Cottages.' Lamorna fanned her face as if she was hot. 'I just came down to grab a couple of pieces of carrot cake. I need the energy from the sugar and Elowen needs something stuffed into her mouth to shut her up.'

Elowen burst into the tearoom. 'Why do I need shutting up, Great-Grandma? You said women need to speak up for themselves and I always speak up.' She carried Oggy Two under her arm. 'I can't wait to go to your house, Grandma. Will Brenda sleep on my bed?' She turned to Tamsin. 'I like Grandma's house best. Grandma has a pet.'

'Where's Zach?' Lamorna asked, to change the subject.

'He's gone home early to take his mum to the doctor's.' Tamsin lowered her voice. 'She has terrible menopause symptoms.'

'So did I.' Lamorna groaned. 'The hot flushes were non-stop and, oooh, you wouldn't believe the night sweats.'

Morwenna pulled a face. 'I don't really remember it.'

'You were too busy fighting with Dad,' Tamsin countered.

Elowen piped up, 'What's the many paws?'

Tamsin opened her mouth, about to ask Elowen if she'd like cake or a scone, when Lamorna pointed to the window. 'There's a suspicious man loitering out there. He looks like he wants to speak to one of us. I hope it's not me.'

Morwenna looked up to where Rick Tremayne, bulky in a beige overcoat, was standing outside the large window, gesticulating wildly. Morwenna pointed at herself. 'Do you want to talk to me?'

He nodded exaggeratedly, and Morwenna was reminded of one of the dog toys that sat in the back of a car, wobbling its head as the engine vibrated. She turned to Tamsin. 'I'll take my tea outside and see what he wants.'

She ignored Lamorna's open mouth; her mother was about to offer to come with her. Lamorna wasn't Rick's greatest fan and if Morwenna was going to back-chat him, she wanted to be there.

Morwenna stepped outside and closed the door behind her, a mug clutched in her hand. 'Rick.'

Rick Tremayne smelled overpoweringly of excessive after-shave. 'Morwenna. I need a word.'

'You're welcome. You can have more than one. Why don't you come inside, take the weight off, have a coffee?'

'I won't come in, not today.' He shook his head, stuck a finger in his ear and inspected the end. 'You've heard about The Cream Tea Killer?'

'Is that what you're calling the murderer at the station now?' Morwenna asked.

'The name's stuck. That's what they're putting in the papers. The person who killed Irina of Rina B's show.' Rick grunted as if he had indigestion. His face was waxen. 'I shouldn't have had the gherkins with my lunch.'

'I haven't had time for lunch, and I'm ready to go home for something to eat,' Morwenna said. 'What can I do for you, Rick?'

'Well, you've been useful in the past.'

'Useful?' Morwenna frowned.

'Helping the police.'

'Oh,' Morwenna said. 'Are you offering to put me on the payroll?'

Rick wiped his forehead. He was sweating. 'I'm under a bit of pressure thanks to the chief inspector from the Met with her modern methods. I need to find out who killed Irina.'

'And it might be good to take a dangerous person off the streets too,' Morwenna added.

'So – if you hear anything.'

'I'll tell you, of course. Or Jane.'

'Jane Choy's just a police constable.'

'And my friend,' Morwenna said.

'If it's important, I want to know.' Rick puffed out his chest. 'I'm DI. I should be the first person you call.'

'Right,' Morwenna said. 'So are you going to start coming swimming with me and Jane on Sunday mornings?' Rick opened his eyes wide. He hadn't realised Morwenna was joking. She patted his arm. 'Don't worry. You don't need to bring your wetsuit just yet. Speedos will do.'

Rick was looking more and more concerned. He still wasn't sure if Morwenna was serious. He said, 'The thing is, I need to be seen to solve this crime. Irina was well respected. And there may be a killer at large.'

'I couldn't agree more.'

'So – do you have any clues?' Rick persisted.

'I'll give it some thought,' Morwenna said. He was still staring at her. 'Will that be all, DI Tremayne?'

'One more thing.' Rick shifted the weight from one foot to another. Morwenna thought he looked as though he had something to hide.

'Name it.'

'I'd be grateful if you didn't say anything about...' Rick wiped his forehead, his hand shaking. 'About Jon being caught on the beach.'

'Of course I won't,' Morwenna said. 'It's a stage he's going through. Many kids try marijuana and don't bother again. Didn't you?' She met his eyes and he looked away.

'No, never.' He was lying.

Morwenna smiled kindly. 'It wouldn't have been for me either. I don't like any kind of smoking. But I won't say anything, Rick.

Kids are just kids. They make mistakes, they give their parents headaches. But we still love them.'

Her mind drifted to Tamsin, coming back from the holiday pregnant with Elowen. The child clearly looked like her father. Whoever he was. She had dark hair and dark eyes, nothing like Tamsin. She and Ruan had offered their daughter nothing but support. She patted Rick's arm. 'Your boys are delightful. I won't gossip – it's not my way. Give Sally my love, and get on home, enjoy some family time.'

'I will,' Rick grunted and turned, shambling away across the road to where his car was parked. Morwenna turned back to the tearoom and exhaled. She felt sorry for him.

Her phone pinged with a message from Jane. She read it quickly and caught her breath.

JANE

> You know what you said about the autopsy? Well there's been a development. I need to talk to you soon. Ring me.

15

Morwenna sat in the living room on the sofa, Elowen next to her, Brenda between them, as she thumbed a reply to Jane.

MORWENNA

> Elowen in bed in an hour. Do you want to come round then?

The phone pinged back moments later with a thumbs up. Morwenna leaned into the cushions. 'How was your dinner, Elowen? Do you like sweetcorn?'

'I like holding it in my hand and chewing the yellow bits and they fall everywhere and I'm just like a dog with a bone.' Elowen was suddenly animated. '*You* think I need a dog, don't you, Grandma?'

Morwenna was ready. This was the perfect moment. She'd been meaning to have this conversation for a while. 'When you can prove you're grown up enough, we can talk about it.'

'I am grown up enough, I'm six. I'm seven on 13 October.'

'So, what do you think being grown up means, Elowen?'

Elowen looked hopeful. 'Being good. Feeding a dog every day.

Taking him for walks.' She thought for a moment. 'Helping Mummy. Not being cheeky to Miss Parker.'

'Mmm.' Morwenna showed Elowen her serious face. 'And do you think you're grown up yet?'

Elowen nodded furiously.

'Don't you think you've got a bit of a way to go?'

'I'm nearly there,' Elowen insisted.

'What do you need to do next?' Morwenna asked. 'To be more grown up?'

'I need to stop hitting Billy Crocker.'

'When did you last hit Billy Crocker?' Morwenna asked tentatively.

Elowen put a finger against her cheek, pretending to think. 'Yesterday.'

Morwenna had heard rumours from Tamsin of a fight – Imelda Parker had phoned home in the usual way. 'Why did you hit him?'

'He said something about my daddy.'

Morwenna paused. This was going to be difficult. 'What did he say?'

'He said he'd heard that my mummy went to the carry out on holiday and she came back with me in her belly.'

Morwenna said, 'She went to the Caribbean on holiday and came back with you in her belly.' She ruffled Elowen's hair. 'That's OK.'

'It hurt my feelings and I felt like thunder and lightning inside.'

Morwenna took Elowen's hand. 'We all feel like that sometimes.'

'So I hit him in the face. It wasn't just me. The thunderstorm in my heart did it really.'

'I get that. I honestly do.' Morwenna looked at the child with affection. 'And being grown up is when you can make the thunder and lightning be quiet and you use your brain to think through the problem sensibly. The way of peace is best. The way of violence never works.'

'Never?'

'Never.'

'But I felt better when I thwacked him.'

'Did Billy feel better?'

'No – his nose bled a tiny bit and Miss Parker sent me outside to calm down, but I was calm because I'd hit him. Grandma?' Elowen's eyes shone. 'Does that mean I can't have a dog?'

'It might mean you're not quite ready for one yet.' Morwenna took Elowen's hand and placed it on the cat purring between them. 'But you can practise being calm and grown up on Brenda until you are ready.'

Elowen nodded furiously. 'I'll try the way of peace. I'll do my best.'

'Good.' Morwenna kissed the top of her head. 'That's all we can ask for. Now it's time you went upstairs, put pyjamas on and cleaned your teeth.'

'Is Grandad coming round, or Jane? Will you sit up till all hours drinking whisky?' Elowen thought for a moment. 'That's another part of being grown up, isn't it?'

'Being sensible about everything is grown up,' Morwenna said. 'Now up you go.'

Elowen slid down from the sofa and planted a huge kiss on Brenda's head. 'Grandma?'

'What is it, my bewty?'

'Billy Crocker told everyone in our class that PC Ploddy Plod's son got arrested on the beach for smoking marinara – is that true?'

Morwenna tried not to smile. 'No, it's not true. Off you go.'

'And...' Elowen was playing for time. 'Can I stop going to school now it's summer? I've learned enough.'

'There are two more weeks until the end of term,' Morwenna said. 'Elowen – no one has ever learned enough.'

'Not even you, Grandma?'

'Especially not me. Now, up you go. I'll follow you in a minute or two, when you have your PJs on.'

Morwenna watched Elowen scurry up the stairs; she leaned over to the bookcase and plucked out Irina's folder. She opened it up again, staring at handwritten notes.

Scatterbee Fruit Farm, 12:00, Thursday.

Scatterbee was where Pen worked and where Tamsin bought her fruit.

Woodpecker camping, 9:30, Friday.

Sheppy lived in a caravan there. He had told her it was a dive with lots of rats. It was always quiet during the day. The rent was about to go up.

Morwenna decided she should visit both places, soon. She might discover a clue about why Irina went there. And it would be easy to snoop around without arousing much suspicion. She glanced at Irina's final entry on the page and read all the dates again. There was one she hadn't noticed.

Elsa Kerr, Saturday, 22:45.

Morwenna had no idea who Elsa Kerr was. A local woman, perhaps. Elsa was the sort of name someone very young would have, or someone very old. She'd research her and see if she came up on the Internet later. But the most important fact was that Irina had been scheduled to meet her the day before she and Morwenna had swum together, the day she had been killed. What had happened between that meeting and Irina's death? Morwenna was sure she could find an answer.

* * *

There was a light knock at the front door at nine o'clock and Morwenna opened it to see Jane and Blessed Barnarde in casual clothes, both wearing jeans and leather jackets. Blessed wore diamond stud earrings. Jane's long hair was loose around her shoulders, the texture of fine silk. Morwenna invited them in and they huddled together on the sofa, each clutching a glass of whisky. Brenda scampered upstairs to Morwenna's bedroom; it was her way of telling her owner it was time for bed.

Blessed came to the point. 'What do you have for us?'

'Nothing yet, not exactly,' Morwenna said, aware that she was concealing evidence. 'A few clues but nothing concrete. My feeling is that Irina was on to something, that her killer is local and that the radio show is somehow involved.'

'And Tom Fox? Where do you think he fits in?' Blessed narrowed her eyes.

'I'm not sure. I think he genuinely cared for Irina.' Morwenna remembered something. 'Mind you, she told me she and Tom had been arguing the night before she was killed.'

'Arguing?' Jane wanted to know more.

'They'd been to The Marine Room. She said he'd been moody and they came away without pudding.' Morwenna was unsure. 'That doesn't mean he killed her, of course.'

'It builds a picture,' Blessed said. 'Jane said you asked if the water in her lungs was sea water. I had it checked. It wasn't.'

'What was it, then?' Morwenna asked.

'The pathologist said it was fresh water, not salt, ordinary H_2O,' Blessed said.

'It could be river water, drinking water,' Jane suggested.

'Ah,' Morwenna said. 'Interesting. So someone drowned Irina first?'

'Yes, and then dumped her body in the sea to make it look like an accident,' Blessed said grimly. 'We're looking for the person who put the bruises on the back of her neck.'

'Any other clues from Pathology?' Morwenna asked.

'The attacker had medium to large hands, strong,' Jane said. 'Probably a man, but not definitely.'

'Do you think Mike Sheridan's involved?' Blessed turned to Morwenna. 'What do we know about him?'

Jane chewed her lip. 'He coined the phrase The Cream Tea Killer. Can you imagine if he was talking about himself? It wouldn't surprise me – he's an odd man. It could be him, glorifying Irina's murder to his listeners on the radio, smug in the knowledge that he did it.'

'I wouldn't rule anything out at this stage,' Blessed said and Morwenna saw a look exchange between them.

Jane seemed pleased with herself. 'We could bring him in for questioning – what do you think, Morwenna?'

Morwenna was surprised to be asked. 'I suppose so. We know that Mike was professionally jealous of Irina. He didn't get on with Tom either. Mike's an old-school sort of DJ – he worked on the radio before Tom took it over and he wants to take on the investigative side of reporting but Tom has said no.' Morwenna was quiet for a while, remembering the conversation. 'I've been assuming Irina died on the Sunday because she didn't show up for our meeting, but could she have been alive longer and prevented from coming? She wanted to share her ideas with me. She said something big – explosive – was happening in Seal Bay.'

'Let's think about that. What might she have meant by it?' Blessed sipped her whisky thoughtfully. 'You don't mind us picking your brain, Morwenna? You have local knowledge.'

'Drugs ring? Prostitution?' Jane wondered. 'Money laundering?'

'It could be any of those,' Morwenna said. 'Fraud?'

'Firearms?' Blessed added.

'We need to find out.' Morwenna reached for her glass. She wondered guiltily if she should tell them that she had broken into Irina's office and that she had taken her folder. It was sitting a few feet away from Blessed, horizontally placed on some books on the bookshelf.

Morwenna had a question. 'Have you found anything useful in Irina and Tom's house? Or at the radio station?'

'Nothing important,' Jane said. 'We checked both out. Their wedding was organised for December, so Tom clearly intended them to marry. She'd even bought a dress – it was in a wardrobe in the spare room. Then I also had a look around her office at Bay Radio.'

'Oh?' Morwenna remembered the open window.

'There was no laptop there. Tom said she didn't use one much, which I thought was odd, given her role,' Jane admitted.

'That's strange,' Morwenna agreed quickly.

'Tom said she committed everything she investigated to paper. We've taken away her notebooks but nothing of interest has come up.' Blessed shrugged. 'What are we missing?'

'What about her phone?' Morwenna asked.

'It was in her handbag, washed up on the beach,' Jane said sadly.

'We got a warrant to request her call records from the mobile phone service provider.' Blessed had finished her drink. 'I'll check the information when it comes through.'

Morwenna decided that she ought to mention Irina's notes soon. She just needed to check once more. 'So – I'm working in the tearoom tomorrow, but I'm going to finish early and look through all the information I've got. Something has to jump out at me.'

'Do you have a lead?' Blessed turned sharply.

'I'm not sure yet. I just feel I'm missing something big that could be staring me in the face. We've got the SWANs swim on Sunday morning. I'll have more idea then,' Morwenna said quickly.

'I'll be there,' Jane added.

'If I can get out of the office, I'll come too – a swim would be good,' Blessed agreed. 'We've got MCIT with us still because it's a murder. Seal Bay will be flooded with plainclothes detectives this weekend.' She almost smiled. 'I thought about moving to MCIT. It's such interesting work. It certainly beats interviewing suspects under caution and taking witness statements.' She was thoughtful. 'I think I'll have a chat to Tom Fox again. And I might wheel Mike Sheridan in for a statement, see how he behaves under questioning.'

Jane gave her a look of pure admiration. 'It's good having Blessed around. I think Rick's struggling at the moment.'

'He does seem stressed.' Blessed agreed. 'He overreacted to his son smoking. He seems desperate to link it to Irina's murder, as if the same person who gave Jon weed had it in for Irina. I told him he has an overactive imagination.'

'Poor Rick,' Morwenna said. 'And Phoenix is the daughter of his new friends out at Pennance Hill?'

'Yes, Matthew and Debra Rice. I went out to talk to them after the incident on the beach, just as a courtesy,' Jane explained. 'Both are professional people, self-employed, from Surrey. They have a holiday home here. He's into digital marketing and she runs an employment agency. They're quite well off.'

'You told me they seemed like responsible parents.' Blessed was quick off the mark.

'They are,' Jane said. 'Debra's genuinely nice, easy-going. She was apologetic about Phoenix's behaviour and said that she's quite an impetuous young woman; lonely, only-child syndrome. She blamed herself – too busy, not enough time spent with her daughter, that kind of thing. Phoenix will be back in Surrey doing A levels in September. Debra said Jon Tremayne's a good influence and the weed was probably all Phoenix's doing.'

'And Matthew Rice?' Blessed asked.

'He reminded me of his daughter,' Jane said. 'A bit hot-headed, outspoken, not quite aggressive – but I sensed he had the potential to be controlling.'

'So how did Rick meet them?' Morwenna wondered.

'Sally and Debra struck up a conversation in the hairdressers. Debra said they were new to the area and invited Sally and her husband to dinner. The friendship grew from there,' Jane explained. 'That's what Rick said.'

Morwenna looked at the empty glasses. 'Do you want a cup of anything? Coffee? Chamomile tea?'

Blessed shook her head. 'We'd better get off.'

'We're both working tomorrow,' Jane said.

'Me too.' Morwenna looked at the clock. It was half past ten. She paused; there was a soft footfall on the stairs; an ominous silence followed. Morwenna knew that Elowen was listening, so she said, 'Come in, say hello to Jane and Blessed. They're just leaving.'

Elowen padded down the final stairs and emerged into the living room in pink pyjamas, clutching Oggy Two in one hand, the other thumb in her mouth.

'Hello, Jane. Hello, Blessed.'

Blessed knelt down so that she was the same height as Elowen. 'You must be Elowen. I've heard all about you.'

'I've changed,' Elowen said smartly. 'I don't hit people any more. The way of peace is best.'

Blessed agreed. 'My job would be a lot easier if everyone was like you.'

'I'm grown up.' Elowen pulled her thumb from her mouth. 'Are you drinking whisky? Can I have whisky?'

'We're just going home to our beds,' Jane said calmly.

'Can I sleep with you, Grandma? I have nightmares.' Elowen looked at Blessed to gauge her reaction. 'I used to call them night-bears when I was little and it made my mummy cry.'

Jane and Blessed exchanged glances. They both knew what had happened to Elowen last autumn, and how Morwenna had solved the case.

Blessed said, 'You're a good girl, Elowen. It's nice to meet you.'

'You too,' Elowen agreed. 'Grandma, is Brenda on your bed? Will she be there all night to keep us safe?'

'Of course she will.' Morwenna ruffled her hair. 'Run up there now and dive in. I'll be up dreckly.'

She watched as Elowen tumbled up the stairs, making for the double bed where Brenda was sure to be stretched out, purring. Morwenna led Jane and Blessed to the front door, opening it, letting in a cold breeze from the sea.

'We'll catch up at the swim on Sunday.'

Jane and Blessed murmured goodnight and made for the gate. A car was parked beyond it, by the roadside. She glanced over to number nine; there was a light on downstairs. Ruan hadn't gone to bed yet.

Morwenna closed the door and locked it, already making plans. After work tomorrow, she'd find an excuse to cycle to the Woodpecker caravan site. Something told her that was where she should start looking.

16

Morwenna arrived at the Proper Ansom Tearooms at eight-thirty, having dropped Elowen off at Ruan's. They were going to Hippity Hoppers, Elowen's favourite trampoline park. Her friend Britney would be there with her mother, Carole, who ran the B & B and her father, Vic, who owned the car showroom.

Tamsin was unusually quiet as she filled the urn and placed condiments on tables. Morwenna watched her as she set up teapots and plates on trays. 'So – was it a good night last night?'

'Not bad.' Tamsin wasn't giving much away.

Morwenna tried again. 'Did you and Becca enjoy yourselves?'

Tamsin gave a short laugh. 'I've no idea how she's going to open the gift shop this morning. She drank a lot of gin. I tucked her up in bed in her flat and left her to it.'

'Do you want to check she's all right?' Morwenna asked anxiously.

'Oh, she's fine.' Tamsin grinned cynically. 'Nothing a fried breakfast won't cure. Becca's a bad influence.'

Morwenna waited for her daughter to say more and Tamsin added, 'She's man mad. She needs to raise her sights, that one.'

'Oh?' Morwenna was intrigued.

'We were getting chatted up by these two lads from Birmingham. One was quiet. The other was a real scally with only one thing on his mind. He thought he was something special, full of all the lines, the innuendo.'

'Such as?' Morwenna wanted to know.

'Oh.' Tamsin reeled a few examples off. '"Are you free tonight, or will it cost me?" "Your clothes would look great on my bedroom floor." And there were worse one-liners – really crude.'

'What did you do?' Morwenna was already concerned for Tamsin.

'I tried to drag Becca away but the two lads kept hassling us. Well, one did and the other just followed.' Tamsin noticed her mother's troubled expression. 'You don't need to worry about me. I can take care of myself, Mum.' They gazed at each other, thinking the same thing: Morwenna had no idea what had happened on the Caribbean holiday – no one ever mentioned Elowen's father.

'So what happened next, Tam?'

Tamsin blew air from her lungs impatiently and arranged coffee cups on trays. 'In the end, we spent the evening with a local man who bought us drinks.'

'Who was that?'

'Tristan Pengellen, and his friend Sebastian who's down from London. Of course, Becca's very keen on both of them.'

'Tristan's nice,' Morwenna said.

Tamsin wrinkled her nose. 'He's a posh, privileged boy. I haven't got time for him. He was trying to impress us with what a great surfer he was and how he has a flat in London.' She shook her head. 'I'm not looking for a boyfriend. Elowen's my priority. It's just good to go out sometimes.'

'And Becca?'

Tamsin laughed. 'She'd have been happy with either of them. I dragged her home at midnight and said no thank you when they invited us back to Pengellen Manor for coffee.'

'Didn't you want to go?'

'I have a business to run,' Tamsin said. The doorbell clanged and Zach came in, hurrying as if he was late. She offered him a warm smile. 'How did your mum get on at the doctor's?'

'She got some pills – thanks for asking, Tamsin,' Zach said breathlessly. 'I'll just rush in and start warming the pastries for breakfast.'

'They're already in the oven,' Tamsin said.

Zach wrapped his apron around his waist, tugged on a cap. 'I'll get started. I expect we'll be busy again.' He hurried into the kitchen. Morwenna followed him.

'Zach, I wonder if I could have a word.'

Zach turned, his face already guilty. 'Of course.'

'You asked me to hold your phone yesterday when you were carrying in the strawberries.'

'I did,' Zach said, flushed.

Morwenna thought he knew what she was going to say, so she got straight to the point. 'I shouldn't have looked at your photos, but I did.'

'Oh?'

'I'm sorry, Zach, but what with you being a student photographer, I just thought there would be some pretty pictures of seals.'

'Ah.'

'But what I actually found were lots of photos of pretty women.'

'I can explain.'

'Go on.'

'I love taking marine pictures.' Zach busied himself with slices of bread. 'But recently, one of the students at uni asked me to take some photos so that she could start a portfolio – she wanted to do some modelling part-time. It was good fun, taking different shots of her, and I thought it might be a sideline, maybe lead to more work. So, I just took a few more.'

'There are photos of Tam on there. Did you ask her first?'

'Sorry.' Zach shook his head. 'I should've.'

'And Irina Bacheva?' Morwenna's eyes met his, examining his reaction.

'I was in town and she was doing some interviews with locals and emmets. I just thought – she was so animated, so full of what she was doing.' Zach reached for his phone. 'I'll delete them.'

'Wait,' Morwenna said quickly. 'Why don't you show Tam her photos? They're really good. Ask her if she wants copies.'

'Will she be angry?'

'Not if you tell her what you just told me.'

'And the DJ?' Zach looked troubled. 'She's been murdered.' He was suddenly awkward. 'You don't think it was me? Like I was obsessed with her or something?'

'I think you should keep the pictures for the time being,' Morwenna said slowly. 'You never know – they may have been the last photos of her doing what she loved. I could ask Tom if he'd appreciate them.'

'Do you think he might?'

'Absolutely,' Morwenna said. 'And in future, the important thing is that you ask first. Of course, you can't ask Irina now. But you're a really talented photographer, Zach.'

'Thanks.' A smile spread slowly across his face. 'And you're right – I need to get permission.'

Morwenna glanced at the clock. 'It's almost nine. The breakfast floodgates will open soon. I'd better leave you to get the pastries out.' She sniffed once. 'I think those croissants are ready.'

* * *

The morning passed in no time; breakfast became elevenses and then the lunch crowds arrived. At two o'clock, Lamorna came in for a cup of tea and what seemed like minutes later, Ruan arrived with Elowen, Britney Taylor, Carole and Vic, who demanded drinks and cake all round. After Morwenna had served home-made lemonade and scones, she took off her apron. 'I'm done, Tam. Can you manage by yourself for the next couple of hours?'

'I'll be fine, and Zach can help out,' Tamsin called from behind a piled tray. 'Grandma will keep Elowen entertained.'

Ruan stood up. 'Do you want a lift back to Harbour Cottages? I can get your bike in the back of the van.'

'Yes, please but—' Morwenna was packing food into containers: pasties, sandwiches, cakes, scones '—I might just ask you to come on a detour first.'

Ruan was delighted. 'Where are we going?' They had reached the door and were about to open it when Morwenna paused. Two burly men stood outside, looking in. They both sported short haircuts, smart jackets and expensive sunglasses. Morwenna had seen them somewhere before but she couldn't remember where.

She pushed the door open and said, 'It's the Blues Brothers.'

Their expressions didn't change. One of them folded his arms. The other barred her way. 'Where are you off to in such a hurry?'

'None of your business,' Morwenna replied smartly. She felt Ruan move closer to her shoulder. The man who spoke had an accent; he was from the London area perhaps.

His tone changed and he became suddenly friendly. 'Is this tearoom any good?'

'The best in Seal Bay,' Morwenna retorted.

The man smiled. 'I might check it out. Do they do cream teas?'

'Of course, in the proper way: jam first.'

The man shook his head as if Morwenna was talking another language. He looked at his friend. 'We'll come back later.'

Morwenna watched them cross the road, striding towards the sea wall. She frowned. 'I wonder what they wanted.'

'It wasn't a cream tea,' Ruan said.

'Who do you think they were?' Morwenna asked.

'Who knows?' Ruan flourished the keys to his van. 'Let's grab your bike. Where are we going to?'

'Woodpecker camping site, up on Polkerris Hill,' Morwenna said.

'Oh, I know where Polkerris Hill is. Beautiful view. I asked someone about Woodpecker in The Smugglers and he said the field is owned by an old farmer. He lets it out to someone who rents caravans to holidaymakers and kids on the cheap.' Ruan paused. 'From what he said, it's a right dive.'

* * *

Ruan drove his van up a steep hill, Morwenna staring at the vast drop down to the sea. The view was stunning; the bay sparkled below, the sunlight bouncing diamonds of light off the waves, frothing surf rolling in. There were small boats on the horizon, pleasure craft with billowing sails. The van turned a sharp left, bouncing down a narrow lane, crowded nettles on either side, then into a wide field where a dozen or so caravans stood, their windows dingy with ragged curtains, their paint peeling. Ruan braked slowly. A sign said 'Woodpecker Caravans' in yellow paint on a wooden post. Another sign said 'No dumping'. It was surrounded by bin bags and empty bottles. A pair of seagulls stabbed at a stray carton that held the remains of a burger. Morwenna clambered out, hugging the basket filled with boxes of food. 'This place is worse than I thought...'

Ruan was next to her. 'So, what are you looking for?'

'Sheppy, the kids' entertainer, lives in one of these caravans – I brought him some food. He's always hungry. But – do you remember? Irina had written the name of this place in her notes – she might have met someone here. I thought a quick visit might shed some light.'

They were walking amongst the caravans, many of them covered in green mould and dirt. There was an eerie silence; if there were any residents, they were keeping very quiet. A mud path had been trodden through the grass, leading to a far gate. There were weeds and nettles straggling around a clump of trees. Morwenna pointed to a caravan. 'That will be Sheppy's. I wonder if he's in.'

'How do you know it's his?' Ruan asked. They were passing an old green caravan that leaned to one side. The acrid smell of stale cooking hung on the air. There was no sound from within.

'The door's open. I can hear music, and I can see a poster on the wall inside – it looks like a magician. That's bound to be him.'

'I'm not so sure,' Ruan said. 'If you're talking about the picture of a man with a top hat, that's Slash.'

'Who?'

'The guitarist in Guns N' Roses. That's not a magic wand, it's a guitar.'

'Oh.' Morwenna blinked. 'My eyes are getting worse.'

They were almost level with the open door of a filthy caravan that had once been painted green. Morwenna noticed the steps were broken. A strong aroma of something musty was coming from inside. Morwenna poked her head round the door. Sheppy was lying on a makeshift bed in shorts, puffing on a joint. He turned like a languid cat and held it out. 'Morwenna. And Mr Morwenna – come in, join me.' He eased himself into a sitting position. 'Do you want a cup of tea? I've got a kettle.'

A cup of tea meant having a conversation. 'Yes, please, Sheppy.' Morwenna beamed. 'This is Ruan. He's Tam's father.'

Sheppy blinked; it was too confusing. He put his joint in the ashtray and stretched his legs. 'Builders' tea with milk all right? I'm out of biscuits.'

'No, you're not.' Morwenna held out the basket. 'I promised I'd bring you some food.'

'Mint. Sit down, make yourselves at home.' Sheppy was all hospitality. Morwenna sat on the bed and Ruan plonked himself beside her. A smell of damp seeped from the mattress.

'How long have you been here?' Morwenna asked.

'Since the beginning of the holiday season.'

'Is it a nice place? I mean – are the other residents nice?' Morwenna opened a container and placed the scones on a cupboard that also served as a table.

'Nice enough,' Sheppy mumbled. 'We don't socialise much. I sometimes hang out in the bars in town with the surfers. Of course, they tend only to stay for a couple of weeks. I've met the odd girl or two, but it's only been one-night stands, that sort of thing.' He laughed once, a little awkward. 'This is a mingin' place to bring a bird back to.'

'How do you get back here at night?' Ruan asked.

'I walk.'

'It must be three miles, uphill.'

'In the dark.' Sheppy grinned. 'If I've had a few drinks, I don't notice. And I just use this place to crash.'

'You're not working today?' Ruan asked.

'It's Saturday,' Sheppy said. 'I've been on the beach since eight. I packed up just after lunch. I was knackered.' He placed two grubby mugs of tea on the cupboard. 'I'm out drinking tonight.'

'Where do you go?' Ruan picked up his tea and drank without hesitating.

'The Packet.'

Ruan shook his head. 'It's rough in there.'

Sheppy smiled. 'Beer's cheap. The local kids hang out there.'

'Come to The Smugglers,' Ruan offered. 'I'll buy you a pint.'

'Thanks, I will.' Sheppy lifted the lid on a box. 'A pasty? Thanks, Morwenna.' He took a huge bite, speaking while chewing. 'I'm always starving.'

'What do your parents think of you being down here?' Morwenna wanted to know.

Sheppy scratched his curls. 'They aren't bothered. They're well rid. I was under their feet.' He stretched his arms. 'I might stay on after the holiday season, pick up some work.' He glanced at Morwenna. 'Do you need anyone in the tearoom?'

'Not really,' Morwenna said. 'It gets quiet in the autumn.'

'There might be something on the boats,' Ruan said. 'I'll ask.'

'Bangin'.' Sheppy crammed the rest of the pasty into his mouth. 'I bet it's damp here in the winter.'

'It's Cornwall,' Morwenna said.

'Same as Levenshulme,' Sheppy agreed. 'I wanted to study acting, but I couldn't get the grades and anyway, my dad said it wasn't a proper job.' He sniffed. 'Neither was working at a petrol station. I did that for nearly a year and I hated it so I bought myself a magician's suit and a juggler costume and I came down here.'

'That's impressive,' Morwenna said, meaning it. 'It takes some nerve.'

'It's not a bad life.' Sheppy stared adoringly at a piece of cake. 'Sponge and jam. Mad for it.' He spoke to Ruan. 'I'm Kyle Sheppard, by the way, but everyone calls me Sheppy.'

'Ruan.' Ruan shook his hand.

Morwenna watched him eating. 'There's plenty more where that comes from, Sheppy. Perhaps you can share food with some of the others who live here.'

'I could.' Sheppy turned to Ruan. 'I don't suppose you've got any tobacco?'

'I don't smoke – never have,' Ruan said.

'Did you ever see Irina up here, Sheppy?'

'The DJ The Cream Tea Killer murdered? Yes, I did, as a matter of fact, once or twice.'

'What was she doing?'

'Getting out of her car.'

'By herself?'

'Yes, she was looking around – knocking on doors. Why?' A grin spread over Sheppy's face. 'Oh, I know – I heard you were a bit of a crime solver. Like Miss Marple.'

'But younger,' Morwenna said. The sound of an engine outside made her sit up. 'What's that?'

Ruan moved to the window. 'A car just drove up. A man's getting out with a young lad. I can't see their faces. That doesn't look good. The man's pulling him by the arm – the kid's being dragged along. We should go and see what's happening.'

'Wait.' Morwenna joined him. Opposite, the door to the filthy black caravan slammed closed. A black Range Rover was parked at an angle. Morwenna turned to Sheppy.

'Who lives there?'

'He's called Taddy,' Sheppy said. 'He's a good kid, but he doesn't say much. He's not home very often.'

'Who's the man with him?' Ruan asked.

'His uncle. He often brings him back. I expect they work together.'

Morwenna frowned. 'The Range Rover's an expensive model – and brand new. So why does the poor boy live in this place?' She made for the step.

'Where are you off? I wouldn't shove my nose in if I were you.' Sheppy was alarmed. 'Taddy's uncle is a bad-tempered bastard. He's always over there, mithering the kiddie for something.'

'I'll find out.' Morwenna clambered down quickly, missing the broken step, and marched across to the black caravan, banging the door with her fist. Ruan was behind her. She waited. No sound came from inside. She knocked again and called, 'Hello?'

Silence. No movement. It was as if the two people inside had held their breath. Morwenna listened, meeting Ruan's eyes questioningly. He shook his head as if to say that the occupants wouldn't answer, but she knocked again.

'Do you think we should just barge in?' she whispered.

'We can come back tonight if you like.'

Morwenna shook her head. 'I have a date.'

'Tomorrow, then?'

'All right.' She knocked once more and put her ear to the door. 'Hello. Is anyone there?'

There was no sound. She knocked again. 'Are you all right in there? Do you need help?'

From inside came a small voice. 'No – thank you.'

Morwenna and Ruan exchanged glances. Without speaking, they both knew they ought to come back.

There was silence, then the sound of a single stifled sob.

17

It was very easy to dress for a date at the funfair. Jeans, colourful trainers and a light jacket. Morwenna thought she'd do fine. She sat on the bed with Brenda, stroking the cat from ears to tail, wondering how the evening would pan out. Brenda rolled on her back, paws in the air, and Morwenna gently rubbed her belly. Brenda closed her eyes, falling asleep.

She continued the smooth motion, soft fur beneath her hand, lost in thought. Her mind moved to Irina. Why had she visited the caravan site? Why had she been interested in the place?

Morwenna wanted to meet Taddy. He hadn't answered the door, but she knew he and his uncle had been inside. It puzzled her why Taddy would live in squalor while his uncle drove such an expensive car. Family problems? She'd go back tomorrow, take more food. Ruan had offered to come along and, in all honesty, she'd be glad of his company. The caravan site was so neglected and silent that it gave her the creeps.

He'd been quiet on the journey home, since she'd told him she had a date. She'd said nothing else. She wasn't sure how Ruan would feel about her dating Barnaby again, but they had spoken about it a few months ago and Morwenna remembered exactly what Ruan had said then. They'd been sharing a meal; he'd told her about Kenzie, the actor from the Spriggan Theatre who'd tried to seduce him and how he'd turned her down. He'd said he and Morwenna were friends now, but no one could predict the future; he'd raised a glass 'To friendship. And to us, to being whatever we will be.'

Morwenna wondered what would become of them. Was what she felt for him simply the residual affection of their years together? Or was it more? And what about Barnaby? She felt some affection for him too. Perhaps a night out at a neutral place like the funfair, where there was no romantic meal, no soft lighting and sweet music, might be just the place to find out.

She removed her hand carefully. Brenda's legs stayed stuck up straight and she was purring contentedly. Morwenna whispered, 'I'll see you later, Bren. I want to talk things over with you about Irina. There might be a few other issues I'd like your opinion on too.' She moved away on light feet.

There was a rap on the door downstairs. Barnaby was bang on time, reliable as ever. Morwenna hurried down the stairs and opened the door. The balmy night air rushed in.

Barnaby was smart in a dark coat; he smelled of spicy after-shave, cinnamon, nutmeg. Morwenna left the house, closed the door and peeked over her shoulder. The harbour lights twinkled, shards of amber against an indigo sea, the sky shot with crimson sunset. She glanced towards number nine and wondered if Ruan had gone to The Smugglers. His van was parked outside.

Barnaby opened the door to his Jaguar and Morwenna clambered in. He offered a charming smile. 'I'm really looking forward to this. It's been a long time since I went to the funfair.'

'Oh? How long?' Morwenna asked.

'I must have been a teenager – it would have been in the seventies,' Barnaby reminisced. 'Out with the other boys, crashing into each other on the dodgems, eating hot dogs and regretting it on the Waltzer.' His eyes sparkled as he started the engine. 'This will be wonderful.'

'I hope so. I remember my schoolfriends used to go in a big group wearing Kiss Me Quick hats, looking for boys to snog. I'd tag along sometimes. I wasn't like them, with their eyeshadow and glamorous clothes – I had a different fashion sense, even then.' Morwenna met his eyes. 'It's good sometimes to rediscover your inner child.'

'It is,' Barnaby agreed. 'It sounds as if you were quite a lonely teenager.'

'Oh, no, I had plenty of friends. I just wasn't one for gadding about. I preferred being out on my bike or swimming. I met Ruan when I was twenty-two.' She smiled at the memory. 'Not much else has changed.'

They were driving down the hill towards the sea.

'So how was the USA?' Morwenna asked.

'Really good.' Barnaby said. 'I did very little but work while I was there, though. Of course, I went sailing with some of the other surgeons a few times. You'd have loved it – the sunshine, the buzz of city life. I wish you'd come with me.'

'It sounds wonderful, but I'm busy here.' Morwenna felt she ought to put things in perspective. After all, if she'd gone to California with him, where would she have stayed? Or, more to the point, where would she have slept? She wasn't even sure she and Barnaby were a proper couple. Tonight was the night when she'd sort out her own feelings and make him clear about their relationship.

They parked opposite The Smugglers, which Morwenna thought wasn't a great idea, as Ruan might be there. As they walked along the seafront towards the entrance to the funfair, he took her hand, holding it gently as if it was precious. Morwenna thought that wasn't good either. Holding hands meant looking like a couple, and goodness knew who they might bump into.

They strolled beneath the glittering archway, flashing lights and the name Collins Funfairs in rainbow colours. The music was already deafening: Slade and T. Rex booming through speakers, the rumbling of engines, the high-pitched scream of excited riders. Morwenna and Barnaby stopped, looking upwards at a Ferris wheel rotating in the bloodshot sky, lights winking. On the ground, on one side, an illuminated carousel of gaudy horses bobbed; on the other, a garishly painted Waltzer slammed forwards and tore away again, the noise of screaming becoming louder and flung away on the air. The air was filled with smells, the aroma of sizzling onions, the sickly-sweet smell of spun candyfloss. Morwenna took in the spectre of a haunted house, the words 'Ghost Train' dripping in blood-red letters from the top of a blue castle, a luminous green skull leering from the woodwork, its mouth open, a demonic laugh echoing from somewhere deep.

Barnaby squeezed her hand. 'What do you want to do first?'

Morwenna looked around, thinking. There was a ride called Out of Control: pink, yellow and red seats that whisked the rider around. Another, Flash Dance, swirled people around too fast in long seats. More neon signs: Sizzler, City Hopper. Morwenna felt dizzy just watching the riders screaming and crashing forwards and backwards. She saw the shooting gallery, Dead Man's Cove; a wooden stall where stuffed dummies of pirates in broad hats sat by barrels. Several tiny targets were strategically placed at intervals behind a line of long brown rifles.

'Let's try the shooting,' Morwenna said.

Barnaby was delighted. He waved at a young man in checked trousers, who held out a languid hand for cash. Barnaby offered his card and a card reader was immediately produced.

'We'll both have a go.' Barnaby picked up a rifle. He leaned forward, aimed and shot three times. The first time he missed the target by inches; the second and third, he hit a pirate.

Morwenna picked up her rifle and joked, 'My eyesight needs testing. This afternoon I saw a poster of Slash and thought it was a magician.'

Barnaby clearly had no idea what she was talking about. She leaned forward, blinking myopically into the rifle sight, and fired, taking aim and firing again. She stood up straight. 'Did I hit anything?'

'You did,' Barnaby said proudly. 'Every time. You're an amazing shot.'

The young man in checked trousers produced a huge soft toy, mostly white, with a dog face and black ears. Its head lolled to one side, as if begging cutely. Morwenna offered it to Barnaby. 'Would you like it?'

'Give it to Elowen.' Barnaby wrapped an arm around her shoulders and they walked on, Morwenna hugging the toy. She hoped she wouldn't bump into anyone she knew now Barnaby was draped around her. They paused at the dodgems and he said, 'Shall we have a go? Can I drive?'

'Go on, then.' Morwenna liked his boyish enthusiasm. The idea filled her with affection that, despite being a responsible surgeon who operated on people, he was still a kid at heart.

The flashing lights slowed and the slamming cars stopped. Suzi Quatro's 'Devil Gate Drive' was blaring, distorted through speakers, the bass thumping. The riders clambered from cars, staggering dizzily away from the arena, and Morwenna's heart sank. Louise and her husband, Steve, were coming towards them. Louise noticed Barnaby and her face was suddenly animated. She shrieked, 'Morwenna!'

'Louise.'

Morwenna was torn two ways; it was great to see Louise – she loved her dearly – but the way her face was shining now meant that on Monday morning she'd be full of questions and Morwenna didn't know the answer to most of them herself yet. Steve Piper, her husband, was a thickset man with a calm face and a dog-eared jacket. He offered a friendly grin. 'Hello, Morwenna.' He was sizing Barnaby up, taking in his expensive clothes, his suave appearance. 'You must be the plastic surgeon from London.'

Barnaby nodded kindly and held out a hand. 'Barnaby Stone.'

Steve gave a single nod. 'You're Pam Truscott's brother – Pam's the one whose—' He was probably about to say *whose husband was murdered*. '—who's got a nice boat.' He bailed himself out quickly. 'I've seen her in it.'

'The *Pammy*,' Barnaby said. 'Morwenna and I have dinner on the boat sometimes.'

That wasn't entirely accurate: she and Barnaby had been out on the *Pammy* once. He'd cooked fish. Louise was still grinning. Morwenna was immediately suspicious.

'I didn't expect to see you here.'

'Oh?' Louise looked guilty. 'I just thought we needed to have some fun.'

Morwenna tried to remember if she'd told Louise that her date with Barnaby was at the fair. Of course she had. It made sense that Louise would have chivvied Steve to come along. 'And are you? Having fun?'

'It's wonderful,' Louise gushed. She clearly meant bumping into Morwenna and Barnaby had made her night.

'The fairground's more expensive than I remember it,' Steve grumbled. 'I have no idea why you wanted to come here, Lou.'

Louise's face showed exactly why she'd wanted to come. Her grin was triumphant; her cheeks glowed. 'You've won a cuddly toy for Morwenna,' she said to Barnaby.

'Morwenna won it,' Barnaby said. 'She has a good eye.'

'It's for Elowen,' Morwenna explained. 'We're about to go on the dodgems.'

'Oh – can we go again, Steve?' Louise asked. 'We can follow each other round. That would be nice.'

'We could smash into each other, make it really fun – that's the whole point.' Morwenna was beginning to like the idea of a four-some. 'We could all go for chips afterwards.'

'Chips sound good,' Steve agreed.

'But we don't want to spoil your evening – I mean, this is a date,' Louise protested.

'You're not spoiling anything,' Morwenna reassured her, ignoring Barnaby's look of disappointment. She tugged his hand. 'You can drive. Come on.'

Barnaby was certainly a good sport. He and Morwenna chose a red dodgem car with yellow flames on the side that seemed to go more quickly than all the others. He, encouraged by Morwenna, managed to smash into Louise and Steve a dozen times, Morwenna urging Barnaby to chase and slam into them at every opportunity, bouncing them towards the edge of the arena. Barnaby was chuckling, enjoying the impact of bumping into Steve, the two men calling out to each other, heckling and laughing while Louise screamed in mock fear and Morwenna waved excitedly.

A fairground attendant in a brown leather jacket leaped on the back of Morwenna's car and muttered in Barnaby's ear, 'You might have a smart coat on, mate, but you're the biggest thug I've seen in ages.'

Morwenna thought it was hilarious. The ride finished; she clutched Barnaby's hand as she staggered out of the car, disoriented, and they clambered down the steps.

Louise had turned a strange shade. 'Shall we find something

quiet to do, Steve?'

'Get some chips?' Steve said hopefully.

'Or maybe have a go on a coconut stall? You can win me a gold-fish. We'll have a wander.' Louise turned to Morwenna. 'You both enjoy yourselves.'

'I liked the dodgems,' Steve said brightly. 'We could go on again.'

'We don't want to be in the way.' Louise shot him a look. 'I'll see you tomorrow for the SWANs, Morwenna.'

'I'll be there.' Morwenna watched Louise drag her husband away; he was still talking about the crashing cars, and how it was the best ride at the fair by miles.

Barnaby said gently, 'What would you like to do now?'

They walked on through crowds, laughing teenagers, families with excited children, so many people with different accents, all on holiday. Morwenna paused by a swing boat ride. 'What's this?'

She read the name – Anchors Aweigh! – and stared at a rocking pirate ship called the *Harry Lee*. The sides of the ride were decorated with images of pirates raising cutlasses, of treasure chests, coiled scrolls of paper with sea maps, tide times, compasses. Morwenna stood still, staring at the artwork with the Bay City Rollers' 'Shang-a-Lang' booming in her ears.

'Morwenna?' Barnaby said gently, touching her arm.

'Uh?' She came out of her dream. 'Sorry, Barnaby. I was just thinking.'

'Crime solving again?' He laughed affectionately. 'Are you thinking about The Cream Tea Killer?'

'Sort of...' Morwenna found it hard to drag herself from her thoughts. A new clue had started to form 'That's just typical of me, to lose myself in the middle of a crowd. So – how about those chips?' She took his hand. 'Cornish fish and chips are the best.'

'I'm looking forward to it,' Barnaby said. 'I've been starving myself all day.'

'Cod, chips and mushy peas coming up.' Morwenna tugged his hand. 'My treat.'

Barnaby was delighted. 'Do you know, I haven't enjoyed myself so much in ages. It's like – letting go of the unimportant things and concentrating on fun.'

'We should let go more often,' Morwenna said and immediately wished she hadn't. She didn't want to mislead him. But she was having a good time too, she had to admit.

The smell of frying fat hung on the air and Morwenna pointed to a stall. There was a queue of people, some walking away, diving into cartons of crispy chips, fish fried in bubbling batter, the tang of vinegar and glistening salt. She felt hungry as she joined the line of people waiting. Ahead, two men had just bought food and they turned, walking past her, speaking loudly in London accents. They were burly, broad-shouldered, in smart jackets. Their hair was short, cut close and Morwenna recognised them instantly.

'The Blues Brothers,' she muttered to herself.

'Who?' Barnaby asked.

She remembered she'd seen them before. In one of Zach's photographs. They'd been in the crowd, watching Irina Bacheva keenly as she interviewed locals. She was sure of it.

They walked past her, one of them turning, meeting her eyes; his stare was steely. He paused for a moment to give her a look that was clearly intended to be a warning.

Then he moved away.

18

'I want to know all about it.' Louise stood on the beach in her red swimsuit and matching cap. 'Was it blissfully romantic?'

Morwenna glanced around. They were all listening: Jane, Blessed, Susan and Barb Grundy, Donald.

'It was nice,' Morwenna said quickly, looking hopefully towards the water, shivering in anticipation, despite the warm weather.

'He's very rich, Pam Truscott's brother.' Barb raised an eyebrow.

'A good catch,' Susan agreed.

Donald looked puzzled. 'I wouldn't have thought there was much call for plastic surgeons around here.'

'Oh, his surgery is in London,' Louise explained. 'He has a flat in Islington.'

'Have you been to Islington?' Blessed asked. 'I just moved from Southwark.'

'We've only had a few dates. It's hardly a relationship.' Morwenna wanted to change the subject. 'Any updates on The Cream Tea Killer?'

'No.' Jane grabbed her arm and her voice was a whisper. 'We'll chat later. I'll message you.'

'Good – there's some stuff I need to talk through,' Morwenna said truthfully. It was time to share all the information she had.

'I heard Seal Bay's crawling with detectives.' Susan turned to Blessed. 'Are you their boss?'

'Hardly crawling – but there's an MCIT presence,' Blessed said. 'And I'm the new chief inspector.'

'So, Morwenna.' Louise hadn't finished with the topic of romance. 'Is it – you know...?'

'Is it what?' Morwenna knew perfectly well.

'Are you and Barnaby in love?'

'He's just a friend, honestly.' Morwenna recalled how she and Barnaby had kissed briefly before she'd wriggled from his car. It had been pleasant. He'd asked her for a date later in the week and she'd said yes. But it was all perfectly friendly, so she wasn't exactly lying. She pressed Louise's hand affectionately. 'Look, I promise the moment we, you know, take it to the next level, which we may not – in fact I really think we probably won't – but if we do, I'll tell you before I tell anyone – other than him.'

Louise's cheeks were flushed with gratitude.

Barb had overheard. 'What's the next level?'

'Snogging. Heavy petting.' Susan covered a chuckle with her fingers. 'Sex.'

'Well, why didn't you say so?' Barb asked, but Morwenna was on her way into the water, enjoying the sharp icy splash against her feet, knees, thighs; she dived in and hooted. 'It's so cold.'

She swam out, away from the others, and turned back to see where they were. Susan and Barb were in shallow water, their mouths open like goldfishes. Louise was splashing, talking to Donald, probably about the supernatural. Blessed and Jane were heading in the other direction, the sun glistening on their arms.

Morwenna flipped over on her back, feeling the icy bite of the waves rush over her shoulders, and she closed her eyes, thinking.

Several images circled in her mind, vying for attention. She recalled the desolate eeriness of the Woodpecker camping site; she heard the jangling music of the fairground and felt the rush of *Anchors Aweigh!*, the swinging pirate ship.

And she recalled Irina's voice, the last time they swam in the sea, her honest, open face, the excitement in her tone. She'd really believed she was on to something big. Morwenna plunged beneath the steely surface and felt the icy water clutch at her heart as she leaped upwards, droplets filling her eyes.

She knew what she needed to do next.

After the swim, everyone else went on to the Proper Ansom Tearoom, where Tamsin was waiting with hot drinks and pastries. Ruan had taken Elowen to the beach. But Morwenna wanted to be on her own. She cycled back to the peace and quiet of her home, where she sat drinking hot chocolate in the living room with only the sound of Brenda's purring. She'd showered and wrapped herself in a fluffy dressing gown, her laptop on her knee, waiting for the screen to brighten.

Brenda clambered onto the keyboard, stretching half her body across the keys, the other half squashing Morwenna's hand on the touchpad. She smirked at Morwenna, as if she was pleased she'd stopped her from working.

Morwenna kissed the damp nose. 'What's the matter, Bren? What do you want?'

Brenda wriggled, flopping over, and immediately the screen changed. Google search came up. Morwenna typed in the name Elsa Kerr. Several photos appeared at once: a snowy-haired woman in her eighties; a smiling woman with honeyed hair and large framed glasses, the photo taken in the nineteen sixties; a sepia picture of a serious nurse in uniform. There were various pages: *Elsa Kerr in the 1940 census. Elsa Kerr, obituary: she will be sadly missed by her devoted husband of sixty-three years. Elsa Lena Kerr, born Elsa Lena Fischer, 1925, in Dusseldorf...*

Brenda disapproved. She stood on all the keys and the page disappeared.

Morwenna typed again: 'Elsa Kerr, Saturday, 22:45'. That was what Irina had written, and suddenly a picture came up. There she was, in all her magnificence: the *Elsa Kerr*.

Of course. It wasn't a person.

She'd been on the brink of knowing it when she'd been at the funfair, and when she'd dived beneath the rushing waves. She clicked on a link and the information floated before her eyes; pictures, details, everything.

'Well, that's a big bit of the jigsaw resolved, Bren.' She picked up her phone, feeling pleased, and messaged Ruan.

MORWENNA

> Can you give me a lift back to the caravan site this afternoon

She didn't have to wait long. The reply pinged in.

RUAN

> Of course. I'll be with you as soon as I've dropped Elowen off

Morwenna rubbed Brenda's ears, watching as the cat closed her eyes and lifted her paws luxuriously.

'Well, we're on the way, Bren. Now let's see what we can find out from Woodpecker.'

* * *

Early in the afternoon, Morwenna and Ruan were again travelling up Polkerris Hill, looking down at the shimmering sea. Morwenna had brought a box of food from her own home, crisps, lemonade, a packet of biscuits, some bread and cheese, a pasty from the tearoom. She wasn't sure if the young man – Taddy, Sheppy had called him – had any cooking facilities. But she thought he might be hungry.

Ruan was chatting as he drove along the bumpy nettle-lined track to the caravan site. 'Elowen was telling me all about the way of peace this morning.'

'What about it?' Morwenna had forgotten.

'You told her not to thump Billy Crocker,' Ruan said. 'I think you're exactly right. Elowen's at that age – she's mixed up, she's got no father figure and Lamorna encourages her to stand up for herself at every opportunity.' He took a breath. 'I was thinking of taking her to football on Wednesday nights.'

'Do you still play football?' Morwenna asked. 'Giss on!'

'Not as much as I used to,' Ruan said. 'But they are starting a girls' team and I thought it would be a good outlet for her.'

'That's a great idea.' Morwenna's face shone with enthusiasm.

'And I might take her to the funfair.' Ruan was looking at the track ahead.

'Who told you I was there?' Morwenna said quickly.

'Damien saw you. And Barnaby Stone's car was outside The Smugglers. It's only a short walk from there.'

Morwenna took a breath. 'You don't mind, do you, Ruan?'

Ruan said nothing for a moment, then he said, 'It's not up to me.' He glanced at her briefly. 'Does he make you happy?'

'I'm not happy or unhappy,' Morwenna replied pragmatically. 'It's just a thing. I go out with him sometimes. He's OK – we get on. We're hardly Napoleon and Josephine.' He said nothing so she tried again. 'Posh and Becks.' He was slowing down near the black caravan, so for effect she said, 'Tristan and Isolde.'

Ruan gave a sad smile. 'As long as you're happy.'

'I'm all right,' she said simply.

'Right. What now?'

Morwenna wriggled out and picked up the box of groceries. 'Let's see if Taddy's in.'

'I've been worrying about him. The uncle's car's not here,' Ruan said. He glanced towards the dirty green caravan. 'And it looks like Sheppy's out.'

'He'll be working, I expect.' Morwenna exchanged a look with Ruan. 'Or drinking in The Packet.'

'Most of the locals go there for the cheap beer. It's not a nice place.'

They'd reached the door of the black caravan and Morwenna knocked. She and Ruan stood still, listening. There was no sound inside. Morwenna rapped again. She whispered, 'What would a young kid be doing on a Sunday, Ruan? Why can't he answer the door?'

'Maybe he's down the beach?'

Morwenna wasn't convinced. 'Do you think he's enjoying leisure time?'

'He could be at his uncle's for Sunday lunch?'

'He didn't look well fed.' Morwenna hugged her box of food. She glanced around. 'It's odd, though. This place is completely deserted and Sheppy said all the caravans were occupied.'

Ruan agreed. 'You'd expect someone to be here, but there's nobody at all.' He peered through the window. 'There's just a bed in here, a few clothes, a cup, a bottle of cola.' He shook his head. 'No sign of Taddy or anyone else.'

Morwenna walked over to a nearby caravan and peered through an opaque window. 'I can't see much – no one's home –

just raggedy curtains, toothpaste, clothes – the bed's unmade.' She turned back to Ruan. 'This place is so run-down. These kids live in squalor.'

'There's not enough affordable housing – no lodgings available. At least they're not sleeping rough. I suppose they have summer jobs in the bay.'

'So where do they go in the winter?' Morwenna asked.

'Home?'

'Then why would they live here?' Morwenna said. 'Imagine if Tam lived in a place like this.'

'It's unthinkable.' Ruan had no answer.

'Oi!'

Morwenna and Ruan turned at the same time. A harsh voice reached them as they saw a man hurrying towards them. He was small, his legs slightly bowed in baggy trousers. He wore a tweed jacket that had seen better days, and a cloth cap pulled down firmly. He reached them, panting, as he spoke directly to Ruan. 'What do you want here?'

Ruan offered him a cheery grin. 'You're the farmer – Mr Rodgers.'

'Ah, that's me, Jeffra Rodgers.' The man didn't seem at all friendly. 'Do I know you?'

'Ruan Pascoe. I'm a fisherman. I fish with your son-in-law, Arthur Lanyon.'

'Our Rose's husband. Ah, he's a lazy tuss if ever I met one. Always down The Smugglers drinking beer...'

'He's all right, Arthur.' Ruan covered a smile. 'We were just looking for someone who lives here. Can you help?'

'Oh, I don't know nobody who lives here.' Farmer Rodgers sniffed loudly. 'I let the field out to someone who puts the caravans in. I just collect the rent for them.'

'Who owns the caravans?' Morwenna asked.

'That's for me to know and no nosey bugger to ask.' Jeffra Rodgers ignored her completely and continued to speak to Ruan. 'The owner comes from up north. They don't live here. I collect the rent and put it in an account and I'm expected to keep nosey so-and-sos like you away.'

'Well, you must know their name?' Morwenna insisted.

'Can't you shut her up?' Farmer Rodgers said to Ruan.

'We're looking for a young man called Taddy,' Ruan said, a little irritable now. 'He lives in this caravan. His uncle oftens comes here with him.'

The farmer's face was closed, hostile. He had no intention of saying any more. 'I don't know who you mean.'

'He drives a Range Rover,' Morwenna said.

'I don't know nothing.' Farmer Rodgers glared at Ruan. 'You won't find nothing here.'

'We're looking for Taddy,' Ruan said again.

'Well, I suggest you don't come here looking for nobody.' The farmer grunted. He rubbed a whiskery chin. 'In fact, if you know what's best for you, you'll get out and stay out. It's no place for the likes of you.'

'What do you mean by that?' Morwenna asked quickly.

Farmer Rodgers looked at her for the first time. His face was thunder. 'I'm telling you, maid, to mind your own business and get off my land.'

Morwenna almost laughed. The farmer's words were ridiculous. She brandished the box of food. 'I'm going to leave this food for our friend Taddy.' She drew herself up to her full height and was still smaller than the farmer, who wasn't tall either. 'Is that all right with you, Jeffra?'

'You can bleddy leave it on the caravan step, then you get out, right?' The farmer turned to Ruan. 'You want to keep that maid under control.'

'And you should talk to women properly,' Ruan said simply.

The farmer glared at him before turning angry eyes on Morwenna. He spat on the ground, walking away past Ruan's van, kicking the side with his boot.

Morwenna laughed. 'Silly tuss.'

'Not a pleasant man,' Ruan said quietly. 'Best avoided if you want to follow the way of peace you told Elowen about.'

'He's covering for someone – I think he was scared,' Morwenna whispered.

'Maybe,' Ruan agreed. 'Shall we leave the box of food and go?'

'For now,' Morwenna said. 'But we'll come back.'

'He said the owner of the caravans came from up north,' Ruan said.

'That could just mean Bodmin.' Morwenna was about to place the box on the bottom step. 'Ruan – what's that?'

She bent down, Ruan beside her. On the metal of the step there were several dark blotches, maroon coloured, almost brown. Morwenna recognised them at once.

'That's blood,' she said, her voice a tiny whisper.

19

A mug of hot tea was waiting for Morwenna when she arrived at the library on Monday morning. Louise was beaming. 'I was talking about you yesterday.' She had a handful of books she was checking in from the trolley. 'We went to my mother-in-law's for Sunday lunch. You know how much she hates me, how she always goes on about how thin Steve looks since he married me – which he doesn't – and how he should have married Patsy Lenton instead. She can be so annoying.'

Morwenna knew Steve was caught between a rock and a hard place. He loved his mother and his wife, who'd never managed to get on with each other.

Morwenna said, 'What about taking some flowers round?'

'She'd start sneezing and say she had an allergy and I'd caused it.' Louise patted Morwenna's arm. 'Steve told her that we'd been to the fair and his mother said that fairs were for common people, so I said we'd seen you there – with the plastic surgeon, and he's not common. And guess what she told me?'

'What?'

'He has a couple of clients in Seal Bay using one of the private surgeries, as a favour. Frances Thacker's husband who works at Korrik Clay had a hair transplant with him a year ago. Barnaby did it while he was staying with Pam, on holiday. Of course, he does most of his work in London but...' Louise patted her cheeks with both hands. 'Do you think I'd benefit from a bit of Botox?'

'No, you look great as you are.' Morwenna said. 'Besides which, you get Botox in cosmetic clinics. Barnaby does reconstructive work. He doesn't do hair transplants often, just for a few people. It's minimally invasive, no general anaesthetic.'

'How do you know all that?' Louise was impressed.

'What else do you think we talk about when we're in his car?' Morwenna winked. 'Right, what do we need to do first?'

'I think I'll clean the desk – look at it. It's very grubby. And there are greasy finger marks on the laptop. I'll give everything a wipe,' Louise said.

'I'll finish putting these books away.' Morwenna turned to the trolley, her mug still in her hand. Louise took off towards the cupboard at the far end of the library. Morwenna stood up for a moment, inhaling the scent of old books. There were several to return to the crime section: M. C. Beaton, Ann Cleeves. She loved the ancient library: the shelves that collected dust, the stained carpet. The high ceilings probably needed the cobwebs brushing, but she felt at home.

'Morwenna!' Louise screamed and came scuttling back. She had two pieces of paper, one in each hand. 'She's been here again.'

'Lady Elizabeth?' Morwenna asked. She loved Louise's enthusiasm for their resident spirit, and the way her eyes widened in complete belief. 'What's she left this time?'

'A newspaper.' Louise brandished the evidence, bubbling over with excitement. 'And a pasty wrapper.'

'Then let's work out what she's trying to tell us.' Morwenna was ever the sleuth. 'So – a pasty wrapper – oh, it's one of ours –

we use those paper bags with a yellow pasty stamp. I suppose the ghost must be telling us she's Cornish – or hungry.'

'Look at the newspaper though,' Louise insisted. 'Look at the headline.'

Morwenna read it aloud. '"Seal Bay Police Taking Oolong Time to Catch The Cream Tea Killer".' She pulled a face. 'Bad pun.'

'But can't you see – cream tea, a pasty?' Louise's eyes were wide. 'It's a direct message to you, Morwenna. She thinks you can catch Irina's killer.'

'Tell her I'm making progress,' Morwenna said. 'I have a theory forming about *Elsa Kerr*.'

'Oh?'

'I just need to check my facts and find out who's behind it all.'

'Giss on.'

'It might be someone who Irina discovered something about, who was angry enough to silence her. It could be anything.' Morwenna frowned. She knew more than she was prepared to tell Louise at this point.

'Isn't it great that Lady Elizabeth cares so much about Seal Bay that she leaves us messages?'

Morwenna pointed to the laptop on the reception desk. 'She's left greasy fingerprints on the screen too.' She chewed her lip and muttered to herself, 'So, who brought a pasty and a newspaper in here over the weekend and ate it, sitting at the laptop? How did they get in – and out? And why were they here? That's what I want to know.'

She glanced towards the far end of the window, where the top pane was cracked open, to let in air during the summer. An animal could get through – Morwenna knew that already – or a person could wriggle in, but they'd have to be agile and compact.

Morwenna's phone rang, vibrating on the desk. It was Jane

Choy. Morwenna was surprised – Jane usually messaged when they were both at work. She rarely phoned. She held the mobile to her ear.

'Hi, Jane.'

'Morwenna – have you heard Mike Sheridan's radio show this morning? He's calling on The Cream Tea Killer to reveal himself – he's going into Seal Bay at lunchtime to talk to locals, and to see if there are any clues. He even said the police were too slow to solve Irina's murder and he'd do a better job himself.'

'He said that on air?' Morwenna was surprised.

'I'm going down to the seafront later to suggest he winds his neck in. I just thought – you'll be in the tearoom. I'll pop in for a quick chat.'

'OK – I'll see you then,' Morwenna said. She pushed the phone into her pocket. 'I wonder why Mike's interfering.' She thought for a moment. 'He wants to be popular; he thinks that'll persuade Tom to give him more investigative work. He was jealous of Irina.'

'If you ask me, he's lonely,' Louise said. 'His wife left him. He drinks a lot. Everyone knows that. He just wants to make himself look bigger to the world because he's been crushed.' She was momentarily sad. 'A broken heart will do that to a man.'

'Right, Louise. Let's clear up all evidence of Lady Elizabeth before the punters come in,' Morwenna said. 'Rain's forecast this week. Everyone in Seal Bay will be wanting to borrow books.'

* * *

Morwenna had been right. From nine-thirty onwards, there had been a stream of people – locals and visitors – waving library cards. Agatha Christie, Stephen King and Val McDermid were very popular – everyone seemed to want to talk about The Cream Tea Killer: was he a local or an emmet? A he or a she? Could it be

Irina's fiancé? Was it a tourist who'd scarpered back up north, never to be found? Morwenna listened, a smile on her face. Five minutes before she was due to leave, Phoenix Rice brought back a sand-filled copy of *Les Liaisons Dangereuses*, announced that Seal Bay was the most boring place on earth and left with a copy of *How to Kill your Family*. She'd given up pretending to be French.

The rain had just started to spatter as Morwenna cycled along the seafront. She slowed down to observe a crowd of people – at a guess, there must have been a hundred – gathered round Mike Sheridan, who was in a pale raincoat and trilby. He was clearly doing his best to look like a detective – Morwenna wondered if he'd produce a deerstalker, pipe and a spyglass. She stopped, watching him talking to locals, thrusting out his phone to record their opinions, his face serious and outraged. Morwenna noticed a police car draw up nearby. Jane clambered out with another officer – she recognised PC Jim Hobbs – and they strode in a professional-looking manner towards Mike.

Morwenna's feet pressed the pedals harder and she took off towards the tearoom. The rain had started to tumble and the skies were the colour of metal. The sea was choppy, forebodingly dark. In the distance, a trawler hovered on the horizon.

Before long, Morwenna was busy. Warm pasties and sausage rolls were the order of the day, then, after two-thirty, everyone wanted hot tea and cake. The tearoom smelled of cooking pastry and warm bodies. Morwenna served laden trays and collected plates, hastening back to the kitchen to load the dishwasher. Zach was busy making sandwiches. He gave Morwenna a sidelong glance and said, 'Do you think it's all right to photograph men without permission? I mean, with me being male?'

'Models?' Morwenna tried not to laugh. 'Or any old person in the street? I'm not sure you should make a habit of it.'

'Will I get into trouble?'

'There is no law preventing people from taking photographs in public, but you need to be careful.' Morwenna offered a reassuring smile. 'What have you done?'

'I was on my break, outside with a coffee. I saw the DJ from Bay Radio down the road and he was talking to a huge crowd. So I took some pictures.'

'You'll make a news photographer yet,' Morwenna said. 'You'll have to show them to me.'

'Here – look.' Zach held out his phone. 'You can see him winding up the crowd, stirring up a right storm. Some man was shouting that the police in Seal Bay get paid for doing nothing and Mike Sheridan said he'd find out who'd killed his friend if it killed him.'

'Did he?' Morwenna said slowly. 'So, he's saying Irina was his friend?'

'Apparently.'

'Oh, will you look at this?' Morwenna stared at the crowd. 'I've seen these bruisers before.' She looked at the two men she'd encountered at the fair and outside the tearoom. They were standing just behind Mike, watching him, just as they'd been watching Irina in Zach's other photo. She was thoughtful for a while. 'And you took these this morning?'

'Yep.' Zach held out a plate. 'Egg and cress for table five. Extra mayo.'

'Thanks, Zach – you've been really helpful.' Morwenna was on her way.

At half-three, Jane came in with Jim Hobbs, both of them looking exhausted. Morwenna brought them cups of tea and slices of lemon drizzle cake without being asked. Jim Hobbs, fresh-faced and keen, leaned back in his seat. 'Wonderful. You're a lifesaver.'

'Was it a tough day?' Morwenna asked.

'It was,' Jane said matter-of-factly, 'Mike has every right to be talking to the crowds unless he's disturbing the peace. We can't limit his speech beyond what's reasonable in a public space. But it was raining heavily and I'd hoped the crowd would disperse. It took longer than expected. And I'm not sure Mike bleating that Irina died because she was beautiful and talented was a wise move.'

'That's not why she was murdered,' Morwenna said quickly.

Jane gave her a look. 'Mike's making her out to be a romantic victim in a crime of passion.' She frowned. 'Tom Fox won't like that.'

Morwenna agreed. 'I'd better get back to work.'

'We'll catch up soon,' Jane called after her. 'I want to know what you've got.'

'Definitely – I've got a few leads.' Morwenna paused at a table near the window, where a family of three had just finished a cream tea. The little girl of about six or seven had a blob of cream on her nose. The child reminded Morwenna of Elowen. She said to the mother, a blonde woman with a leather raincoat, 'Are you enjoying your holiday? It does rain a lot in Cornwall.'

'It chucks it down in Liverpool too.' The woman had a strong accent. 'We're not really supposed to take Freya out of school, but it's only for a couple of days, and it's so good for her to be here. All the prices go up in mid-July.'

The father ruffled his daughter's hair. 'You love Cornwall, don't you, Freya?'

'It's boss. Especially the pasties and the scones and playing on the beach.' The child grinned. 'Can I have more scones, Dad?'

'Can she have a couple?' The man smiled indulgently just as Morwenna glanced up. She jumped, stepping back. There they were again – the two familiar faces staring through the window, cropped hair, smart raincoats. Morwenna stood her ground as one of them tried to stare her out. Finally, they moved away.

The woman at the table said, 'They look like shady characters. What were they looking at?'

'You get some dodgy types in Cornwall.' The man shook his head. 'We've just been hearing about The Cream Tea Killer from some fella on the seafront. Is that a real thing or just a local myth?'

'Oh, I shouldn't worry about it.' Morwenna glanced at the child, who was licking her fingers. 'Just enjoy the rest of your holiday. I'll bring more scones.'

'We will, thanks, love,' the woman said with a smile. Morwenna lifted her tray and was off back to the counter when something caught her eye. A figure moving furtively just outside the door, peering in through the window. A scruffy looking young man, hair dishevelled and damp.

'What's going on?'

She placed the tray on the counter and rushed outside into the rain, the door clanging behind her. A lad in jeans and a thin black T-shirt was on the run. She wondered if he'd been trying to unlock her bike. Morwenna watched him race down the road and disappear around the corner of a parade of shops. She shook her head, unlocking the bike with the intention of taking it inside the tearoom. She could keep it in the stairwell that led to Tamsin's flat.

She hesitated. The boy was there again, peeping around a wall, watching her, a skinny kid – he couldn't be more than sixteen. It was hard to see him properly with her bad eyesight.

As quickly as he'd appeared, he was gone again.

Morwenna paused, the rain drenching her hair. If he wasn't a thief, who was he, and what did he want?

20

Early on Tuesday morning, Morwenna was eating breakfast, lost in thought, when she heard a knock at the door. She recognised it as Ruan's and wondered if he'd knock again or use the spare keys. She'd have let him in straight away but Brenda was sitting on a chair with one paw raised, the adorable begging that she knew she shouldn't reward.

Morwenna pushed the last morsel of toast into her mouth as the second rap came. Her heart started to thump – she wasn't sure why. It could be bad news, even at this hour – she wasn't expecting to see Ruan. Her thoughts went straight to Tamsin and Elowen, and her heart raced faster. Lamorna was in her eighties – what if something had happened to her? But why would Ruan receive a message about her mother before she did?

By the time Morwenna reached the door, she was imagining all sorts of awful things. She threw it wide. It was a bright day, the bay glistening in the distance like a sapphire.

'Ruan?'

'I'd better come in.'

'Why – what's happened?'

'Did you hear the news?'

'What news?'

Ruan was in his oilskins, on the way to the trawler. 'Mike Sheridan.'

'What about him?'

'You know he was doing the roving reporter bit yesterday down by the seafront?'

'I saw him.' Morwenna was becoming impatient. 'What's happened, Ruan?'

'Hasn't Jane messaged?'

Morwenna rummaged in her jeans pocket and tugged out her phone. There were three messages from Jane Choy. She opened them up. 'Oh, no.'

'Mike was found beaten up in a shop doorway yesterday evening.' Ruan took a breath. 'He's in hospital.'

'Is he conscious?'

'Not yet. I just got a message from Damien on the fishermen's WhatsApp group.'

'Who beat him up?'

'No one knows.' Ruan frowned. 'But you can be sure someone thinks he overstepped the mark.'

'So, The Cream Tea Killer has tried to shut him up.'

'What does Jane say in her messages?'

'Only what she's allowed to. She's down at the hospital now with Rick. Blessed's there too. Mike's been severely beaten – broken limbs, facial injuries, head injuries. Jane thinks a blunt instrument was used.' Morwenna was reading the text. She looked up. 'It's been a week since Irina's body was found and the police are drawing a blank. They're bringing more MCIT officers to the bay. She wants a catch-up to find out what I know. I'll message now – oh, hang on, what's this?' Another message pinged and

Morwenna jumped nervously. 'Perhaps this is an update. No, it's Barnaby – he wants to take me out.'

Ruan made a sound that might have been disappointment and offered a smile to compensate. 'Well, it's not all bad news, then.'

'He's asked me to be his plus one at a dinner tonight in Seal Bay. Some old client of his is having a dinner party.'

'Anyone we know?'

'I doubt it.' Morwenna shook her head. Most of her friends were Seal Bay born and bred; Ruan moved among the fishing community. Morwenna imagined Barnaby's clients would be the people who'd come from outside and bought the more expensive homes. It might be fun, though.

'You should go,' Ruan said and Morwenna wondered why he was encouraging her.

'I will – it's interesting to meet new people.' Morwenna texted back that she'd love to be his plus one and then immediately she wondered if she'd sounded a bit too keen. But a dinner with some of Seal Bay's newer residents might be just what she needed to cheer her up. She lifted her phone. 'I'll message Jane and tell her we need to talk, and ask her to keep me in the loop. Poor Mike.' She was thoughtful for a moment. 'What if he doesn't come round?'

'Damien said that whoever beat him up did a proper job,' Ruan said grimly. 'Someone clearly wanted to shut him up.'

'And Jane says the police are going to talk to Tom Fox again. He'll be short of a DJ for the breakfast show this morning.'

'He will.' Ruan frowned. 'Do you think Tom's mixed up in all this?'

'He's Mike's boss, Irina's boyfriend. He could be.'

'But why would Tom kill his fiancée?'

'And beat Mike up?' Morwenna shook her head. 'It makes no sense.'

'I'd pop round later but you're busy.'

'Text me, Ruan,' Morwenna said and he turned to go. She called after him, 'Take care on that boat.'

'You always used to say that.' Ruan grinned. Then he was gone.

* * *

All the talk in the library was about Mike Sheridan. Morwenna stood with Louise and Pawly Yelland, drinking tea. Louise insisted that the ghost of Lady Elizabeth wanted her to get involved in finding The Cream Tea Killer.

'She knew what was going to happen to Mike.' Louise turned earnest eyes on Pawly. 'She leaves us messages because she cares about people in Seal Bay.'

Pawly wasn't so sure. 'I spent the day at Pengellen Manor yesterday. Julian and Pippa were very helpful. They showed me round the house – it's beautiful, with a grand view of the bay, lots of fascinating historical design. And Tristan's been really good – he's read my book and he knows the sort of thing I'm after.'

'So, what are you researching exactly?' Morwenna asked.

'All that history.' Louise sighed.

'And the family scandal. Readers will love it. Who slept with who, illegitimate babies, masters and servants,' Pawly said. 'I think all that personal-interest stuff will bring my book to life – it links well to the historical period, the morals and privileges, the exploitation of the poor.'

'And Lady Elizabeth's at the centre of it all – her husband broke her heart and she took poison,' Louise said dreamily.

Pawly disagreed. 'Julian thinks that's unlikely. He was saying how Lady Elizabeth was very fond of laudanum, an opiate dissolved in alcohol. He thinks that was what hastened her death, by all accounts.'

'Oh?' Louise looked disappointed. 'Maybe her cheating husband drove her to it.'

'Perhaps he told fibs about the affairs he had.' Morwenna caught Pawly's eye meaningfully.

'Oh, I'm sure many men indulged in affairs in those days,' Pawly said, making light of it.

'Then and now, I imagine,' Morwenna said. She moved closer to Pawly and her voice took on a persuasive tone. 'You knew Irina, didn't you?'

Pawly seemed to be about to deny it but instead he said, 'Did she tell you?' Morwenna nodded and he gave a low groan. 'It was a long time ago.'

'When she was a student, at Plymouth,' Morwenna urged him on, noticing Louise's shocked expression.

'I was a visiting writer. Over ten years ago – I was forty-something and she was twenty.' Pawly shook his head. 'I should have known better, but she was young and beautiful and I was a foolish man who needed reassurance. For a while it seemed to work, but I went back to my wife and Irina moved away.' Pawly seemed resigned. 'The wife thing didn't work out either. I'm not good with relationships.' He met Morwenna's eyes with a hopeful smile. 'You'd know all about a troubled love life, from what I've heard.'

'Oh, no, Morwenna has a boyfriend – and her ex is still in love with her.' Louise was ever the romantic.

'Ruan and I are good friends,' Morwenna insisted. 'Same as Barnaby and me, and that's all there is to it.'

Pawly chuckled. 'You're in demand.' He looked sad again. 'I don't like to talk about Irina. It's in the past. And I didn't behave well.' He was quiet for a while. 'I hope they find who murdered her.'

'Oh, they'll be found soon,' Morwenna said determinedly. She heard footsteps at the door. 'Donald – you're early.'

Donald Stewart hurried in. He was holding up a copy of Pawly Yelland's book *Hidden Secrets of Seal Bay*. 'I heard there was a meeting about our ghost – and I hoped Pawly would sign this for me.'

'Of course.' Pawly was clearly delighted.

Morwenna glanced at the wall clock. 'Well, if you're happy to look after things here, Donald, I'll pop out for a couple of minutes – it's gone eleven. There's someone I'd like to call on. I'll leave my bike in the corridor and pick it up when I'm done.'

'OK,' Louise said, collecting mugs. 'We'll see you tomorrow. I can't wait to hear about your date.'

'Right,' Morwenna said quickly and made for the door, grabbing her bag and jacket.

She hurried down the street, passing loitering shoppers and browsing tourists, then headed around the corner, stopping outside Bay Radio. She was about to press the buzzer when the door opened.

Tom Fox appeared; he was ready to go jogging in a T-shirt and tracksuit bottoms. Morwenna gave him her most persuasive smile. 'Tom – do you have a minute?'

'Maria Mutton.' His face filled with recognition. 'No, it's Morwenna, I remember. Hello.'

'I was just coming to see you,' Morwenna said. 'I heard about Mike. How is he?'

'No change,' Tom said sadly. 'DI Tremayne has just been for a chat.'

'What did Rick want?'

'To talk about Irina. There were bruises—'

'I heard.'

'The night before she died, we argued. I grabbed her arm in a fit of temper.' Tom looked flustered. 'But that's all.'

'I'm sure Rick isn't accusing you,' Morwenna said gently, watching his face.

'He wants me to make a statement on air, asking The Cream Tea Killer to give himself up,' Tom said.

'But you don't have any DJs left – just yourself.'

'I do Irina's afternoon show,' Tom said forlornly. 'But someone's stepped forward and offered to take Mike's on, while he's...' His voice trailed off.

'Who?'

'A local man. He's staying in Seal Bay for the summer but he's done hospital radio in London, just for a hobby, and he's offered to fill in, which is so kind.' Tom seemed resigned, as if there was little he could do. 'Rick Tremayne said the bay's flooded with MCIT and that they'll find the killer soon, and a statement from me would make people vigilant. But I really don't want to talk about Irina. It's too painful.'

'I'll do it,' Morwenna offered.

'You? Why?'

'Because I can. I knew her. And Mike, a bit. I'm fairly well known in Seal Bay.'

'You could.' Tom was coming round to the idea.

'What time do you want me tomorrow? I work in the library in the morning. I can pop out for half an hour.'

'Ten-thirty?' Tom looked relieved. 'I'd be glad not to have to do it. The DI will be here, of course.'

'Of course,' Morwenna said kindly. She took in Tom's joggers. 'You're off for a run, then?'

'I am,' Tom said sheepishly. 'I need to keep fit, and keep myself busy now Irina's—'

The door opened and Trudi, blonde ponytail and Lycra clothes, stepped out, all smiles. 'Tom, I'm ready. Are we running down the seafront or—?' She saw Morwenna and stopped.

'Hello, Trudi,' Morwenna said. She pressed Tom's arm kindly. 'How are you managing?'

Tom looked miserable. 'I'm trying my best – it's what Irina would have wanted.' His eyes filled with tears.

Morwenna felt sorry for him. She thought for a moment how swimming in the sea always improved her mood, how the release of endorphins helped the body deal with stress. 'Of course. Take care, Tom. I'll see you tomorrow.'

She turned her back, on her way to the library, to her bicycle, examining her feelings. Irina had been dead for a week and Tom was out running with Trudi. It was probably innocent enough. After all, they were colleagues – and relationships were complex things.

Who was she to judge?

* * *

The afternoon in the tearoom was so busy, Morwenna had no time to think about relationships, Tom Fox's or her own, despite the fact that she was going out to dinner with Barnaby that evening. She was serving at tables, clearing empty plates, loading the dishwasher, helping a frazzled Zach in the kitchen. Tamsin had shared a pasty with her earlier during a quickly snatched break, and Morwenna promised to take Elowen for a sleepover on Thursday night while Tamsin had a night out with Becca. She had hardly any time to talk to Lamorna when she popped in with Elowen at four o'clock. By five, the tearoom was almost empty but for a young couple lingering over tea. She collected her bag and jacket from behind the counter.

'I'll get off now, Tam.'

'Right, Mum.'

'Off to get ready for your big date?' Lamorna called

mischievously from a far table where she was helping Elowen colour animal pictures.

'Have you got a big date?' Elowen asked. 'Can I come, Grandma?'

'You and I will have our girls' night on Thursday,' Morwenna said.

'Is Mummy going to get pissed with Becca again?' Elowen sucked the end of her pencil. The romantic couple gazing at each other over empty teacups didn't seem to notice.

'We don't accept bad language, Elowen,' Morwenna said firmly.

'Sorry, Grandma.' Elowen looked apologetic. 'I heard Great-Grandma say it to Britney's mummy at the school gates. She said Mummy and her friend go on the pull and get pissed.' She frowned. 'What does on the pull mean?'

Lamorna cringed. 'Oh, me and my big mouth.'

'Elowen.' Tamsin was next to the table, a whirlwind holding a tea towel. 'You don't copy what people say, do you understand?' She met Lamorna's eyes. 'Especially your great-grandma.'

Elowen nodded energetically. 'I'm sorry. I'm trying my best. And I didn't hit Billy today because Grandma told me about the way of peace.'

'Good,' said Tamsin. 'Now finish your colouring and I'll make macaroni cheese for dinner. Great-Grandma's staying for a few hours, then she'll get the last bus.'

'Can you stay too, Grandma?' Elowen called, brown eyes pleading.

'She has a date with the plastic surgeon,' Lamorna explained.

'Grandma told me he's not a real plastic man, but it's from a Greek word *plastikos*.' Elowen was full of herself. 'Even Miss Parker didn't know what it meant so I told everyone in the class.'

'What did you say?' Morwenna was mortified.

'That *plastikos* meant plastic and my grandma was having sex with a Greek man,' Elowen announced at the top of her voice.

'That will be all over Seal Bay by breakfast.' Lamorna cringed.

'Time for a quick exit, I think – I'll see you all tomorrow.' Morwenna leaped for the safety of the door and stepped thankfully outside.

Then she saw the skinny kid, standing next to her bike.

He was wearing the same crumpled black T-shirt, dirty jeans. He had dark hair, dark eyes and a swollen lip, as if someone's fist had landed a heavy punch there. He stared at Morwenna and she stared back.

He started to run, his face genuinely afraid, disappearing around the corner, behind the parade of shops.

Morwenna frowned. It was the second time she'd seen him near the tearoom. She was sure who he was now, and why he was following her – he had something he needed to tell her. And she had a good idea what it was. If she could get him to confide in her, she hoped he'd provide all the evidence the police needed.

21

Morwenna was still thinking about the young man with the swollen lip as she sat in Barnaby's Jaguar, being driven up Pennance Hill. She thought about the blood on the step, how he hadn't been in the caravan when she'd called round. She had her suspicions about what was going on there. And she still hadn't told Jane about Irina's notes – she had so much to tell her. Now she just had to find proof.

She turned her attention to Barnaby, who was looking suave in chinos and a crisp shirt, the spicy nutmeg aftershave filling the car. Morwenna was feeling confident in her purple jumpsuit and her favourite patchwork velvet coat, dangly earrings, matching necklace, and her silver hair was freshly washed, tied up in a high ponytail. She'd sprayed Fleur de Patchouli all over herself before she left and was pleased that it equalled Barnaby's aftershave in pungency.

Barnaby was in a great mood. 'I took the boat out this afternoon. Pam was desperate to get on the water. She's off to the Caribbean next week. Simon's in Barbados. You remember him?'

'I do.' Morwenna remembered him well. 'Is he still working in a bar?'

'He is. You wouldn't recognise him. He's taller, more confident – he's grown his hair,' Barnaby said. 'So, Pam's off to visit him and I'm going back to London for a few days. I have some clients. Then, mid-July, I'll come back to house-sit Mirador.' His eyes gleamed. 'You'll have to come over.'

Morwenna knew Mirador, a double-fronted red-brick house with high gables and a grand oak door, with a spectacular view of the bay. Louise said it was her favourite house in the world and she'd give anything to live there. Lamorna often called it Mordor by mistake.

She said, 'I might.'

'Perhaps you could take some time off?' Barnaby was full of plans. 'We could go sailing during the day and in the evening, we'd have dinner...' His voice trailed off.

'Mmm, sounds good. If only...' Morwenna knew Tamsin couldn't manage without her. Donald had arranged to take over Louise's library work while she and Steve had a holiday at the end of the month. It was unlikely she'd be able to take time off to be with Barnaby.

She peered through the window just as Barnaby was slowing down. 'I know where we are. This is the house Beverley – Damien's fiancée – used to live in. Half Moon Cottage.'

'Matthew bought it. It's his holiday home,' Barnaby explained. 'You'll like Matthew and Debra.'

'Oh – Rick's here.' Morwenna recognised his car.

'Dinner for six,' Barnaby said. 'The Rices are friends of the Tremaynes. Debra and Rick's wife are thick as thieves.'

They clambered out of the car, Barnaby clutching two expensive bottles of wine, and Morwenna hugging the two bottles of sparkling Cornish elderflower she had brought. She said, 'I've met their daughter, Phoenix.'

'Oh? Where did you cross paths?'

'She – borrows books in the library.'

'Seal Bay's a small world,' Barnaby said. He knocked at the door. It was opened immediately by a narrow-shouldered man with a slightly rounded belly and thick light brown hair. He grabbed Barnaby's hand and shook it hard.

'Barnaby, I'm so glad you could come.' He turned to Morwenna and she noticed a look of surprise pass over his face – he'd clearly expected someone very different. Matthew Rice composed his expression. 'And you must be Morwenna. Pleased to meet you – do come in.'

They stepped inside and Morwenna looked around. The last time she'd been in the cottage, it had been crammed with paintings, easels, half-filled canvasses. Now the room was painted fresh white, furnished with two plush white sofas and a low table. Matthew said, 'Come on through to the dining room.'

Morwenna had never been in Beverley's dining room, but she could see this one was freshly decorated. The oak kitchen looked new, as did the solid wood table in the centre. Rick and Sally Tremayne were seated, drinking wine. Sally waved a cheery hello to Morwenna and Rick stared, horrified – he clearly wasn't expecting her. A slender woman with honey hair in a chignon, wearing a linen dress, whirled round from the gleaming red Aga.

'Barnaby – and your guest – wonderful. Do sit down. Matthew – wine, please. I'm Debra, by the way.' The woman seized Morwenna and kissed both her cheeks.

'So – something smells amazing.' Barnaby smiled.

'Oh, I'm so glad you think so,' said Debra, pretending to be modest. 'I've done a salmon en croute with a cream cheese and dill sauce. But do leave some room for the chocolate fondant. It's rather special, with a molten middle of caramel and coffee.' She placed a hand over Barnaby's and offered him a dazzling smile. 'I hope that sounds tempting...'

'It does,' Barnaby agreed.

'I want the recipes, Debra,' Sally Tremayne cooed.

'I tried to get Phoenix to help me, but she's not interested.' Debra Rice said. 'She's upstairs right now, with Jon and Ben, up to goodness knows what.' Her laughter tinkled, as if she didn't care.

'They were playing Call of Duty when I looked in. I've no idea what Phoenix sees in those games.' Matthew stood at a quartz worktop and began to pour wine.

Barnaby indicated the soft drinks. 'I'm driving.'

Matthew guffawed. 'He'll be all right with a couple of glasses – won't he, Rick?'

'No, thanks.' Barnaby shook his head and Rick looked awkward.

Debra didn't notice. 'Phoenix worked so hard at her GCSEs. I'm glad she has some down time. She loves Seal Bay.' She smiled at Morwenna, then Sally. 'She'll miss it when we go back to Reigate. She's doing A levels in the sixth form college – Psychology, History and Biology. She's very clever.'

'She takes after me,' Matthew said glibly.

'Oh, Jon's waiting for his GCSE results,' Sally said nervously. 'We're hoping he'll pass them all, take Maths A level and go on to university.'

'I hope he doesn't join the police force.' Rick grunted. 'It's not what it used to be.'

'Perhaps he'll be a surgeon?' Debra said with a glimmering look towards Barnaby as she placed a tray of pastry-crusted salmon on the table. 'I hear you're a grandmother, Morwenna. Your daughter has a child.'

'She does – Elowen. She's a little heller.' Morwenna inhaled the cooking. It smelled wonderful.

'Your daughter's not married?' Debra asked.

'No – we have no idea who the father is,' Morwenna said breezily. 'He's not important. Tam, my mum and I bring her up.'

'But every child needs a father figure,' Matthew said emphatically.

'I agree.' Rick folded his arms.

'I'm sure Phoenix and Jon profit from the good influence of a male parent,' Morwenna said simply. 'Oh, this looks great. I love salmon.'

'Dig in,' Debra sat down.

Sally said, 'I've been meaning to come to the library, Morwenna – I want to get some holiday reading.'

'Do you still work, Morwenna?' Debra wrinkled her nose. 'I would've thought you'd be retired.'

'I run the teashop with Tamsin and Lamorna as well as helping out in the library,' Morwenna said.

'She's marvellous.' Barnaby topped up her wine glass and helped himself to more sparkling elderflower.

'My business runs itself – I'm in recruiting,' Debra said. 'And Matthew's digital marketing has gone from strength to strength. That's why we can take time out to come here.'

'It sounds like the perfect life.' Sally pretended to swoon. 'I wish I'd kept working – but looking after Jon and Ben has always been a full-time job.'

'It's a priority for a police officer, having a woman in the home,' Rick said firmly.

'Jane Choy seems to manage by herself,' Morwenna murmured.

'My ex-wife's a writer of historical novels,' Barnaby said. 'Even when Dom was young, she worked. It kept her fresh. I'd never have stood in the way of what she loved.'

'Oh, have I heard of her?' Sally asked.

'Mickie writes under the pen name of Cassandra Hill,' Barnaby said.

'Oh yes – she wrote *The Sixth Wife* and *The Lady of Doves*. I think she's amazing,' Debra said, passing dishes of cooked potatoes in herbs, and buttered green vegetables.

'I don't think I've ever seen you read a book.' Matthew grunted and Debra shot him an evil look. 'I'm just saying.'

'You have no idea what I do, Matthew,' Debra snapped back.

'Morwenna's always busy. She cycles everywhere, swims in the sea.' Barnaby leaned back in his seat.

'Oh, isn't that dangerous?' Matthew leaned forward. 'Wasn't a local woman washed up in the sea this week? She drowned, didn't she?'

Rick cleared his throat. 'We believe her death wasn't accidental.'

'Oh? Was she murdered?' Matthew scratched his scalp. 'Yes, I remember now. I heard about The Cream Tea Killer.'

'Not at the dinner table, Matthew,' Debra said sweetly. 'I'm sure Rick doesn't want to talk shop.'

'But it's fascinating.' Matthew winked at Rick. 'Caught anyone yet, have you?'

'We're getting close,' Rick lied.

'It's horrible having another murder in the bay – Rick comes home exhausted. All the long hours,' Sally said.

'Morwenna's helped the police a few times,' Barnaby said proudly.

'Oh, do you do secretarial work?' Debra asked. 'You're a woman of so many talents.'

'Morwenna's a local businesswoman.' Rick shifted awkwardly in his seat. 'She often passes on information.'

Debra's laughter pealed. 'So, you're a snitch – a police informer?'

'I just keep my eyes open,' Morwenna said simply.

'This food's divine, Debra.' Sally tried to change the subject.

'I'm so glad you like it, Sal.' Debra's face shone with pleasure. 'I was meaning to ask – shall I book us both in for a lava shell massage at the spa hotel tomorrow?' She gave Morwenna an overly sweet look. 'You could come along too, if you have time.'

'That might be nice,' Barnaby said kindly.

'Oh, I'm on Bay Radio with Rick,' Morwenna said, noticing Rick sit up in surprise out of the corner of her eye.

'You could come with us instead, Barnaby,' Debra cooed. 'The massage is so relaxing and often Sally and I have a swim before we go in.' She offered a tantalising expression. 'I bet you look good in Speedos.' Her gaze swivelled to Morwenna. 'Does he?'

'Barnaby looks good in everything,' Morwenna said, digging into the salmon.

'Or nothing at all?' Debra's laugh tinkled. 'I'd like to see that.'

Matthew ignored his wife and finished the wine in his glass in one gulp.

Sally turned to Rick. 'I don't think I've ever seen you in Speedos.'

'I get no time for hobbies.' Rick sulked. 'I'm working every hour there is.'

'And you still haven't caught the crumb cake killer.' Matthew laughed. 'More wine, anyone?'

* * *

It was past midnight as Barnaby drove Morwenna back to Seal Bay. It had been a long evening. Morwenna said, 'The food was incredible.'

'It was lovely,' Barnaby agreed. 'What did you think of Matthew and Debra?'

'Honestly?' Morwenna took a deep breath. 'They both strike me as being a bit unhappy.'

'Why would they be? They have just about everything.'

'Mmm,' Morwenna said. 'He's unsettled, she flirts and there's not much of a spark between them.' She grinned. 'But it was a nice evening. I enjoyed it.'

'You're so perceptive.' Barnaby glanced at her.

'How long have you known them?'

'I don't know them well at all. I've met them twice socially. Matthew is a client, so I know him better than Debra.'

'Hair?'

Barnaby nodded. 'I try not to talk about client's treatments. It's confidential.'

'Is that why you said you didn't know Irina?' Morwenna asked. 'Because you did some work on her chin?'

'Ah.' Barnaby looked like a rabbit in a headlight. 'I suppose it's all right to say now. Irina wanted a chin implant. I put a dimple in for her. She was a good-looking woman.'

'She told me she'd had it done,' Morwenna explained.

'I try to keep these things quiet,' Barnaby said. 'I know Matthew would be appalled if I'd mentioned his hair transplant. I think you're right about him and Debra. I'm not sure their marriage is happy.'

'Some people prefer an unhappy marriage to none at all,' Morwenna said.

'Not you and me though. Mickie and I were fine for a long time because we had Dom, but then we drifted apart.'

'How long were you together?'

'Twenty-five years.' Barnaby steered the car towards the hill that led to Harbour Cottages. 'You and your ex were together even longer than that.'

'We were,' Morwenna remembered. 'Thirty-something years. A long time.'

Barnaby turned the corner, slowing down outside number four, switching off the idling engine. They looked out to the bay; it was pitch dark, little lights zigzagging, dancing on the water. He inhaled. 'May I ask you something?'

'You may.'

Barnaby didn't pause. 'Are you completely over Ruan?'

'What makes you ask?' Morwenna wasn't sure how to answer.

'Mickie has a new partner now. We have Dom, the grandkids – we get on. But things improved so much between us after she met someone else.'

'Oh?' Morwenna wanted to avoid talking about Ruan.

'It used to be all bickering and arguments, even after we split up. Mickie remarried and now we get on fine. She even asks me who I'm dating. I've told her about you.'

'What did you say?'

'That I've met someone,' Barnaby said cryptically. 'The thing is, though – sometimes I suspect you're not completely over your ex.'

Morwenna said, 'We do still get on.'

'Morwenna.' Barnaby took her hand. 'I've been thinking of ways to say this.'

'The best way is just to say it,' Morwenna replied, wondering what he was about to announce.

'When we go out together, when we date, if you like, we have a great time. But I bring you back home and – the evening sort of ends there. A quick kiss and a quicker goodbye.'

Morwenna felt caught out; perhaps she hadn't been completely honest with him. She was relieved that they were discussing it now. 'Is that a bad thing?'

'You want to take things slowly, I know.' Barnaby squeezed her hand in both his. 'But if it's your ex, if you still love him, just tell me and I'll walk away.'

'I'm fond of Ruan,' Morwenna admitted.

'Of course you are – he's Tamsin's father.' Barnaby took a breath. 'But what about me? Could you be fond of me too?'

Morwenna didn't know. 'I might...'

'So, what if...?' He brought her hand to his lips. 'What if we go at your pace? I'm ready to take things further. If I'm honest, I could throw myself into a relationship with you with both feet.' He gave a muffled laugh. 'I've never met anyone like you.'

'That's kind,' Morwenna said. 'And I like you too. But I'm not really ready to—'

'Of course, I completely understand,' Barnaby interrupted quickly. 'Let's just date and see.' He smiled at his joke. 'What do you say?'

'Is that all right?' Morwenna felt a surge of affection. 'I mean – it might take some time for me to work it all out.'

'I sense that. After all, you had a lot of years with Ruan.' Barnaby kissed her cheek. 'I'm happy to wait, if that's what it takes.'

'Thanks, that's kind,' Morwenna said.

He wrapped an arm round her, his lips brushing hers. 'I'm going back to London soon. Will I see you before I go? Maybe dinner on the boat?'

'That would be nice.' Morwenna kissed him back briefly. 'I'll text you.'

'I'll look forward to it,' Barnaby said and, on impulse, Morwenna kissed him again, then she scrambled out of the car. He started the engine, waved and drove towards the glimmering lights as Morwenna watched him go.

He was a nice man. She wondered if that was enough.

She glanced over towards number nine. A lamp glowed from the bedroom. A shadow stood at the window, watching her. It was Ruan.

Morwenna lifted a hand in acknowledgement and moved towards her front door, her mind crammed with thoughts.

Life was full of difficult decisions.

22

The next morning, Morwenna managed to avoid questions about her date with Barnaby. Louise was more interested in the book that had been left on the keypad of her laptop. It was a copy of *Hidden Secrets of Seal Bay* by Pawly Yelland that had been returned yesterday afternoon. Louise was sure she'd put it on the trolley, but there it was, on her laptop. Proof that the ghost had left another sign.

Morwenna was about to dash off to the radio – she'd just have time to get there before the show began with the new DJ and Rick. She shrugged on her velvet patchwork coat. 'Maybe you just moved it to the laptop to remind you to put it away?'

'No,' Louise protested. 'I know I didn't – the ghost is telling us Seal Bay needs your help to solve the secrets.' She picked it up and a folded piece of paper floated out. 'What's this?' Her eyes were wide. 'Lady Elizabeth has left us a note?'

Morwenna picked it up and smoothed it. Something had been scrawled in pen. She read the words and handed it to Louise.

Louise stared. 'It doesn't make sense. "Else Ker Sunday 22:55".' Louise turned to Morwenna, amazed. 'Is it a note from the ghost?

Who is Else Ker?' She gasped. 'It's The Cream Tea Killer's next victim – he's going to kill poor Else on Sunday...'

Morwenna puffed out air, giving herself time to think. 'I'll research it online and let you know.'

It wasn't easy to lie to Louise. Morwenna knew already – Irina had written 'Elsa Kerr, Saturday, 22:45' in her folder, the spelling different, and the time. But it was just the information Morwenna needed. Now she had a date, an appointment, and she was fairly sure where the place might be. She couldn't let Louise know, not yet, but she ought to tell Jane, and soon. She grinned to cover her second lie. 'If the ghost were to send a message to the people of Seal Bay, she'd use Pawly's book as a sign. Leave it with me. I'll look up Else Ker and tell you what I find out. She might be someone local.'

'Oh, what if she was and we could warn her and save her life? Pawly could put it in his next book.' Louise was delighted. 'I thought you didn't believe in Lady Elizabeth.'

'I'm a sceptic, but I'll definitely research the name.' Morwenna hugged Louise quickly. 'I'm late – I'd better get off to the radio studio. I won't be long.'

'Will you be all right on air, live, with all Seal Bay listening?' Louise's face was etched with friendly concern. 'I can't think of anything scarier than being on the radio, except being on the radio with Rick Tremayne.'

'I'll wing it,' Morwenna said with a wink, and rushed for the door.

Ten minutes later, a guilty-looking Trudi let Morwenna in, ushering her to the inner door, swiping her card. 'We're ready for you. Rick's in the studio with Tom and the new DJ. We have your mic set up. It shouldn't take long to get you comfortable. We won't need you to talk for more than a minute or two.' She eyed Morwenna suspiciously. 'Have you written a speech?'

'I don't need to.' Morwenna tapped her head. 'It's all in here.'

She followed Trudi into the room with the green carpet. A familiar voice came through the speakers. 'Coming up soon is a live message from DI Rick Tremayne, who wants to update everyone on The Cream Tea Killer and what local people can do to keep themselves safe. He'll be joined by Morwenna Mutton, who'll also have some important words about Bay Radio's very own Irina. But first, let's have a bit of "Whiskey in the Jar" from 1972, a classic brew from Thin Lizzy.'

'I know who that is.' Morwenna grinned with delight. 'It's Tristan Pengellen.'

'He's very good – he lives in London most of the year,' Trudi said as she led the way into the larger room where several people were hunched over laptops. She indicated the studio where Tristan was sitting in shorts and a loud T-shirt, headphones over his tousled blond hair. Morwenna waved. Tom rushed to the door, ushering her inside, sitting her on a revolving chair with a high back, next to Rick Tremayne.

Tom fiddled with some wires while Rick met Morwenna's eyes and grunted in recognition. He leaned over to whisper, 'Just let me do all the talking – you can say a word or two. Tell people to leave things up to the police, not to do anything stupid or panic.'

Morwenna gave him the thumbs up. Tristan winked, a complicit signal that she'd be fine. He seemed confident she'd be more likely to say the right thing than Rick would. Tom was visibly nervous as he hesitated in the doorway. He met Morwenna's eyes and mouthed, 'Everything OK?' Morwenna nodded. The final notes of Thin Lizzy faded.

'So,' Tristan said, his tone suddenly hushed. 'As you all know, Seal Bay recently lost a wonderful woman and a talented DJ from Bay Radio. Everyone who knew Irina Bacheva loved and admired her. And here on Bay Radio today, we've invited in DI Rick

Tremayne from the Devon and Cornwall Police to give you the latest update on the so-called Cream Tea Killer. Rick?' Tristan smiled encouragingly. 'Naturally, the people of Seal Bay, both residents and visitors, are concerned after what happened to Irina. But what's rumour and what's fact? What can you say to put our minds at rest?'

'Well.' Rick swallowed hard. There were seconds of dead air, then he said, 'I can guarantee everyone in Seal Bay that the police are doing their utmost to catch Irina's killer. We have leads, suspects. The town is full of extra officers, all keen to bring the perpetrator to justice. People in Seal Bay have nothing to fear. And we are working hard as a unit to bring this case to a close. And...' he chose his words carefully '...as DI, I can absolutely assure you that the killer will be found soon and dealt with severely.'

'Do you have a timescale for this?' Tristan asked smoothly.

'We do.' Rick grinned smugly, then he realised he hadn't answered the question fully. 'I mean, my men – and women – expect to bring the killer in very soon. It's an absolute priority. But...' An idea had occurred to him. 'The public are asked not to approach any strangers who are acting suspiciously. We believe Irina's killer is dangerous and if approached, he may react violently. So – stay safe at all times and if in doubt, ring 999 or contact your local police station.'

'Right.' Tristan turned easily to Morwenna, indicating that it was her turn. 'Many of the people of Seal Bay know Morwenna Mutton, our other studio guest this morning. Morwenna works in the library and owns a share in her family business, the Proper Ansom Tearoom. We've asked her in to say a few words about Irina. Morwenna, you knew her quite well, didn't you?'

'I did. She was lovely.' Morwenna spoke steadily. 'She was a person I admired greatly for her keen mind and her sense of justice. The day before she – was discovered on the beach – we'd been swimming together. She was a strong sea swimmer. So, on Irina's behalf, I'd like to say a few straight words to The Cream Tea Killer, just in case he or she is listening.'

'Go on,' Tristan encouraged. Rick sliced a flat hand in front of his throat, a sign for Morwenna to shut up.

'So, to the so-called Cream Tea Killer, whoever did this dreadful thing to Irina.' Morwenna moved closer to the microphone. 'The people of Seal Bay won't put up with it. We're proper Cornish people, and that stands for something. It means that we'll hunt you down, we'll find you and we will put you behind bars for what you did.'

'Well said, Morwenna.' Tristan applauded, drawing Morwenna's attention to an expensive metal watch and several colourful cord bracelets on his wrist.

'And that's not all.' Morwenna saw Rick's eyes bulge in horror, but she continued, undaunted. 'I keep my wits about me and I have a few clues about what's been going on. The police and I have a theory about who killed Irina and we're working on it as we speak. And although DI Tremayne can't give you an exact timescale to catch this cowardly Cream Tea Killer, I'll try my best. Not that I'm Mystic Morwenna, but I think our friends in the police will have caught the murderer by...' Morwenna remembered the scribbled note in the library. Sunday, 22:55. 'By next Monday morning. That's 15 July. By next week, The Cream Tea Killer will just be a few stale crumbs on an empty plate.'

Rick's face was thunderous. Tristan continued, his voice smooth. 'Some reassuring words – thanks for that, Morwenna. Seal Bay residents will be pleased to hear it. And while we pause a moment to remember Irina, I'd like to play something in her memory. Here's "Nothing Compares 2 U" by Sinéad O'Connor.'

The music began and Rick stood up, face red with fury. 'What was all that about, Morwenna? How can you promise people we'll catch the killer? The police have hardly anything to go on.'

Morwenna smiled sweetly. 'Nor do I yet, but I'm working on it, and when I do, I'll share it with Jane and Blessed – and you, of course.'

'I could take you in – charge you with obstructing—'

'I'm not obstructing anyone,' Morwenna said. 'Quite honestly, Rick—' She thought to herself, here goes another lie... '—I just said it to draw the killer out. If he or she thinks we have suspicions about them, they'll come to us, maybe, or put a foot wrong.' She shrugged. 'I was only trying to help.'

'Well, don't interfere.' Rick folded his arms grumpily. 'Let me handle this.'

'Of course, whatever you say. But – I thought we were friends.' Morwenna turned to Tristan and Tom, Trudi watching from the door, her mouth open. 'We had dinner together last night, didn't we, Rick? It was lovely.'

'I'm a busy man. I don't have time to chit-chat.' Rick flung his chair back and stormed towards the door. 'If you'll excuse me – I have a killer to catch.'

Trudi scuttled after him.

Tom looked upset. 'Thanks, Morwenna – for what you said about Irina. It was really lovely.'

'Do we know when the funeral is?' Morwenna asked gently.

'The police haven't released her—' He stopped, putting a hand to his face. His eyes were filled with tears.

Morwenna placed a hand on his shoulder. 'I'm so sorry. Let me know when, will you?' She turned to Tristan. 'You're doing a great job. Pop into the tearoom. There's a cuppa and a slice of cake with your name on it.'

'Ansom,' Tristan said, and Morwenna waved a hand. It was time to get back to the library.

She stepped outside into bright sunlight, blinking. Her bicycle was back at the library; she'd hurry back, stack a few books, tell Louise about her date with Barnaby. She'd probably go sailing with him in a day or two.

Something blocked the light from the sky.

To her left, a broad man with very short hair and a smart jacket stood in front of her and folded his arms. To the right, another one, almost identical, stepped from a doorway. They filled the pavement.

Morwenna glanced around. There were a few people, shoppers, browsers, a family. Morwenna had no intention of screaming for help. She wouldn't show any fear. She stared at the first man, then his companion. 'Excuse me.' Her voice was businesslike, although she was shaking.

'Morwenna Mutton?' one said in an estuary-accented voice.

'You've just been on the radio. We heard you.' The second man stood close to her, filling her space. Morwenna could smell sweat mixed with cologne.

'That's me.' She stood her ground, but her body was tense and her legs were trembling. She expected one of them to grab her.

'You're a local, aren't you?' the first man said.

'Do you know much about what goes on around these parts?' The second was closing in too. He had bad breath. Morwenna's mind raced.

'Who are you?' Morwenna said, but not too confidently.

The man with bad breath leered. 'We're the CID.'

'That's right, the CID.' The sweaty man agreed. 'So, you should be a bit careful about what you say on the radio.'

'Oh?' Morwenna met his eyes.

'Just watch your mouth.'

Morwenna looked baffled. 'I thought the job of the police was to protect the public – not to threaten them.'

'Oh, we're not threatening you.' The second man spat on the ground, just missing her foot.

'We're looking out for you,' the first man added.

'What does Blessed think of your tactics?' Morwenna asked.

'We don't answer to no Blessed.'

'Best you stay out of things, you hear?'

They both stared a little longer, then the pair of them strode away, strutting like roosters. Morwenna didn't move. Her heart was thumping. She was terrified.

They weren't CID. Or MCIT. No way.

She decided to hurry back to the library. She'd call Jane – she needed to tell her so much now; she needed her help. It was her own fault. She shouldn't have said what she did on air. It was reckless.

She saw a shape, a face, poking around the corner of a brick wall, dark hair and eyes, a swollen lip.

The young lad shook his head once, his eyes fixed on hers, a brief warning. Then he turned quickly and was gone.

23

As she cycled to the tearoom for her afternoon shift, Morwenna had to concentrate hard on road safety. Her mind was buzzing, filled with other things. It would have been far too easy to ignore the steady stream of cars, the thundering Korrik Clay lorry, the blundering pedestrians. She stopped to let a woman pushing a pram pass on a pedestrian crossing when the lights flashed. She pressed the pedals down again, her mind full of Else Ker or Elsa Kerr. It didn't matter that two people had spelled the name differently – she knew about Sunday night, at 22:55. And she was sure the killer knew too. That was why the two men had threatened her. They'd been quick off the mark.

They knew she knew. She'd have to watch her back now.

She almost forgot to stop at a junction. A car whizzed in front of her, blaring a horn; she turned right and cycled along the seafront as her mind wandered again. She was fairly sure she knew the connection between Irina and the killer now. But who was behind it all?

Morwenna slowed down outside the tearoom. A van from Scatterbee Fruit Farm, with its colourful logo of bees and fruit on the side, was badly parked by the kerb. She thought about securing her bicycle – most people knew it was hers – but something made her change her mind. It would be safer inside, in the stairwell.

A man blustered out, a cap firmly pulled down, followed by Zach, who greeted Morwenna with a cheery smile. 'I heard you on the radio. You were great.'

'Thanks, Zach.' Morwenna turned to the man, who was handing a tray of fruit to Zach. '*Myttin da.* How are you, Pen?'

'Proper teazy.' He scowled, waiting until Zach had gone back inside, then he lowered his voice. 'In fact, I'm jumping. This will be my last week at Scatterbee. I've been here fifty-seven years, man and boy, and they are finishing me off on Friday.'

'You're leaving?' Morwenna asked.

'I've been let go.' Pen had tears in his eyes. 'After all I've done for that place.'

'That's awful. Why?'

'I got no idea. None whatsoever. I ain't done nothing wrong,' Pen said. 'The life up at Scatterbee's used to be all right when old John Trebullet owned it. But things are changing.'

'How?'

'Now we got these new people come, they're expanding. More fruit, more veg, more workers on the plot, and most of them won't have nothing to do with you.'

'Oh?'

'I know people have got to live somewhere, but I'm old school, Morwenna. Cornwall used to be for the Cornish. Now all sorts come here and it ain't the same. You might call me a teazy old tuss, but I speak as I find.'

'I disagree. The world's a better place when it's inclusive, Pen.'

'Your world may be, maid.' Pen frowned. 'But now I got let go, mine's a whole lot worse. I don't know who'll be delivering your grub next week, but don't be at all surprised if it's some bloke who don't know his strawberries from his purple plums.' He sniffed. 'There. I said what I think.'

'I'm sorry that's happened.' Morwenna placed a hand on his arm. 'I'll miss you.' She offered a grin. 'Come in any time – there's a cuppa with your name on it.'

'I might just take you up on that – just to have a look at your Tamsin in those shorts she wears.' Pen managed a grin as he clambered onto the van.

'Some things don't change,' Morwenna said as she watched him pull away.

The tearoom was busy, a typical Wednesday lunchtime, the aroma of heated pasties filling the air. Tamsin was busier than ever, waiting on tables. Morwenna pulled on her apron and noticed Sheppy, in his magician's costume, looking pleased with himself. He tugged off his top hat in greeting and ruffled his curls.

'Tea and cake, please, waitress – it's Magic Sheppy day.'

'Coming up,' Morwenna called back. Moments later, she placed a tray in front of him.

Sheppy flourished a ten-pound note. 'Here. Takings are good on the beach this morning – there are more kids now.' He puffed out his chest. 'I made sixty quid.'

'That's really impressive.'

'If business carries on like this, I'm moving to Camp Dynamo. It's nearer the beach where all the surfers hang out. The caravans there are lovely. It's a bit more expensive but – hey, I'm raking it in.'

'So – you'd turn your back on Woodpecker?'

'In a flash. It's mingin'.' Sheppy slurped his tea and made a loud sound of contentment. 'The farmer's put a big sign up, "No Entry Except for Residents". And the place is like a morgue.'

'Is it?'

'There's no one there half the time, and the rest of the time they're all asleep. And you know Taddy, the lad you gave the box of food to?'

'I remember.'

'He's gone.'

'Gone?'

Sheppy stuffed cake into his mouth. 'He runs away all the time. He gave me a few bits from the box you left for him and he told me a couple of things. That man who comes round isn't his uncle. He slaps him, shouts at him, and he hits some of the other kids who live in the caravans. It's like he's keeping them in order.'

Morwenna was intrigued. 'How many people are there, do you think?'

'Twenty, thirty. Mostly my age – some of them are younger. There are four people packed in some of those bigger caravans. Taddy said they are bringing some more caravans in and expanding the site. But I don't think it'll be any cleaner. And the atmosphere's not great.'

'Oh?'

'The bloke who brought Taddy back came over and banged on my door a day or so ago, shouting that he'd done a runner and had I seen him. I didn't answer. I keep it locked – not that the lock's up to much. A fist would open that door. But I think he's dangerous.' Sheppy finished the last of his tea and handed the ten-pound note to Morwenna. 'That was nice. I'll have another. And have you got a hot pasty? I'll treat myself and go back to work. The more kids that flock to Seal Bay, the more money I can make.'

'Coming up.' Morwenna turned to go. 'You're sure Taddy's gone?'

'Oh, he always runs off. But this time he's been gone for a few days. I expect the man will bring him back and give him a belting before too long.'

'I might mention it to Jane,' Morwenna said quietly. 'I owe her a text.'

'Your friend the copper, who's always in here?' Sheppy frowned. 'Don't tell her I told you. And if she's coming up, give me a nod first – I'll hide the weed.'

Morwenna winked and walked away. She moved to the counter, picked up her phone and texted Jane. She needed to talk to her. Things were taking shape.

Then she texted Ruan. She needed his help.

* * *

Later that evening, Ruan and Morwenna drove up Polkerris Hill in the white van. She had outlined their plan. They were dressed in black, with torches and phones in their hoodie pockets, soft trainers on their feet. Ruan pulled into a space in front of a five-bar gate, a field of barley waving in the breeze, and they clambered out into the cool air. They stood in the semi-darkness, the sea breeze in their faces.

Ruan said, 'You need to tell Jane about this.'

'I must. I'm meeting her tomorrow to give her an update. The MCIT haven't come up with anything yet. Rick Tremayne's still harping on about Tom Fox being the killer.'

'At least Mike Sheridan's conscious.'

'Jane said he couldn't shed any light on who'd beaten him up. Several men, he'd said, but that was about it. They hit him from behind.' Morwenna lowered her voice, even though there was no one around. 'Jane thinks he's too afraid to tell the police what really happened.'

'He was threatened?' Ruan said anxiously. 'You need to be really careful. Who do you think those two men were who spoke to you outside Bay Radio? MCIT?'

'No.' Morwenna tugged up her hood, tucking in her silver hair. The sky was almost dark. 'They'd heard the broadcast. I didn't get the feeling that they spoke to me because they were Rick's fan club.'

'Morwenna.' Ruan was worried. 'We should leave this alone. Tell the police what you know.'

'I will, as soon as I can. I just want to check this place first.' She met his eyes.

'I know what you're like when you get a bee in your bonnet. Right. It's best if we approach the campsite from the trees at the back, and that means crossing the field.' He glanced back at the van. 'I hope it'll be safe left here.'

'We'll be quick. And who's going to come up this hill late at night?'

'We could be a courting couple,' Ruan said, almost hopefully.

Morwenna ignored the remark. 'Come on – we need to have a good look round and get back before anyone sees us.'

They crossed the field together, shoulders hunched against the night breeze. The sky was grey and starless, the rising moon casting silver light on clouds. Morwenna said, 'Should we use our torches?'

'Not yet – we can just about see,' Ruan advised. 'And we don't want anyone to notice us coming.'

'Right.'

There was a clump of trees in the distance, tall shadows moving in the wind. The grass was damp, Morwenna felt moisture around her ankles. She shivered. They reached the fence and Ruan stopped. 'This used to be just hedges. Someone has put barbed wire up.' He frowned. 'That's not good.'

'It's to keep people out – look.' Morwenna noticed a sign had been hammered into the ground. It simply said, 'Woodpecker Camping. Residents Only'.

Morwenna found a gap in the hedge and heaved a leg over the barbed wire. 'Come on.'

He followed her and they stood in the field. The caravans were crammed in front of them like rows of rotten teeth. Some were crooked, leaning to one side. Morwenna moved forward, edging towards them.

'There are no lights on, Ruan.'

Ruan looked around. 'There's a dim light coming from that one – and the one at the far end.'

'That's Sheppy's, I think. I spoke to him today. He's keen to move out.'

They stood close to an old white caravan that smelled of damp and mould. 'I'm not surprised.' Ruan peered through a window. 'There's no one in there. This place is desolate.'

'That's what Sheppy said.' Morwenna led the way as they moved forward, closer to the black caravan where Taddy lived. There was no light, no sign inside. Opposite, low music came from the green caravan, the sound of a jangling guitar. Morwenna whispered, 'Sheppy…'

'We shouldn't disturb him,' Ruan said. He grabbed Morwenna's arm. A vehicle was approaching, headlights blazing as it juddered through the entrance and over the bumpy grass.

Morwenna huddled against the side of the black caravan, out of sight. She hissed, 'I can't see anything from here, Ruan.'

'If you can see anything then you can be seen,' Ruan hissed in reply.

'Right.' Morwenna dived onto the ground and scrabbled on her knees until she was flat on her belly beneath the caravan.

'It's not safe.' Ruan was next to her, following her as she edged forward on the damp grass so that she could see what was happening. Her fingers dug into moist earth and stones and water seeped through her clothes, but she wriggled forwards. There was a stench of mould and mud.

A vehicle was idling outside the caravan, some sort of minibus. Morwenna tugged her phone from her pocket in an attempt to photograph the numberplate, but she couldn't see it in the dark. Ruan put his mouth close to her ear. 'It's a Ford Transit.'

She was glad of the warmth of him next to her. The minibus door opened and several people clambered out, one set of trainer-clad feet after another, so close to where Morwenna lay, doing her best to breathe steadily. A gruff voice said something. 'Get yourselves to bed. It's a busy day again tomorrow.'

Morwenna inched along again on her belly like a frantic worm. She wanted to see more. Several youngsters were clambering out, hurrying towards caravans, dispersing quickly, talking in hushed voices. Two men remained behind, arms folded. Morwenna recognised them even though it was dark: their shaven heads, dark overcoats over muscled bodies. They could easily pass for bouncers. Or MCIT.

She dragged herself along the ground to hear better, her heart thumping in her ears. One said to the other, 'Time for a whisky in The Lugger.'

'Make mine a double,' the other replied. 'I hope that brat's freezing to death out there, slippery little bastard.'

'I left my mark on him, then we lost him again. We'll find him tomorrow,' the first man said. 'We need to get him moved on. He's too much trouble.'

'It's in hand,' the second one said cryptically. He moved back to the minibus.

The engine revved and headlights blazed. There was a rotten smell of sulphur as diesel smoke spluttered from the exhaust and the van chugged away.

Morwenna breathed out with relief. She turned to Ruan, her eyes wide. 'They were talking about Taddy.'

'He's got away?' Ruan whispered, 'So where is he? And why do the others stay?'

'We need to find out. What's going on with those two men? They're the same ones who warned me off this morning.'

'We know where they're staying,' Ruan said. 'The Lugger Bar is in The Fisherman's Knot Hotel, on the edge of town.'

'That's an expensive place.' Morwenna's eyes flashed. 'Someone's making big money.' She squirmed backwards until her feet protruded from the caravan, dragged herself out and upright. Ruan joined her. There were dim lights glowing from most of the caravans now. Cooking smells filtered through gaps in doors, the smell of burned toast or fried egg.

'We should head off,' Ruan said. 'We don't want to be seen.'

Morwenna was aware that her clothes and her hands were caked in mud, her shoes too. 'We should.'

They scurried back the way they had come, ducking past cara-vans, finding the hole in the hedge and lifting their legs high over barbed wire. The route back through the field of barley led them to Ruan's van, parked by the gate. Morwenna flicked on a torch, staring at Ruan. His face was muddy. Hers must be the same.

He said, 'Let's get home and talk about what we've just seen.'

'Right, and I need a brandy.'

'Oh no,' Ruan said. 'Someone must have seen us.'

'What's happened?' Morwenna whispered.

Ruan was shining the beam of his torch on the wheel. The tyre was flat on the ground. She knelt down and examined it with her fingers.

The rubber had been slashed.

24

Morwenna stood in the library feeling tired, listening to Louise chattering about something she'd seen on television the night before. She was replacing books, trying her best to put them in order, to remember that P came after O and before R. She'd been up until two o'clock talking to Ruan about what they had seen at the Woodpecker site, and how it might tie in with Irina's notes. They had arrived back well after midnight, once Ruan had put the spare wheel on.

Two things preyed on Morwenna's mind. One was that, although she felt confident she was on to the killer, he or she was on to her too: they'd marked her card. The other concern was Taddy, what had happened to him. Morwenna imagined him being found washed up by the seashore, just as Irina had. The idea made her shudder.

Louise was still talking about the television programme. 'The documentary said that Pablo Escobar was the seventh richest man in the world.' She was shocked. 'Do you know he even entered Colombian politics? A drug lord... imagine that!'

'Really?' Morwenna was doing her best to join in. 'It was on TV last night?'

'And El Chapo – he was so rich, and he kept escaping from the authorities.' Louise was fascinated. 'Can you believe things like that go on around the world – cocaine and opiates and millions of dollars and so many lives lost?' She folded her arms. 'Thank goodness we have a quiet life in Seal Bay. Do you want a cup of tea?'

'Ansom,' Morwenna replied. 'No sign of Lizzie today?' Her eyes moved to the open window at the far end of the library, to the carpeted floor below. She saw a dark spot on the ground. 'What's that, Louise?'

'What's what?' Louise joined her, kettle in hand.

Morwenna placed a finger to her lips. She approached the window above the store cupboard at the end of the library. She knelt on the carpet, Louise just behind her, and pointed at the dark blotch. She mouthed 'Blood?' It was damp, fresh.

'Is it our ghost again?' Louise whispered, wide-eyed.

'Not this time.' Morwenna shook her head. She moved to the cupboard and tugged the door open. Louise shrieked, but Morwenna knew exactly what lay behind it. A skinny young man in a grimy black T-shirt and jeans sat huddled in the corner, gnawing on a piece of bread. His lip, once swollen, was still red. There was a bruise on his cheek and he had a cut below his eye, which had been bleeding. He stared at Morwenna with wild eyes. She said, 'Taddy.'

He was on his feet, terrified. 'Please.'

Morwenna held out a soothing hand. 'It's all right. You're safe.'

'No, not safe, not anywhere.' The young man looked around nervously.

'Just tell us what's happening,' Morwenna said kindly.

'I hide here.' The young man's face puckered. 'I am sorry. I don't want trouble.'

'Oh, don't worry—' Morwenna began.

But Taddy darted past her, calling, 'I'm sorry,' again, then he weaved through bookshelves, towards the library entrance.

Morwenna called after him, 'I live at Harbour Cottages – number four – if you need anything.'

But he'd gone.

'What just happened?' Louise asked, puzzled. 'Who on earth was that?'

Morwenna was thoughtful. 'The poor boy. I think he's on the run. I need to talk to Jane.'

'Why? What's going on?' Louise grabbed Morwenna's hand. 'He was bleeding – someone had hit him.'

'I know.'

'And did you see the bruises on his face? He looked like he'd recently been beaten up.' Louise gaped. 'You knew his name. And what type of accent did he have? He wasn't from Cornwall.'

'He's in danger. Louise—' Morwenna grabbed her friend's hand '—if some hefty men come in here in smart clothes claiming they're MCIT, don't tell them you've seen the boy.'

'There were two of them in yesterday afternoon, very expensively dressed. I forgot to say.' Louise looked bewildered. 'Like you said, they were from the MCIT and they asked me if I'd seen anything suspicious and told me to keep an eye open. Oh – and I almost forgot – they asked when you worked here.'

'What did you tell them?' Morwenna asked urgently.

'That you were here in the mornings.' Louise was shocked. 'Did I say the wrong thing?'

'Don't worry,' Morwenna said kindly. 'If they come in again, don't say anything at all. They aren't who they claim to be. I think we're really close to finding Irina's killer.'

'And what about Else Ker? Did you find out who she was?'

'Oh yes,' Morwenna said quietly. 'I'll be seeing her in a day or two. I need to tell Jane what I'm up to and get her to help. Sorry, Louise – I can't say anything, not yet. Just in case the Blues Brothers come back.'

'Those men?' Louise was about to laugh but she stopped herself. 'They're dangerous, aren't they?'

Morwenna nodded once. 'Say nothing to them, all right?'

'Right.' Louise shivered. 'This is really scary. Will you be OK?'

'I'll be fine,' Morwenna said determinedly. 'I'll just keep my head down. We'll go swimming as usual on Sunday morning and by Monday morning, it will all be over.'

She placed her hands behind her back and crossed her fingers, as she did when she was a child, although she wasn't sure if it was a lie yet. After all, she was working on a hunch, nothing more.

* * *

By the end of the afternoon shift, Morwenna was ready to put her feet up. But Elowen came back to Harbour Cottages for a sleep-over and Lamorna had invited herself too. It would have normally been lovely to spend an evening together, three generations of Mutton women – Elowen might be a Pascoe and have a Caribbean father, but she was more Mutton than anything else. Morwenna wished she could be on her own, just this once – she had things she needed to do. Jane was calling round later. There was so much they needed to talk about.

They were squashed on the sofa, Elowen between Morwenna and Lamorna, Brenda curled in a ball on the little girl's knee. Elowen was hugging Oggy Two and Oggy Three, the toy Morwenna had won at the funfair, Elowen's new favourite.

Lamorna was clutching a cup of tea and eating Cornish fairings one after the other. She'd baked a batch earlier specially for the evening; sweet, spicy biscuits made with syrup. Elowen was munching too; even Brenda sniffed a biscuit, wanting to try.

Morwenna said, 'What are you two like? I fed you plenty for dinner.'

Lamorna agreed. 'I love rice, but it always leaves me hungry, so I need something sweet.'

'Great-Grandma and I have sweet teeth.' Elowen reached for another.

Morwenna glanced at the clock. It was almost eight. 'It's time for bed now, Elowen.'

'Great-Grandma said I could stay up late specially.' Elowen looked from Morwenna to Lamorna to check their reaction, to gauge her success.

'Can't she stay up for a bit?' Lamorna wrapped an arm around the child. 'We only get to see each other when I pick her up from school. I was looking forward to an evening with my little munchkin.'

Morwenna frowned. 'This munchkin has school tomorrow.'

'But it's Friday,' Lamorna insisted. 'It only counts for half a day.'

Morwenna met her eyes determinedly, wondering whether she was in fact worse than Elowen at procrastinating. She'd put her foot down.

'Right, Mum – here's what we'll do. You take Elowen upstairs, give her a bath and read her a story. That's your quality time together. When you come down, we'll do whatever you want.'

'Ruan promised me he'd run me home. He's coming over at ten.' Lamorna folded her arms. 'I can always rely on Ruan. He's so good to me, to all of us.'

Morwenna knew what was coming; she stemmed it quickly. 'You'd better get Elowen in the bath.'

'Just another few minutes,' Elowen begged, making her cutest face.

'No,' Morwenna said firmly. 'Take Oggy Two and Oggy Three up with you. A quick bath, a quicker story, and bed.'

Elowen slunk towards the stairs, her lower lip stuck out. Morwenna heard her mutter something like, 'I like my great-grandma better than my grandma.'

She ignored it and glared at Lamorna. 'Mum?'

Lamorna got up slowly. 'It'll kill my aching hip, standing over that bath.'

'I'll go, then?'

'No, you rest,' Lamorna said. 'Or you can make another cuppa. I want to tell you about these two men I met outside the school today. Charming, they were, ever so well dressed, and they spoke so nicely.'

Morwenna's blood froze. She watched Elowen clamber up the stairs, an Oggy toy in each hand, and murmured, 'Did they say they were from the MCIT?'

'Yes – have you met them? Lovely men.'

Morwenna felt her heart miss a beat. 'Did they speak to Elowen?'

'No, I was waiting outside the school with the other mums and dads. They came straight up to me, asked me if I'd seen anything suspicious around Seal Bay. Of course, I told them everything was suspicious around here until they arrested The Cream Tea Killer, but I said my daughter was very clever and— What? Apparently, they are looking for a skinny lad, dark hair and dark eyes.'

'Mum, they aren't MCIT. You mustn't say anything to them.'

'Who are they?'

Morwenna sliced a hand across her throat and glared again. 'Avoid them. Don't mention me. And you haven't seen anything.'

'Well, I haven't.' Lamorna stood up, groaning. 'Oh, my poor

sore hip. You need to tell Jane there are some dodgy men asking questions.'

'I know.'

'Well, giss on.' Lamorna tutted. 'In my day you knew who was who. The police wore uniforms and the baddies all looked suspicious. Now they all look the same.' She wandered up the stairs, her gait exactly the same stroppy roll Elowen had just done. 'I don't know. I'm only useful for picking up kids and giving them baths now.'

'I'll put the kettle on, Mum.' Morwenna reached for a Cornish fairing and decided against it. Brenda looked up hopefully before settling down again, closing her eyes. The phone buzzed on the sofa arm. It was Barnaby. Morwenna was momentarily annoyed with herself – she'd promised to ring him and she'd forgotten. She picked the mobile up and put on a welcoming smile, even though he couldn't see her.

'Hi, Barnaby.'

'Morwenna – how are you?' He sounded happy.

'I'm fine. I meant to ring. I've been so busy.'

'And I've been doing nothing, sailing in the *Pammy*, chilling.' He chuckled quietly. 'Do you need a break? We've been invited out.'

'Oh, when?'

'Tomorrow night,' Barnaby said. 'Matthew Rice rang me. It's his wedding anniversary. He's hired a boat and invited lots of people. Damien Woon recommended the party boat – he'll be there. There will be food and drink, music. Would you like to go?'

'I'd love to,' Morwenna said.

'We'll cruise around the bay with the stars above us and the sea below.' Barnaby's voice was husky. 'I'll pick you up at seven. Make sure you have something warm to wear – it will be chilly on board.'

'Thanks – I will.' Morwenna recalled that last time she'd been on a boat with Barnaby, she'd been unsuitably dressed against the cold sea breeze. This time she'd wear sensible shoes. 'I'll see you.' She placed the phone back on the sofa arm and heard a soft rap at the front door. She eased Brenda into a comfortable position and stood up. 'It's Euston station here tonight.'

No sooner had she opened the front door than Jane and Blessed barged in. Morwenna pointed to the ceiling and placed a finger against her lips. 'Mum and Elowen are upstairs.'

'We'll be quick as we can,' Blessed said, taking a seat in the chair. Morwenna and Jane plonked themselves down on either side of Brenda.

'Jane told me you'd been warned off after the radio show.' Blessed kept her voice low. 'These men who are posing as MCIT – they definitely aren't ours.'

'I know,' Morwenna said. 'They're involved with what's going on at Woodpecker caravan site. They're staying at The Fisherman's Knot Hotel.'

'So, what exactly *is* going on?' Jane narrowed her eyes.

'I'll go down to The Fisherman's Knot, have a look at the guest list, run some checks,' Blessed said.

'Mike Sheridan has been no help – there's something he's afraid to tell us,' Jane muttered. 'We're still keeping tabs on Tom Fox. He's admitted that the bruise marks on Irina's arm were caused by him, but not the one on her neck. And the marks are different. But we could call him in again.'

'You have to track down the men posing as MCIT.' Morwenna's eyes gleamed. 'You could use them as bait for the bigger fish.'

'What do you mean?' Blessed wanted to know.

'Irina gave me this. I've been meaning to give it to you but I kept forgetting.' Morwenna reached for the loose-leaf folder, hoping that she'd get away with small lies. She didn't want to say that she'd stolen it. 'Take a look at what she's written on the pages.'

Jane moved next to Blessed and they inspected the folder together. Jane said, 'Weather forecasts – dates and times – is this what I think it is?'

Morwenna nodded. 'Yes, and look at the final entry. "Elsa Kerr, Saturday, 22:45". It's a boat.'

'Meaning?' Blessed asked.

'Meaning that Irina knew about the boats that were coming into Seal Bay. Perhaps someone found out what she knew and wanted her kept quiet.' Morwenna pushed a hand in her pocket and handed over a folded scrap of paper. 'There's this too – I found it in the library. It was left by the young lad I told you about, Jane.'

Blessed opened the paper and read, '"Else Ker Sunday 22:55".'

'I checked tide times for the bay,' Morwenna said, pleased with herself. 'And I believe that's this Sunday night.'

Jane frowned. 'Why would the kid in the library leave you a piece of paper with the time of a boat's arrival?'

'That's what we need to find out,' Morwenna said. 'He's trying to tell us something important – about what's on board.'

Blessed looked up sharply. 'So we could be waiting at the appointed time and—'

'We'll be there just as the boat comes in, with back-up.' A smile spread on Jane's face. 'We'll catch Irina's killer red-handed.'

'Exactly – because whoever killed her will probably be on the boat, with its haul,' Morwenna said with a flourish. 'We won't just reel in the tiddlers, we'll get the one we're after as well.'

'Well done,' Blessed said. 'But there will be no "we", Morwenna. Understand?'

'I know – I'll stay at home and leave it to the police,' Morwenna said brightly.

'But the girl done good,' Jane said. 'This is perfect. Sunday night, we'll make the swoop and net the lot of them.'

'This calls for a celebration.' Morwenna held out Lamorna's plate of biscuits. 'Anyone for a Cornish fairing?'

'I don't mind if I do,' Jane said.

Blessed had already beaten her to it. 'Mmm.'

'Are you wolfing my biscuits down? You'd better save one for me.' Lamorna was thundering downstairs, rushing into the room, despite her sore hip. 'And if we're having a party, Morwenna, you'd better get that bottle of Prosecco out the fridge that you were saving for tomorrow night. You won't be needing it. I just heard. You're out on a date with Barnaby Stone again.'

'You can't keep anything from these Mutton women.' Jane rolled her eyes. 'It's a good job they're on our side.'

25

It was the hottest day of the year so far, and the busiest. Morwenna gave Elowen breakfast before taking her back to the tearoom, wheeling her bicycle downhill with the little one perched on the saddle. She dropped her off with Tamsin, who listened to her read before Carole Taylor arrived with Britney to walk the girls to school.

Morwenna rode to the library through building Friday traffic. Pawly Yelland had organised a meeting about the Victorian Pengellens, how they'd built Seal Bay library for the local people, and Louise spent the entire morning chattering with him and Donald while Morwenna checked books in from people who'd borrowed them during the wet weather. By lunchtime, she was glad to cycle through the sunshine to the tearoom, where a steady stream of customers came and went.

Tamsin was full of beans after her night out. 'Thanks for looking after Elowen, Mum. Becca and I had a whale of a time.' Her eyes shone. 'We went dancing. They had an eighties night at the Duck Dive. It was great, bopping to all the old music.'

'Old music?' Morwenna laughed. It seemed like only yesterday that she'd bopped to Michael Jackson and Wham!

'We had Fish Bowl Cocktails – Becca had about six Sin Cities. She can't hold her drink, that one.'

Morwenna closed her eyes but the images were still there, Tamsin and Becca in glittering dresses, dancing, falling about drunk, being held up by shady men with bad intentions. It was hard being a mum.

'Don't worry.' Tamsin laughed. 'We were fine. Becca's still got this thing about Tristan Pengellen, especially now he's a temp DJ, and his friend Seb was there too – they bought us drinks, so it was a great night. And you'll never guess who else was there?'

Morwenna groaned. She imagined Rick Tremayne and his officers, raiding the surfer dance hall for drugs. 'Who?'

'Sheppy, the magician, who comes in here. He sent you his best.'

'Oh, that's nice. He's going up in the world. I thought he spent his evenings in The Packet.'

'The Packet's horrible.' Tamsin pulled a face. 'Sheppy's in with a surf crowd now. He told me to tell you he's moving out of the dive – he's got a place at Camp Dynamo on the beach with two other lads. He said it's tons better than Woodpecker.'

'I can imagine.' Morwenna recalled how desolate the place was. 'I'm surprised anyone uses it. It's very isolated.'

'Far from it – Sheppy says they are bringing more old caravans in, a dozen of them,' Tamsin said.

'I remember him saying that.'

'The rats will have a field day up there. It's a wonder the council doesn't do something.'

'Perhaps they'll clean it up if they're bringing in more residents,' Morwenna suggested.

'Maybe.' Tamsin thrust a tray in her hand with plates of steaming pasties, cups of tea. 'This lot's for table three.'

'Tam.' Morwenna held the tray but didn't move. 'What do you know about Scatterbee's Fruit Farm?'

'I get my fruit from there, and some veg. The van driver's a bit of a lech, but the produce is good and it's cheap.'

'Pen said he'd just lost his job,' Morwenna said quietly. 'Who else works there?'

Tamsin shook her head. 'I've no idea – local people, I guess: students, working mums. I don't know.'

'Right – table three.' Morwenna was in motion, the tray in her hands, placing pasties in front of delighted faces. 'Enjoy.' As she passed Tamsin she said, 'And I'm off out tonight myself – you're not the only one who can gad about. It's an anniversary party. On a boat.'

'Tristan told me. It's the people up at Pennance Hill. They asked him to DJ. Of course, he said no. Who'd want to DJ for a load of—?' Tamsin was pouring tea. She looked up, a grin on her face. 'You'll have a great time, Mum. Are you going with Barnaby?'

'I am.'

'Dad'll be impressed.'

'Oh?' Morwenna considered Tamsin's expression. Of course, she was joking. 'What did he say?'

'We were talking, Mum. Dad and I often talk.'

'What about?' Morwenna felt a sharp pang. She and Ruan had lost the knack of meaningful conversation along the way. They'd lost each other.

'About you and Barnaby. Dad thinks he's a nice enough man, that you'll be all right with him.'

'Is that what he said?'

'Yep.' Tamsin turned on her heel, placing a pot of tea on a tray. 'But that's not what he means.'

'What does he mean?' Morwenna frowned.

'Ask him yourself.'

* * *

Morwenna was still thinking about Ruan as she sat in Barnaby's car, heading for the quay. At least she was warm in the patchwork coat, stars and stripes leggings and her Cornwall hand-knitted cardigan that she'd bought in aid of the Lifeboats from the pop-up shop. Ruan loved her taste in clothes – he'd always said she was unique, a one-off. Barnaby was wearing chinos and a smart jacket, and he hadn't commented on her attire, although he'd glanced twice at the vibrant colour-block trainers. Morwenna snuggled back into the warmth of the leather seats. She was looking forward to the evening, listening to the low thrum of the engine and the huskiness of Barnaby's voice.

'So, Pam's off to Barbados next Friday. She'll stay for a month. I'm leaving for London first thing tomorrow.'

'Good.' This meant that he'd be absent for the Sunday swim and the subsequent police swoop later – she didn't want him involved or asking questions. In a flash, she realised it sounded as though she was pleased he was going, so she tried again. 'I mean, it's good that you're travelling on a Saturday – it'll give you time to relax when you get back.' The next question came easily. 'How long will you be in London?'

'I'll stay for the week – I have appointments until Friday morning, but I was hoping to be back here by the end of next weekend to house-sit for a while.' Barnaby was waiting for her reaction.

'That's nice.'

'We can go out on the *Pammy*. I'm so glad you enjoy sailing.'

'Water always draws me,' Morwenna admitted. 'I'm never happier than when I'm up to my neck in it.' She was quiet a moment, remembering. 'I want to go to Irina's funeral. It won't be for a few weeks.'

'Are they any closer to finding the killer?'

'No, I don't think so.' Morwenna didn't like lying. 'I hope they find them soon.'

'You said on the radio that they would.' Barnaby had listened to Tristan's show. 'I thought you spoke well.'

'Thanks. Jane and I decided that if the killer thought they were on the verge of being caught, they might slip up.'

Barnaby reached out a hand and covered Morwenna's. 'Be careful, won't you?'

'I'll be right as ninepence,' Morwenna said. 'Oh, look!' They had reached the quay and Morwenna pointed to a powder-pink and blue boat adorned with coloured lights. 'They've hired *The Aquaholic*.'

Barnaby was confused. 'The what?'

'*The Aquaholic*.' Morwenna laughed. 'It's always used for big parties in the bay. I've seen Damien working on it at the boatyard. I can tell you – it's not cheap to hire.'

They clambered out of the Jaguar and stood on the quayside, looking at the huge pleasure boat, twinkling lights reflecting zigzag patterns in the dark water. People were already on board; a song was playing. Morwenna recognised 'Purple Rain' by Prince and smiled. Tamsin would call it old music.

Barnaby took her hand. 'Shall we go aboard?'

Morwenna nodded. 'I can't wait – where will we sail to?'

'The boat just goes out to sea a little way – we'll just cruise around the bay,' Barnaby said. 'I asked Matthew when he invited us.'

Moments later, they were on deck. Someone offered Morwenna a glass of champagne but she wanted to keep a clear head; instead, she reached for a tempting canapé from the plate that someone held beneath her nose. She looked around to see if there was anyone there she knew.

Rick and Sally Tremayne were talking to a group of people; Sally waved cheerily. Damien Woon and Beverley Okoro stood together, staring out to sea, her long hair blowing in the breeze. Damien noticed Morwenna and nodded curtly. He was Ruan's friend; Morwenna expected nothing more than an acknowledgement, now they weren't together. Jon and Ben Tremayne were talking to a sulky-looking Phoenix, who wore a glittery dress. Morwenna recognised most of the people on deck from the library, people who'd pop in from time to time to borrow books. Tom Fox was with a group of young men and women, drinking and laughing. Morwenna noticed that he stood next to Trudi from Bay Radio. Pawly Yelland was also there, talking to Pam Truscott, Barnaby's sister. She waved eagerly.

Morwenna said, 'I didn't know Pam was coming.'

Barnaby said, 'I'm glad she's getting out a bit more now, after Alex...' He gave her his full attention. 'Shall we go downstairs?'

'OK.' Morwenna didn't mind.

A cool voice said, 'Barnaby – glad you could come. And – Morwenna, isn't it?' Matthew Rice, smart in a black dinner jacket, looked her up and down, a smirk on his face. Morwenna expected him to make a comment about it not being a fancy-dress party. But he gave his full attention to Barnaby. 'Pam tells me you're back in London next weekend?'

'I am.'

'I might pop up.' He glanced over his shoulder. 'Debra's having a few days away with the girls from tomorrow and Phoenix wants to go back to Reigate to see some friends, so I might make it a trip and call in. Can you – fit me in?' He raised an eyebrow and pushed a hand through his hair.

'I'd be glad to. Phone me at the office.' Barnaby gave a professional smile. 'Morwenna and I are going to dance.' He wrapped an arm around her and led her downstairs into a throng of people, all wearing evening dress, swaying to Marvin Gaye's 'Sexual Healing'. Morwenna put her head against Barnaby's shoulder and wished it had been a different song; this one was far too seductive. She was sure Barnaby had his eyes closed as he pressed her close. She tried to concentrate on the music, but she found herself checking to see if there was anyone else she knew. She recognised Pippa and Julian Pengellen, who were dancing, of sorts: Julian had his arm around Pippa's waist, more of a formal waltz than a smooch. Morwenna tried not to smile.

The music ended and she pulled away. 'Shall I get us a drink?'

'Great.' Barnaby looked as if he needed one; his face was flushed. 'I'll just pop over and say hi to Pam.'

'Right – give her my best,' Morwenna said. She negotiated the crowd. Damien and Beverley were locked in an embrace. She patted Pawly on the shoulder and said, 'Hi,' as she passed him; he opened his mouth to invite her to stay and chat, but she was making a beeline for a young woman in a black dress who was holding out glasses of orange juice. She needed to quench her thirst.

Then she froze. A man in a dinner jacket shoved past her in the crowd and disappeared from view. She was sure it was the sweaty man who had accosted her with his friend outside the radio studio. Perhaps she was wrong. She reached the tray of juice and took two glasses, making sure to tell the waitress how much she appreciated her being there.

As she turned, she was greeted by Debra Rice in a turquoise satin evening dress. She offered a friendly smile. 'I just wanted to say, Morwenna, how nice it was meeting you the other night.'

'Thanks,' Morwenna said. 'We had a great time. The food was gorgeous.'

'You know, I was saying to Matthew, I think you're really good for Barnaby.'

'Am I?'

'I've never seen him look so happy.'

Morwenna didn't know if Debra had met him enough times to make such a remark but said, 'That's nice.'

'Matthew thinks the same. He knows Barnaby professionally. Of course, Barnaby's a wonderful surgeon but he doesn't ever let his hair down. You've really made him happy.' Debra raised her champagne flute. 'Long may it continue.'

'That's kind.'

'And—' Debra's smile widened '—I often get away with girl-friends – a spa weekend, you know, all the treatments, lots of champagne – and I hope that you'll come too at some point.' She placed a hand on Morwenna's arm. 'It would be great fun.'

'Thanks.' Morwenna wasn't sure if she'd enjoy being with Debra and her friends, but she was grateful for the gesture. She lifted the glasses of orange. 'I ought to get these to Barnaby.'

'I saw him go up on deck, all by himself.' Debra said. 'He was looking very lonely. I think he's missing you.'

'Oh right – I'll go and find him.'

'You should. Nice to see you, Morwenna. We'll catch up later.'

'Definitely – great party.' Morwenna made for the steps and clambered up to the top where people were leaning against the rails, staring out to sea. She passed Tom Fox, talking quietly with Trudi. He didn't notice her. She searched for Barnaby, but he was nowhere to be seen.

Morwenna gazed around the deck. It was crowded, people talking and drinking. She moved to a quiet place where the lights were dimmer and she leaned against the rail, closing her eyes, feeling the cool sea breeze lift her hair. She inhaled the sharp salt of the sea, enjoying the moment of peace that came with it. The sea was in her blood, the ice water, the whispering of the waves. Her mind drifted to Ruan, to the time they'd taken a small boat out when Tamsin had been a little bit older than Elowen was now. It had been an open sixteen-foot tiller-driven boat in the old clinker style, built by Damien Woon and his father: It was called *The Kraken*. They'd had such fun as a family. Morwenna could picture them now, laughing, enjoying the rise and jolt of the waves, spotting dolphins and seals in the bay. They'd been the best times.

She realised what was happening a split second too late as the stench of sweat filled her nose, the sharp tang of too-strong cologne. Someone had their arms around her. Morwenna twisted, trying to turn, but she was heaved up over the rail, and shoved hard. She screamed as her body fell through the air and hit the water with a crash. There was nothing she could do. She sank below into the depths, plummeting down, her clothes waterlogged and heavy, her arms flailing. The cold took her breath away as she closed her eyes for a moment, then she surfaced and gasped for air.

It was important to be calm, to think straight – she reminded herself that her heart rate was increasing, reducing blood vessel size, increasing blood pressure... What should she do next?

Think...

She fought the urge to thrash around in the water – the initial shock would pass in less than a minute. She summoned all her strength, tried to focus her mind and floated on her back, breathing steadily.

She flipped over, treading water, keeping herself afloat, staring up at the side of the ship, her breath coming in huge gulps. A loud horn blared from somewhere high above, voices shouting. Someone was yelling from the rails, throwing a lifebelt. It fell in the water and a spotlight picked it out, orange in a bright yellow beam. She swam towards it, her heart thumping in her ears, and grabbed hold tightly. A voice shouted again, loud instructions, and someone threw a rope.

It was Rick Tremayne.

Morwenna hung on for dear life, staring up at the ship through water-filled eyes, shivering violently.

She had a hunch who'd heaved her over the rail. But who had told them to do it? Who was the person on board who wanted her dead?

26

Morwenna was trembling, teeth clacking, hugging a rough blanket that was almost as damp and dripping as she was. She was confused and dazed. Voices came from all around.

'Morwenna, are you all right? Can you hear me?' That was Barnaby – there was a strangled concern in his tone.

'I didn't see her fall in... She must have been leaning over the rail. I didn't see what happened but I heard the scream,' Rick Tremayne said. 'There was a splash and I raised the alarm straight away.'

'It's a good job you acted quickly,' a woman said. Debra perhaps.

'She was probably drunk and fell.' That was almost certainly Matthew Rice.

'Let's get the TPA round her.' Damien Woon wrapped her in a thermal protective aid and she heard a low chuckle. 'You're fond of falling in the water, aren't you, maid?'

Morwenna could hardly move her mouth. She wanted to say that she'd been thrown overboard. No one had seen who'd hauled her over the rail – she hadn't seen him either. It was surely a man – she'd smelled the heavy cologne.

Barnaby was next to her now, his arms around her. The warmth of another body was what she craved most. She was so cold.

'Drink this.' Debra handed her a glass of brandy. 'It'll warm you up.'

'No,' Barnaby said. 'We need to get the wet clothing off and give her dry ones. And she'll need warm fluids to drink and food to eat.'

'I'll help.' Pam Truscott put a hand on Morwenna's shoulder. 'Let's get her into something dry, then you can take her home, Barnaby.'

Morwenna muttered, 'Thanks.'

'I'm so glad you're all right.' Barnaby's concerned face seemed to blur. 'What on earth happened?'

'I don't know,' Morwenna lied as she closed her eyes. 'Can I go home, please?' she whispered. At least she'd be safe there.

* * *

She sat in her living room in pyjamas and a dressing gown, wrapped in a fluffy blanket, clutching a mug of cocoa. Brenda had crawled onto her knee, doing her best to keep her human warm. Barnaby was holding her spare hand, stroking it as if it would bring her back to life. Jane Choy sat at her feet, still in uniform.

'Rick sent me straight round. I have to say, this beats the normal Friday night patrol around Seal Bay. How are you feeling?'

Morwenna grunted, 'OK.'

'It was very quick-witted of Rick to raise the alarm and throw you a line,' Jane added. 'So, what happened?'

'He didn't see it?'

'See what?'

Morwenna took a breath. 'Someone threw me over the rail.'

Barnaby frowned. 'Are you sure?'

'Definitely. There were a lot of people on deck. I was standing a distance away, in shadow, but someone came up behind me. He smelled like one of those two men who were pretending to be MCIT.'

Jane asked, 'Did you see them on board, at the party?'

Morwenna was still confused. 'I'm not sure. I hoped Rick might have noticed something but—'

'He only saw you fall,' Jane said.

'When I think of what might have happened.' Barnaby's brow creased. 'Look, I won't go back tomorrow, I'll stay on.'

'No, it's fine,' Morwenna protested. 'You go – it's only for a week.' Her eyes met Jane's – they both knew what was happening on Sunday evening and Barnaby was certainly not included in the plan.

'We'll take good care of her,' Jane soothed. 'And when you're back, she'll be relaxed and well again.'

'If you're sure,' Barnaby said.

'Of course,' Jane replied briskly. 'Give her some time to rest. You shouldn't go into work tomorrow, Morwenna – can Tamsin find someone else for the tearoom?'

'Not at this late notice,' Morwenna fretted.

'Jane's right.' Barnaby patted her hand. His voice was husky. 'Do you really think someone tried to harm you? Jane – do you think that's what happened to Irina? Could it have been The Cream Tea Killer?'

'No – maybe I was a bit confused.' Morwenna knew instinctively that if Barnaby was worried about her, he'd want to stay. 'Maybe someone knocked into me and I lost my balance. I was standing on a rail.' She gave a high laugh. 'Silly me.'

Barnaby stood up. 'You remember that?'

'I do.'

'You should probably go,' Jane told him. 'She needs to sleep.'

'Are you sure you'll be all right, Morwenna?'

'I'll stay and look after her for a bit,' Jane offered.

'She can look after herself.' Morwenna grunted, forcing half a smile, and eased herself to her feet and kissed Barnaby's lips briefly. 'I'm glad you were there. It was quite an evening.'

His eyes were full of affection. 'I was so worried when Matthew told me. I'd been waylaid by someone asking about corrective surgery.'

'Weren't you talking to Pam?' Morwenna asked.

'I was, earlier.' He kissed her again. 'I'll ring you.'

'Good.'

'Take care.'

'I will.'

Jane stood up. 'I'll show you out, Barnaby.'

Morwenna stroked Brenda from ears to tail, five, six times before Jane was back in the room, watching her with an anxious face. Morwenna gave her a sidelong look.

'I'll be all right for Sunday.'

Jane folded her arms. 'You're not coming on Sunday. It's a police matter.' She flopped next to her on the sofa. 'You promised.'

'I meant the swim,' Morwenna said and Jane pretended to glower.

'It's dangerous. You've done your bit for the police.'

'I know.'

Jane patted her hand. 'One of those men tried to kill you?'

'Definitely.' Morwenna said. 'I smelled him.'

'You didn't get a good look?'

'He was too quick.'

Jane watched her with a thoughtful expression. 'Do you mind if I call in at Ruan's on the way out? Tell him what happened?'

'He'll know,' Morwenna said. 'Damien will have messaged him on the fishermen's WhatsApp.'

'I'll call round anyway.'

'Right,' Morwenna said, glancing at the clock. It was half past eleven. 'He'll be back from The Smugglers by now.'

* * *

Morwenna slept heavily beneath a warm duvet, Brenda on the pillow next to her, and woke to the sound of someone moving downstairs. She was about to call out, 'Ruan...' He'd have his spare keys. But she paused; the feeling of someone gripping her from behind, heaving her in the air and hurling her towards the icy black waves was still foremost in her thoughts.

There was a soft footfall on the stairs; she reminded herself that she ought to keep a heavy implement next to her bed, a paperweight or a hammer. After last night, it wasn't the silliest idea. Ruan stood at the door holding a mug of tea.

'All right?'

Morwenna sat up. 'Not so bad.' She took the tea. 'Thanks, Ruan – I suppose my moonlight swim's all over WhatsApp?'

Ruan nodded. 'Damien said Rick Tremayne was a hero.'

'He was,' Morwenna admitted. 'He reacted so quickly. I'm very grateful.'

'There are beans on toast downstairs when you're ready. I thought you'd need the protein.'

'Thanks – I'll get up.'

'Take your time,' Ruan said. 'I'll be here.'

Morwenna glanced at the clock. 'It's nearly ten – I'm supposed to be at the tearoom.' She whisked her pyjamaed legs out of bed. Her feet were still ice cold.

'You don't need to worry – Tam and I sorted it,' Ruan said. 'I rang her and she's got a fill-in waitress.'

'Since when?'

'Since this morning. One of the surfers Tam goes dancing with was looking for part-time work. She's waited on tables before, so she's working Saturdays for the summer season to give you a break – Fridays too, if you like. She's called Imogen.'

Morwenna flopped back on the pillow, causing Brenda to open one eye. 'Thank goodness.'

'No worries.' Ruan winked. 'The beans on toast are ready when you are.'

'Right.' Morwenna closed her eyes, counting her blessings. When she opened them, Ruan had gone downstairs.

* * *

Wrapped in a blanket on the sofa, Morwenna woke up with a start, as if she'd just hit the cold water again. It was almost three o'clock and she was exhausted. She was still shivering, her feet full of pins and needles. Ruan had left shortly after he'd washed up the breakfast dishes. He was taking Elowen to Hippity Hoppers, promising to call in on Morwenna as soon as he returned. She knew he'd cook something for their dinner. Her eyelids were heavy and she was overwhelmed with feelings of thankfulness. She reached for her phone and found a dozen messages, all from people enquiring after her health. Ruan had texted encouragement and a photo of Elowen grinning and bouncing, her arms in the air, dark curls over her eyes. Lamorna overreacted, as expected; her mother wanted to come round on Sunday evening and cook her dinner –

how would Morwenna manage without her? She was properly worried sick.

Morwenna took a breath. Sunday wasn't the best day – she'd have to put her mother off, ask her to delay it until Monday. Jane and Blessed had both told her not to meddle in police business, but she had to be available for when the *Elsa Kerr* came in.

Tamsin had sent messages from the tearoom; she, Imogen and Zach were doing absolutely fine, she wasn't to worry.

Jane had messaged, just checking in.

Louise had heard about Morwenna falling in the water from Susan and Barb in the pop-up shop. Apparently, it was all round Seal Bay that she'd been dead drunk, slipped on a rail while being sick in the sea and would have drowned if Rick Tremayne hadn't stripped down to his boxers, leaped in and rescued her. Morwenna actually laughed out loud. The idea was ridiculous.

Barnaby had messaged; he was back in London and thinking of her. He hoped she was feeling better and he was missing her. He'd phone later.

Morwenna replied to everyone, filled with gratitude. She was loved by so many people; family and friends were so important. Then, overcome with tiredness, her eyelids heavy, she fell asleep again. The last thing she remembered was Brenda clambering on top of her, kneading her chest with hard paws and settling down with a furry flop.

She woke to the smell of frying onions. Ruan was in the kitchen, cooking tea. Morwenna opened heavy eyes. 'I'd love a glass of wine.'

'Should you drink after last night?' Ruan asked.

'What are you suggesting?' Morwenna laughed.

'I mean – is alcohol good for your recovery?' Ruan said simply.

'I don't know, but my body's asking for it,' Morwenna called back. She could hear him uncorking a bottle with a soft plop and wine glugging into a glass. He brought two glasses through, one for himself, handing the other to her. She took a grateful sip and closed her eyes. 'That's better.'

'I'm cooking vegetable satay with noodles,' Ruan said.

Morwenna met his eyes. 'You don't have to be so nice, Ruan. But I'm really grateful.'

'You shouldn't be,' he replied lightly. 'It's what I'm here for.'

'You don't owe me anything.'

'I do,' Ruan said. 'I'm only across the road. We're family.'

Morwenna paused, thinking about it for a moment. She heard a muffled sound at the front door and frowned. 'That's not the postman.'

'No. I'll go.' Ruan padded into the hall and Morwenna heard him talking to someone with a light voice. He reappeared, holding a heavy bunch of flowers. 'These came – for you.' He handed them to her.

Morwenna eased herself upright and read the label. 'Barnaby.' She sniffed the petals. 'I'll put them in water.'

'I'll do it,' Ruan offered. 'He's a good man.' He busied himself with finding a vase, taking the flowers from the wrapping, handing her the affectionate message on the florist's card. 'He thinks a lot of you.'

'I suppose so,' Morwenna said. 'I don't know what I feel. Sometimes I think it's going well and sometimes I'm not sure.' She glanced at Ruan. 'I shouldn't be telling you this.'

He smiled. 'You know you can tell me what you like.'

'Well...' Morwenna took a deep breath. Then it all came out too quickly. 'The problem is, it will take a very special man to follow you, Ruan. And I can't tell if Barnaby is that special man or not.'

'Give it time,' Ruan said. 'Don't rush it.'

'How would you feel if I – if I was serious about someone else?'

'It's not my business. I care, obviously. I'll always look out for you. But I suppose, inevitably, one of us will find someone else.' Ruan exhaled. 'It's a shame.'

'What is?'

'You and me – we were great. We let things get away from us. We took each other for granted.'

'We did. It was like going over a bump in the road. We argued over silly things and then we didn't speak at all.'

Ruan met her eyes. 'You argued, I didn't speak.' He almost smiled. 'But I know for sure I'll never care for someone the way I cared for you.'

Morwenna was a little surprised. 'How does that make you feel?'

'I'll live with it.' Ruan lifted his shoulders, placid, ever pragmatic.

'It's not easy to move on, though,' Morwenna admitted.

'It's not,' Ruan said. He looked as if he was about to say something meaningful but instead he muttered, 'I think the food's ready.'

'I'm starving,' Morwenna said, as Brenda sprang from her knee and hissed, staring at the window.

Morwenna turned, following the cat's gaze. There was a face at the window staring through. Dark hair, shining eyes. All of a sudden, he was gone.

Ruan was on his feet, rushing towards the door, leaving it wide open as he went out. Morwenna followed him, listening to a scuffle on the path, at the gate. Then Ruan was hauling a dark-clad figure back to the door, heaving him up to face her.

Morwenna took in the young man's split lip, the bruised face, and she said, 'Taddy. I knew it was you.'

27

'My name is Tadas Kazlauskas,' the young man said. 'I come from Klaipéda.'

'In Lithuania. Of course.' Morwenna nodded. 'How long have you been living in Seal Bay, Tadas?'

'Six weeks. But I run away. It is not nice.'

'You speak good English,' Ruan said kindly.

'My father and mother speak it. I learn from them. It is good to know it. But I don't like to live here.' He stared at his grubby hands, his dirty nails. 'I want to go home.'

'Who hit you?' Ruan asked, examining the young man's swollen face.

'I work for two men. I don't like to be there, so I run away. They bring me back to the caravan and tell me to stay, but I run again.'

'Ruan, take him upstairs and show him where the bathroom is.' Morwenna decided that they could speak later. 'Tadas, have a nice hot bath and when you come down, we'll eat some food.'

Tadas's eyes shone. 'I am very dirty. And hungry.'

'Go and have a long soak, then we'll eat,' Morwenna said kindly. 'Not all people in Seal Bay are bad.'

'Thank you.' Tadas turned to Ruan. 'If the men come for me, you will not tell them I am here?'

'Of course I won't,' Ruan said. 'You're safe.' He led him to the stairs, glancing over his shoulder to Morwenna. Ruan's expression was one of compassion for Tadas and indignation at how he had been treated.

Morwenna eased herself up from the sofa. 'I've sat here long enough. I'll go check on the food. And I need to call in a favour.' She picked up her phone. 'Hi, Rosie, it's Morwenna. I don't suppose you have any old clothes of Tommy's you don't want? I know you pass them down to the boys – yes, I have a bit of an urgent situation – no, it's nothing to do with me falling into the— No, I wasn't drunk. Yes, I'll ask Ruan to pop over dreckly. That's proper nice of you, Rosie, thanks.'

An hour later, Tadas was sitting at the table eating noodles, dressed in a clean shirt, hoodie and jeans that had once belonged to Tommy Buvač, Rosie's eldest. Ruan had rushed round in the van and come back with two changes of clothes, a pair of old Star Wars pyjamas, some recycled trainers and a brand-new pair of boxers that Tommy had been given for Christmas and never taken from the wrapper. Tadas's eyes had filled with tears.

Morwenna said, 'People of Seal Bay are kind and thoughtful. We're not like those men you've met.'

Tadas was clearly hungry, but he ate slowly, chewing carefully. Morwenna asked gently, 'What were you doing in my garden?'

'I follow you sometimes when you are in the cafe – I see you work there. I know you are kind lady. You leave food for me by the van and I am very hungry. You tell me four Harbour Cottages and I see a map in town showing the way to places.' Tadas exhaled. 'One time I am in the street and I hide when I see the two men come to talk to you. I am afraid they will hurt you. They are wicked men. I hear them speak and you tell them some clever words. You are not afraid of them. So I think, perhaps I can ask this lady for help.' He turned to Ruan. 'And you are a kind man. I am grateful.'

'How old are you, Tadas?' Ruan asked, his fork in mid-air.

'I am seventeen years.'

'Who brought you here?'

'It is a mistake,' Tadas said. 'At home, a man promises me a good job in England and I make money for my family. I work two years in this country, then I come back to Klaipėda a rich man and I help my parents with their life. My father is sick and he cannot work – I have two brothers and a sister younger than me.'

Morwenna understood. 'And how did you get here?'

'Boat, a big truck, and another boat. It is very hard. There are many of us, from many cities. We all hope we will do well here. We live in a dirty van and the work is many hours. The men tell us we owe them for the transport from Lithuania and we must pay it first, and they are not good to us. We are hungry and I want to go home, so I try to run.'

'You worked at Scatterbee's Fruit Farm?' Morwenna asked gently.

'Many of us work there. Others go far away to do other things. I hear someone tell me that one girl goes to be a servant for a rich family, and another goes to a man in a city who likes to keep young women in his home for his friends when they have big parties.' Tadas shook his head. 'I wish I had not come here.'

Morwenna leaned forward. 'You've been here for six weeks?'

'It seems like all my life.'

'And in that time have any more people come to join you?' She met his eyes. 'At the fruit farm?'

'No, but I hear that some will come soon.' Tadas squeezed his eyes shut. 'I feel bad for them. They do not know what waits. They think they will return to their families and make them happy.'

'Tadas, we can help you get home,' Ruan said.

'How will you do that?'

'You can stay with me, in my house – it's just across the road,' Ruan explained. 'And we have friends who can help you get back.' He raised an eyebrow to Morwenna. 'I think you should message Jane after we've eaten.'

'I'll do it now. My friend Jane works to help people and she'll make sure you can go home.' Morwenna reached for her phone and she saw Tadas flinch. 'Is that all right?'

'I can trust you?'

'I promise you can,' Morwenna said gently. 'When I've called her, we'll have some ice cream. And you can stay with Ruan tonight.'

Tadas frowned. 'You do not live here with your wife?'

'It's complicated.' Ruan placed another spoonful of noodles on Tadas's plate. 'But you'll be safe.'

'What if the men come after me again?' Tadas's eyes were wide.

'They won't find you,' Morwenna said calmly. 'Now finish up your food and I'll get you some ice cream. Do you like plain or chocolate chip?'

'Chocolate, please.' Tadas's expression was one of blissful happiness.

Morwenna thumbed a quick message to Jane.

MORWENNA

> One of the kids from Woodpecker is here – he's being hunted down – can you advise – we can keep him somewhere safe until he can go home.

She got to her feet, cleared the table, scurried to the kitchen and filled bowls with ice cream. She placed the largest one in front of Tadas and he attacked it with a spoon.

'Mmm. This is good.'

'I had a funny feeling that you were never far away, Tadas. You hid in the library, where I work,' Morwenna said. Her phone buzzed with a message. 'That was Jane – she said she'll come over.'

Tadas spoke between mouthfuls. 'A window is open and I get in and out. It is warm and dry in the cupboard. I look at books sometimes and I sit at the laptop. One time I look at pictures of Lithuania because I miss my family and I see that your Queen Elizabeth who died has some ancestors from Lithuania. I am happy to know it. I hope the people of England might help me, like you help me.'

Morwenna remembered. Louise would be disappointed that Lady Elizabeth's ghost hadn't been behind the disturbances. 'And you left me a message on a scrap of paper?'

Tadas nodded. 'I write Else Ker. Sunday night. I hear the men talking about the boat. More people will come as I did.'

'The *Elsa Kerr*,' Ruan said. 'I've heard of that boat – I don't know who it belongs to though.'

'You remember looking at Irina's folder? There were tide times, weather forecasts. I'm sure Irina found out about the boat before she was killed. That's what she was going to tell me – and who was responsible.'

'So the *Elsa Kerr* is bringing a cargo on Sunday?'

'Right.'

'And Jane knows?'

'The boat will be met, Ruan,' Morwenna said, giving him a look that suggested Tadas needed to know nothing more.

'Please – stay away,' Ruan said. 'It will be dangerous.'

'I'll leave it to the police,' Morwenna assured him. 'I don't want to have anything to do with it.'

'It will all be finished and I can go home to Klaipėda?' Tadas finished his ice cream. He looked truly calm for the first time. 'Thank you.'

'It's a pleasure to help,' Morwenna said.

There was a clatter at the front door and Morwenna stood up. 'That will be Jane. I expect she's brought Blessed.'

'Or Rick?' Ruan said. 'He's your new best friend.'

'I want to say thanks to him,' Morwenna said. 'He was very quick to help – and I mightn't be here without him.' She turned to Tadas. 'My friend is at the door. She's a police officer. She'll keep you safe.' She patted his face, touching the swollen cheekbone gently. 'But I think you should go upstairs just in case. Stay in the bedroom until I call you.' She watched Tadas's eyes widen. 'It'll be fine. But it might be a neighbour or my mother.' She laughed. 'My mum would eat you alive.'

Tadas didn't understand, but he headed up the stairs, two at a time. Morwenna padded through the hall and opened the door, expecting to see Jane.

Instead, two short-haired men in smart jackets filled the space. 'Where's the kid?'

One of them propelled her hard into the house and before she could react they were in the hall, slamming the door behind them. Morwenna rushed into the living room, where Ruan was standing, barring the entrance to the stairs. He'd heard their voices. Brenda leaped from the sofa, all narrowed eyes and raised fur, and rushed upstairs to keep Tadas company.

The men moved apart, filling the room. 'Where is he?'

'Who are you?' Ruan asked.

Morwenna was amazed how calm his voice was. Her pulse was racing, blood singing in her ears. She could hear herself breathing heavily.

One of the men said, 'You know why we're here. He was spotted hanging around. Just give him to us and we'll go without smashing your faces in.'

Morwenna sized them both up. Squat, arms that bulged beneath their sleeves. She glanced at Ruan, muscly but slender, and she was five feet three in her socks and tired out from half drowning – she didn't fancy their chances. She'd have to use guile.

She took a deep breath. 'A small kid came to the door begging. We sent him on with a fiver. He went off into Seal Bay.'

One of them lurched towards her, a fist raised. 'You're a lying bitch.'

Ruan caught the arm. 'You should go.'

The man's eyes narrowed. 'Don't tell me you weren't warned.'

'It's time you left,' Ruan said again, his voice still steady.

The other man roared, rushing at Ruan, forcing him to the ground. The first one aimed a kick at him and Ruan rolled away. Morwenna was on her feet, dashing into the kitchen, breathing fast. She came back with a cast-iron frying pan and whanged it as hard as she could, hitting the man in the mouth. She watched blood bubble. He touched his face, his lips twisting in anger as he spat a swearword. She hit him again and shrieked, 'Ruan!'

Ruan lurched towards the fireplace, picking up a shovel that Morwenna had once used for coal. She used it nowadays to sweep up rubbish from the hearth: Ruan was using it as a bat. She heard it crash down on one of the men's heads.

The other had her arm in a vice grip. She bit into the flesh of his wrist and slammed the frying pan into his face again. He twisted her arm hard and she yelped.

The front door sprang open. Jane and Blessed hurtled in. Morwenna thought she saw a baton raised, a taser. Everything seemed to happen in slow motion. The man she'd hit was missing several teeth; blood was pouring from his mouth. He rushed at Jane and she tumbled backwards as he pelted towards the door, dragging his friend behind him, a gash on his cropped head. Morwenna reached for Ruan. He was standing now, leaning to one side, holding his ribs. Blood seeped from his cheekbone, the flesh already puffy. The two men's feet thundered as they ran out into the dark night.

Jane clutched a baton as she said, 'Are you all right?'

Ruan groaned. 'I think a rib cracked.'

'Morwenna?' Blessed was at her side.

'I'm fine – it's just a bruise.' Morwenna held up her wrist where the flesh was already swelling. 'At least Tadas is safe. Thanks for coming so quickly.'

'I got your text,' Jane said. 'We'd have come quicker if we'd known they were here.'

'You ought to get checked over,' Blessed said efficiently.

'We can look after the young lad,' Jane added.

'No, please.' Tadas was standing at the bottom of the stairs. 'I want to stay here. I am safe with these people,' he said quietly.

'I'm glad you came when you did, Jane.' Ruan was exhausted. A second bruise was swelling on his cheek. 'I was a bit worried.'

Jane was radioing for officers to come round, speaking in a calm voice, giving directions, location, descriptions of the men. She wanted them apprehended immediately. She turned to Morwenna. 'I'd be happier if you let me take you down to A & E. And I'll need a statement.'

'No, we're fine for now.' Morwenna wrapped an arm around Tadas. 'Will you get those men tonight, Jane?'

'There are officers all over it – and if we don't pick them up now, we'll certainly apprehend them tomorrow at the boat,' Jane said grimly.

Blessed was full of admiration. 'Well, Morwenna, Ruan – you both know how to take care of yourselves, for sure,' she said. 'Those men are a nasty pair. But we have their number.'

'You did well,' Jane agreed. 'So – can I take you down to A & E now?'

'I'll pop in tomorrow if I need to,' Ruan said.

'Yes, let's stay here for a bit and see how we feel.' Morwenna looked at Tadas. 'A cup of tea and some quiet time among friends will make this one feel a lot safer.'

Tadas was troubled. 'What will happen to me?'

'Leave it all to us.' Blessed offered him a kind smile. 'By tomorrow night, it will all be over. No more worries for you, young man.'

'That's a relief.' Ruan turned to Morwenna, his face full of concern. 'I certainly didn't expect to spend my Saturday evening fighting. Are you all right?'

'I think so. Just don't tell Elowen that we were exchanging blows with two thugs, and that I hit one over the head with a frying pan,' Morwenna said, breathing deeply. 'I've just spent the last six months trying to convince her of the way of peace.'

28

The Sunday SWANs wild swim was very well attended. Morwenna knew why: news of her fall from *The Aquaholic* at the Rices' party had spread like wildfire around Seal Bay, thanks to the fishermen's WhatsApp and local gossip.

Louise wrapped a protective arm around Morwenna. 'I'm so glad you're all right – you could have drowned.'

Jane and Blessed exchanged smiles. Jane said, 'It pays to be a strong swimmer.'

Morwenna shivered in her swimsuit – Irina had been a powerful swimmer and that hadn't helped her survive.

Susan Grundy stood on the sand in her brown swimsuit, a pale towel around her shoulders. 'I heard Rick Tremayne dived into the sea and rescued you.'

'Did he throw himself in from the ship's rail and tug you out of the ocean?' Barb asked.

'Everyone is saying that he flung off his clothes and dived in like Superman,' Susan added.

'And according to half of Seal Bay, he gave you the kiss of life.' Lamorna, in floral swimsuit and cap, folded her arms dubiously.

'Everyone in the supermarket was talking about it. Of course, I told them that's a load of old rubbish. You'd rather drown than get kissed by Rick Tremayne.'

'Didn't Barnaby try to save you?' Susan asked.

'I heard he's gone back to London with his tail between his legs,' Barb added. 'He must feel very put out, watching Rick play the big hero.'

'I expect he can't swim – these London types never see a drop of the ocean.' Susan grunted.

'No, he's always here, going out on that boat, the *Pammy*,' Barb countered.

'He's very fond of Morwenna,' Louise said, closing her eyes in a mock swoon.

'It's good to see you here this morning, Morwenna – we didn't expect you to turn up.' Donald spoke up, hugging a towel around his pale chest and baggy swim shorts.

'But you've hurt yourself. How will you swim?' Louise indicated Morwenna's bruised wrist. 'Did you do that falling in the sea?'

'No, I had an accident with a frying pan,' Morwenna mumbled. 'We should get in the water.'

'And afterwards, we'll get hot chocolate.' Jane glanced towards Blessed. 'We've a busy day today.'

'We have,' Blessed agreed, offering Jane a cryptic look.

Susan overheard. 'Oh? Have you got a lot of criminals to catch?'

'Have you found The Cream Tea Killer?' Barb asked suspiciously.

Blessed, tall and sturdy in a red swimsuit, offered a professional smile. 'You can leave all that to us. Now – are we going in?' She offered Jane a smile. 'I'll race you.'

Everyone ran across the sand towards the rolling waves apart from Lamorna, who stood her ground, and Morwenna, who asked, 'Will you come in the water and have a little swim today, Mum?'

Lamorna frowned. 'I know that look on your face, Morwenna Mutton.'

Morwenna presented an innocent expression. 'What look?'

'That look. You're up to something.'

'Me?' Morwenna asked. '*Moi?*'

'Right, I want to know what's going on. It's that Barnaby, isn't it?' Lamorna's eyes blazed in triumph – she was sure she was right. 'You're sleeping together.'

'We're not,' Morwenna replied.

'Well, what is it, then? I know that guilty face. Ever since you were a kid and peed in your toy box.'

'Mum, let's get in the water. We can talk about anything you want there.'

'I'm coming round to yours tonight. You can make me dinner and tell me all about it then.'

'About what?'

'What you're up to. Romance. Barnaby?' She glared at Morwenna. 'Or is it Ruan?'

'I'm busy tonight – I have plans. Come round on Monday.'

'What plans?'

'Come on, Mum – let's get into the water.'

'My hip's playing me up.'

'A swim will help.'

'You go in – I'll follow.'

'Right.'

Morwenna knew it would be no good trying to persuade her mother to swim so she rushed towards the tide. The other SWANs were already splashing and squealing with the shock of the sudden low temperature. She joined them and felt the familiar sensation of something gnawing at her flesh – the cold was intense. Morwenna recalled the ice of the ocean when she fell overboard from *The Aquaholic*. She had never felt so numb. The Sunday swim was easy in comparison. She dived beneath the surface, remembering her swim with Irina two weeks ago. Morwenna was filled with a strange feeling of relief – she'd been lucky in comparison.

But Irina had not drowned in the sea. Fresh water had been found in her lungs. Tap water? Morwenna surfaced, spluttering. She recalled hiding under the table in Irina's office, watching someone in jogging bottoms and trainers wiping water from the carpet, and marks had been found at the back of Irina's neck; fingerprints.

Irina had been drowned in the handbasin of her own office.

Morwenna blinked water from her eyes as Jane swam towards her and started to tread water.

'Where's Tadas now?' she asked.

'With Ruan, having breakfast,' Morwenna said. 'Poor kid. What he must have been through. What will happen to him now?'

'We have a duty to notify the Home Office, once we've done the swoop tonight.' Jane said. 'Tadas isn't automatically eligible to stay in the UK.'

'He wants to go home,' Morwenna explained.

'There's a system in place to support victims, a national referral mechanism that will get him all the help he needs. I'm focused on the arrest right now. We have a team ready to be at West Point beach.'

'West Point?'

Jane nodded. 'Tadas identified it as the place he was brought to. We'll wait for the *Elsa Kerr* to come in and we'll make arrests.' She beamed, her face shining with water. 'Well done, Morwenna.'

'And do you think one of the two men who attacked me and Ruan is The Cream Tea Killer?'

'Probably,' Jane said. 'But there will be others. We'll bring them all in. I'm hoping it's a real coup, finding The Cream Tea Killer and arresting a gang of human traffickers at the same time.'

Morwenna wasn't sure. 'Tadas said some of the victims have been taken beyond Cornwall – he said some of the young people who came with him were used for domestic slavery, sexual exploitation.'

'We'll interview the culprits when we catch them and follow it up.' Jane spluttered. 'Modern slavery is an adult safeguarding concern, and we have legal duties to provide support for victims.'

Morwenna said, 'I wish I could come with you.'

Jane gave her a 'police look'. 'Please don't. We'll have enough to contend with.'

'I know. I'll stay at home.' Morwenna shivered. Her wrist ached from the effort of swimming. 'I think I'll go back.'

'I'll join you.' Jane kicked her legs. 'Hot chocolate's on me. I still can't believe how brave you and Ruan were yesterday, faced with those two men – I'm looking forward to making the arrest later. You owe us a statement about the face-off at Harbour Cottages last night.'

'I'm still a bit dazed by it.' Morwenna shuddered at the memory, her eyes on Lamorna, who was still standing on the beach. 'I'll do your statement on Monday, when you've arrested them all, if that's OK? Let's swim for shore. I'm freezing now, and Mum looks like she needs a hot drink.'

* * *

Ruan and Morwenna decided it was wise to take Tadas out of the house all day, in case the two men came back. Tamsin was busy with Elowen; they were spending the afternoon on the beach with Becca, who apparently was going to wear her most alluring bikini in case a certain Pengellen surfer and his friend were nearby. Tamsin was more interested in having quality time with Elowen.

They drove around Seal Bay in the van, up to the clifftop over-looking Pettarock Bay, showing Tadas all the local beauty spots, stopping to buy ice cream. Tadas was clearly still hungry, devouring everything he was offered: sandwiches, Cornish pasties. He didn't refuse a proper Cornish cream tea either when Ruan and Morwenna took him to The Happy Kettle by the seafront at Pettarock Bay.

They drove back at six o'clock and Tadas wanted more food. When presented with carb-rich pizza, he ate the lot and looked for seconds. By ten o'clock, he was almost asleep on the sofa, Brenda sprawled across his knee.

Ruan and Morwenna sat on the carpet with cups of tea. Ruan gestured with a smile. 'Look at him. I ought to take him over the road, let him sleep in a soft bed.'

'Stay for a bit, until we get the all-clear from the police,' Morwenna suggested.

Ruan's eyes were still on Tadas. 'That's how it should be for a seventeen-year-old, spending a Sunday with friends and family, chilling.' He shook his head. 'He's been through hell.'

'He has,' Morwenna said sadly. 'Jane said it might take up to forty-five days to arrange to get him back home.'

'I wonder if they'll let him stay with me for a bit?' Ruan asked. 'I can get him some work on the trawler. It would be some money in his pocket to take home to his family.'

'That's a nice idea, Ruan.' Morwenna kept her voice low. 'I think he'd like that.'

'I'll ask,' Ruan said.

'How's your sore rib now?' Morwenna asked kindly.

'I just need to rest it. An ice pack and painkillers will help, but I'll give it time. How's the wrist?'

'Same.' Morwenna glanced at his swollen face. 'We were lucky to get away with just a few bruises last night.'

'You were so brave,' Ruan said. 'I always knew you were. Do you remember when we had Tamsin, when the midwife said she was struggling in the womb and you had to have a C-section? I saw the epidural go in and I was terrified. But you were smiling.'

'I'd had so much gas and air, I couldn't have cared less,' Morwenna said, remembering. 'They were good times.'

'I cried when I held her for the first time – she was just a little scrap,' Ruan admitted.

'An eight-and-a-half-pound little scrap,' Morwenna said. 'We were happy then, Ruan.'

'We were.' His eyes glimmered. 'We could be again.'

Morwenna felt a pang of nostalgia for the good times they'd shared. Ruan was right. 'We could.' Then she remembered the bickering, the silences. 'I don't know how we lost each other.'

'Perhaps we didn't, not really,' Ruan said.

Before he could say any more there was a sharp knock at the door and they exchanged nervous glances.

'Who can that be, at this time?' Morwenna whispered. 'The front door's locked – the security light's on outside. Jane says to ring 999 if the men come back, and not to open the door.'

'I'll go,' Ruan said. 'I won't let anyone in.'

Morwenna listened carefully, feeling sure that Ruan was checking the shape in the glass to see if there were two men behind it. She heard the door open and a woman's anxious voice said loudly, 'I had to come round, Ruan. I was so worried. I didn't think you'd be here though – it's late.'

'What's up, Lamorna?'

'Something's going on. I can feel it in my waters. Ever since Morwenna fell in the sea, I've been worried sick. And this morning at the swim, she was proper shifty...' Lamorna, in a red check jacket and green felt hat, sauntered into the living room and saw Tadas asleep on the sofa. 'Who's this?'

Tadas sat up sleepily, rubbing his eyes. Morwenna said, 'Tadas, this is my mum. Mum, meet Tadas. He's a – house guest.'

Tadas was only half awake. *'Malonu tave vėl matyti, močiute...'* He shook his head. 'I am sorry. I thought I am home again and my grandmother comes to see me. But she is not alive now.'

Morwenna ruffled his hair. 'You rest, Tadas. My mum has just come round to say hello.'

Ruan frowned. 'It's late, Lamorna. Did you walk all the way here? You could have texted.'

'I wanted to see Morwenna. I was sitting watching TV and it was nearly time for my bed, but I couldn't relax. It kept preying on my mind and I thought, I won't sleep, I'll just go round – it's a bleddy long walk, mind, it nearly killed me – but I *have* to know. I'm sure she's up to something, that maid. I knew you'd give me a lift back home, Ruan. So I get here and now you've taken in a young man from goodness knows where.' She looked him over. 'Lovely eyes he's got, mind.'

'You didn't see anyone hanging around Harbour Cottages, Mum? You weren't followed?'

Lamorna was suddenly suspicious. She turned sharply, grabbing Morwenna's sore wrist with her ringed fingers. 'What's going on? I knew you were in danger, falling in the sea, hurting your arm. It's my maternal instinct that told me. And look at your face, Ruan – you've been in a fight. My hunch was right – something terrible's going on. It's The Cream Tea Killer, isn't it? Now – spill the beans.'

'All right, Mum. There's been some human trafficking in Seal Bay,' Morwenna said quietly. 'Tadas is safe with us. Jane's on it – I expect the police will just be getting in position to make arrests now.'

'Human traffic in Seal Bay? Whatever do you mean by that?' Lamorna asked. 'Where are the police to?'

'They've gone to West Point Bay, where they are going to arrest the criminals who have been bringing people into the country as modern slaves,' Morwenna said.

'West Point? Is that where they've gone?' Ruan asked.

'Yes – that's where Tadas was brought to.' Morwenna faced him. 'What's wrong?'

'The police should've asked a fisherman,' Ruan said. 'The *Elsa Kerr* won't come into West Point tonight. The tides aren't quite right. They'll sail into Pettarock Bay.'

Morwenna glanced at the clock. 'Oh no, they'll get away – the new kids will be up at Woodpecker site before we know it and the police will have a harder time proving their case. They need to catch them red-handed.' She grabbed Ruan's arm. 'Can you drive with a cracked rib?'

Ruan's hand was already in his pocket for his keys. 'Can you ring Jane with a bruised wrist?'

They were tugging on their coats.

Lamorna wailed, 'Where are you going?'

Morwenna kissed her mother's cheek. 'Look after Tadas. Make him hot chocolate, with cream and sprinkles.'

'What?' Lamorna was shocked. 'Can't I come?'

'No, absolutely not.' Ruan turned to Tadas. 'Stay here. You'll be all right with Lamorna.'

'No, please.' Tadas was on his feet. 'I come with you.'

Morwenna glanced at Ruan. 'Shall we take him along? At least we'll know where he is.'

'Please – I am safe with you.' Tadas's eyes were huge.

'All right,' Ruan said quickly. 'But we'll have to hide you in the van – you can't be seen.'

Tadas almost smiled. 'I am good at hiding.'

'Mum, you'll be OK by yourself for a while,' Morwenna said. 'Stay overnight if you want. But we won't be long...'

'I'll watch TV for a bit.' Lamorna looked confused. 'Where did you say you're going?'

'Pettarock Bay,' Morwenna said quickly, throwing an arm round Tadas. 'Just hang on for us.'

The three of them hurried towards the door as Lamorna frowned from the sofa, arms folded.

'I've still no bleddy idea what's going on,' she grumbled. 'That maid will be the death of me.'

29

Ruan drove the van as fast as he could, Morwenna speaking furiously on the phone to Jane that she needed to divert the officers to Pettarock Bay, that West Point was the wrong beach and the *Elsa Kerr* would be disembarking any time now. Tadas was huddled in the van behind them, staring out of the windows, his face anxious.

Ruan said quickly, 'When we stop the van, Tadas, stay in the back, out of sight, and hide.'

'We shouldn't have brought him,' Morwenna said.

'He was desperate to be with us. He feels safer – he's been through so much. We'll keep him out of harm's way.' Ruan took a deep breath. 'The poor kid's in shock. He trusts us. He'd have been terrified, waiting in the house with your mother.'

They hurtled along the road in darkness, past the glow of street lights, towards the place where the beach came to a natural end. There was no one around. Morwenna stared through the passenger window; she must have imagined a movement further down the road. She whispered, 'Look – over there.'

A minibus drove up, parking by the kerb. It was a Ford Transit, with just the sidelights on. The glimmer picked out moving shapes. Then a group of figures emerged from the shadows, clambering up the steps towards the road. A beam shone from a torch as a group of young people were shepherded towards the road.

'It's them,' Morwenna muttered. 'They're bringing new people to the minibus. Ruan, do something.'

'Right.' Ruan accelerated, driving forward at a furious speed, then he braked hard, his van careering, stopping horizontally against the bumper, barring its way. The headlights illuminated several faces in the darkness, huddled close to the minibus. Morwenna recognised the two men with cropped hair and heavy coats, who turned towards them.

'Stay in the van,' Ruan said hoarsely. 'Don't get out.'

One of the men scurried towards the minibus. He came back, carrying something. Morwenna's heart sank – it was a crowbar, raised in his huge fist. He shouted expletives, a warning, then the crowbar came crashing down on the windscreen, again and again, the safety glass cracking with each blow.

Morwenna whirled towards Ruan. 'What do we do now?'

Ruan locked the doors and revved the engine, ready to reverse. 'We'll slow them down for a few more seconds, then we'll drive backwards.'

Morwenna was on the phone again, her voice raised with urgency. 'Jane – where are you? You have to be here now. We can't hold them off. Make it quick.'

Cracks were all over the glass, a hole had appeared and still the man continued to beat the windscreen. Now the other man was at Morwenna's door, tugging at the handle, swearing. He noticed Tadas in the back of the van and increased his effort. Ruan reversed quickly, manoeuvring backwards in a circle, accelerating forward again, back, and forward like a performing pony.

'Jane's on her way,' Morwenna said.

'I hope she gets here soon,' Ruan muttered. 'Any minute, they'll be off. I don't want to lose them.'

Morwenna stared through the cracks in the windscreen. She leaned forward and a figure stepped into the road. She recognised who it was immediately and shouted, 'Stop, Ruan!'

He braked a distance from the minibus, and Morwenna said, 'I'm getting out. Just be ready. The moment I'm worried, I'll get back in and we'll drive off – right?'

'What are you doing?'

Morwenna took a breath. 'I can hold them up until Jane gets here.'

'I don't think you should,' Ruan said, but Morwenna opened the door, standing behind it as a shield. She stared at the figure in front of her, who was shining a torch directly in her eyes.

Morwenna said, 'I knew it was you.'

There was a clacking of heels as a woman walked a few paces towards her, elegant in a dark coat. The wind blew strands from her honey hair, tied in a chignon.

Debra Rice said, 'Well, doesn't that make you the clever one? The snoop. The sleuth.' She took another two steps forward. 'So, come on, let's hear it. What made you suspect it was me?'

'You sent me up on deck, where your man followed me and shoved me into the sea,' Morwenna said. 'What did you say your business was in Surrey? A recruitment agency? That's a cover for what you're doing with all these kids – placing them on farms, in homes, to work for a pittance while you exploit them.'

Debra's voice came from the darkness. 'Go on. Tell me more. This is all fascinating. And very flattering.'

Morwenna took a shaky breath. 'I suppose having a holiday home here was a great cover. But you dropped breadcrumbs, you made some mistakes. You told your husband that you were away for a girls' spa weekend. Is that what you tell him when the boats come in?'

'Matthew has no idea what I do.'

'So, is it just you behind this little business venture?' Morwenna asked. 'You and the Blues Brothers?'

The man with the crowbar had taken his place behind Debra, arm raised, ready to hurl himself forward. She held out a hand to stop him – she was in charge. 'You should be grateful – we provide a service to this pathetic little backwater.' Debra snickered. 'We employ the foreign workers up at Scatterbee's, we employ others to run the place. The farmer gets rent for his field, and the fruit is picked and packed. Cornwall does well, thanks to me.'

'But it's slave labour,' Morwenna said.

'That's what Irina said too. She *had* to meddle, just like you're meddling.'

'Did you kill her?' Morwenna asked.

'You think I'm The Cream Tea Killer?' Debra laughed openly. 'You think I lured her to a meeting and drowned her. Well, that's a compliment.'

'Did you order one of your men to do it?'

'They do as they are told – they're paid a good wage,' Debra said smartly, with a nod to the man at her shoulder. 'Irina was warned to keep her mouth shut. But she had to keep sticking her nose in. Fortunately, she kept all her information on her laptop. That seems to have gone missing. What a shame.'

Morwenna wished Jane would hurry up – she couldn't keep Debra talking forever. There was a cold breeze coming from the sea, the sinister whisper of waves. She couldn't see the boat; the entire beach was in darkness. She looked up. Stars twinkled, chips of diamond.

'So – my turn to ask questions.' Debra's brow wrinkled. 'How did you guess we'd be here tonight?'

'Skill, research,' Morwenna said. 'Putting two and two together.'

'You mean the kid told you? The one who ran away?' Debra was suddenly angry. 'He's mine.'

'You can't own people, Debra.' Morwenna couldn't help herself.

'He's my property.' Debra's face was hard in the half-light. 'Hand him over.'

'Who are you talking about?' Morwenna knew it was pointless to protest her ignorance, but she hoped it might waste more time. She willed Jane to hurry up.

'He's in the back of the van,' Debra said.

'He's staying with us.'

Debra's voice was icy. 'Send him over. We'll drive away. You've seen nothing. It's your only way out.'

'He's staying here,' Morwenna began.

'You were warned.' Debra's hand moved to her coat pocket. Ruan revved the engine and Morwenna whirled back into the van, slamming the door as he drove backwards, swerving in a half-circle, making the van roar. A shot rang out, a single crack.

Ruan whisked the van round, facing the other way, and began to drive blindly just as police cars screamed past him, lights flashing. He edged the van around again slowly. It was difficult to see through the shattered windscreen.

Morwenna turned to Tadas. 'Are you all right?'

He nodded, wide-eyed.

She reached a hand to him, patted his cheek. 'The police are here now. There's nothing to worry about.'

More sirens wailed, more police cars arrived, sirens whooping and flashing blue lights. There was a lot of shouting, people running. Morwenna clambered out of the van into the darkness and blinked hard, trying to see what was happening.

Blessed leaped athletically from a squad car and in an instant, she had Debra on the ground, face down, and was shouting a caution. 'You do not have to say anything. But it may harm your defence if you do not mention when questioned something which you later rely on...'

There were so many officers Morwenna had never seen before; in the dark it was hard to pick out anyone she recognised. The man with the crowbar and his friend were handcuffed; she could hear them protesting loudly. Jane was herding the confused young people into a group, trying to explain that they were safe, that she was there to help them and that they would not come to any harm.

Morwenna closed her eyes and felt the cool sea breeze on her face. Ruan was next to her, his arm gently around her. Morwenna realised she was trembling; her legs shook. She felt a hand take hers, a cold, dry palm pressing against her own. She looked into Tadas's brown eyes, the whites gleaming. 'Thank you,' he murmured.

She stifled a sob and Ruan pulled her close. 'Are you OK?'

'I think so.'

'You kept her talking,' Ruan said, his face full of admiration.

'I did.' Morwenna gave a small laugh, trying to make light of it all. 'Jane took her time, though – I was running out of words.'

A tall, broad man walked towards her; he was wearing a long coat. He held out a hand, took hers and shook it heartily. 'Thank you, Morwenna.' He turned to Ruan. 'You've both been a great help.'

Morwenna exhaled, exhausted now. 'I'm glad we could do something useful, Rick.'

'We're lucky to have you as our resident sleuth, Ms Mutton.' Rick met her eyes.

'Amateur. But I'm learning.'

Rick gave a small cough. 'I don't hold with meddling in police matters but I have to admit, you've been very useful. I don't know where we'd be without you.'

Morwenna felt Ruan's arm tighten around her as he said, 'It's nice to hear you say that, Rick.'

'I know I haven't been your biggest fan in the past but—' Rick shrugged '—thanks.'

Even more squad cars arrived, blue lights whirling. Morwenna watched as uniformed officers ran past. She shook his hand again. 'Thank you, Rick, too – you saved my bacon the other day, on the boat.'

'I saw you fall – I wish I'd seen who pushed you over,' he said. 'I knew you were on to something. Apparently, the force has been trying to haul this little gang in for a while.' He looked pleased with himself. 'You'll all have to come into the nick and make a statement.'

'I'm getting used to giving statements,' Morwenna said. 'I'll be in tomorrow.'

'Right,' Rick said. 'Well, it's late. I'll be working on into the early hours – Sally won't be best pleased with me. No change there.'

'She'll be proud of you,' Morwenna said kindly.

'To be honest, I'm a bit annoyed with myself.' Rick said. 'Debra Rice made a friend of Sally to get me into her friendship group. Having the DI on her side was useful, I suppose.'

'It was.' Morwenna had suspected it.

'I should have seen through it.'

'You just did, Rick.' Morwenna patted his shoulder. 'Right, we'll leave you to it. I'm tired now.'

'Jane will give you a lift up to Harbour Cottages. Reinforcements have arrived,' Rick said. He indicated the van with its smashed windscreen, the hole on the side of the metal door where the bullet had skimmed. 'I'll need to hang onto this for a while.'

'Thanks, Rick.' Ruan's hand went to his sore rib. He looked exhausted. 'I think we'll get this young man home – we all need to sleep.'

'Of course.' Rick waved a hand, calling over his shoulder, 'Jane, we've got it from here. Can you grab a squad car and get these good people back to Harbour Cottages?'

Morwenna watched as Jane emerged from a mêlée of police officers, talking kindly to the muddled new arrivals, organising two handcuffed men and one woman into police cars. Lights continued to flash, and there was the occasional whoop of a siren. Morwenna closed her eyes and thought she'd fall asleep where she stood.

Jane arrived, efficient and energetic. She said kindly to Morwenna, 'Come on – let's get you home.'

Morwenna sat in the front seat next to Jane with Ruan and Tadas huddled behind. The youngster was asleep, his head on Ruan's shoulder. Morwenna said very little, except for the occasional grunt when Jane asked if she was all right.

Jane was delighted with the night's outcome. 'We'll get a conviction. Debra Rice won't see the light of day for a while. If she's found guilty, the maximum sentence is life imprisonment.'

'I see.' Morwenna couldn't really take it all in.

'They'll throw the book at her – forced or compulsory labour, human trafficking, exploitation,' Jane continued. 'She'll go away for a long time.'

Morwenna closed her eyes and listened to the thrum of the engine. Finally, she felt the lurch of the vehicle and steady braking. They were home.

She clambered out, watching Ruan and Tadas tumble from the back seats, only half awake. She leaned towards Jane, who had the window open.

'Are you done for the night?'

'Are you inviting me in for coffee?' Jane joked.

Morwenna rolled her eyes. 'I'm too tired – sorry.'

'I'm off back to the station now. I won't finish for hours yet. Not with the little group we have to process in the nick, after Operation Elsa Kerr.'

'I'll text you, Jane.' Morwenna managed a smile as Jane drove off. She turned to Ruan. 'I'm all in.'

'Me too,' he said, looking at Tadas, whose eyelids were already drooping.

Morwenna glanced towards number four. 'Oh no – there's a light on in the lounge. I forgot, Mum's still there.'

'I promised I'd take her home,' Ruan said. 'But I haven't got the van.'

'It's fine – she can stay over,' Morwenna said.

'Right.' Ruan closed his eyes for a moment. He was tired. 'Come on, Tadas – I'll show you where you're sleeping. Then I'll pop back here, just for a few minutes. Shall we have a nightcap?'

'I'll get the kettle on.'

'Good idea. It's been a long night, and we need a brandy. I think I need a couple – I'll bring a bottle. We'll explain to Lamorna what's happened. Is that all right?' Ruan met her eyes. 'To be honest, I don't want to leave you alone after all this.'

'It's fine by me. Yes,' Morwenna said. Ruan was always practical. 'I could do with a stiff drink and I'd rather you tell Mum all about what happened – she'll only grumble if I tell her that I've been investigating again. She'll say I'm raising her blood pressure.' She smiled. 'Thanks, Ruan. We've both been through a—' she considered the words '—a lot, and we need to recover. Yes, that would be nice.'

His eyes met hers. 'I'll just be a minute.'

'I don't want to be alone.' Tadas looked anxiously at Ruan. 'I can come with you?'

'Aren't you tired?'

'I want to stay with you. Please.'

Morwenna touched Ruan's arm. 'He'll feel safer.'

'Of course,' Ruan said kindly. 'You go into the house with Morwenna and I'll catch you up. You can doze on the couch if you need to.'

'Thank you,' Tadas muttered.

'Come on. It's only for half an hour. And I'm sure you won't mind a slice of cake, young man.' Morwenna wrapped an arm around Tadas, shepherding him towards the door. 'I'll see you in five, Ruan. Wish me luck with Mum if she's still awake. I bet she's fast asleep with Brenda on her knee.' She tugged the keys from her pocket, pushing the door open.

She walked tiredly inside.

30

Morwenna stepped into the hall, Tadas beside her. From there she could see her mother sitting in the lounge, bolt upright on a chair. Something was wrong. Morwenna had expected her to be upstairs asleep, or at least slumped in front of the TV watching an old film, but Lamorna was staring ahead blankly, her face anxious.

Morwenna was about to close the door behind her when a deep voice called, 'Come in, Morwenna. I've been waiting for you.' She froze.

Lamorna said weakly, 'He's got a gun.'

Morwenna couldn't see who it was but she recognised the voice. The man laughed lightly. 'We have unfinished business and I'm in a hurry.'

'Right, I'm just coming.' Morwenna turned to Tadas and placed a finger over his lips. She mouthed, 'Find Ruan. Get help. Get Jane.'

Tadas nodded, bolting away into the darkness. Morwenna closed the door with a deliberate bang. She walked slowly into the living room.

'Someone was outside and I thought it was you and Ruan come back, so I let him in.' Lamorna was trembling.

Morwenna moved gingerly, sitting down on the carpet in front of her mother. From the sofa opposite, Tom Fox pointed a firearm.

His voice was cold. 'I thought I'd pay you a visit. I expected you to be home. But it seems you were out, meddling again.'

Morwenna wasn't sure what to say, so she said nothing.

'Interfering in my affairs. I can't have that. I've called round to settle the score. So, what happened at Pettarock Bay? Did you tell the police where the cargo was coming in? Did they arrest Debra?'

'I don't know.' Morwenna shook her head.

'Your mother said the police went to West Point and you went to Pettarock Bay, where the *Elsa Kerr* was due.'

'I didn't see anything. There wasn't anyone there,' Morwenna said, trying to keep her voice calm.

'Liar.' Tom raised his voice. 'I asked you what happened.'

'I think there were people on the beach but I couldn't see properly – it was dark. I don't know what happened after that. It's not my business.'

Tom sneered. 'You make everything your business. You're a nosey old bitch. I never liked you when you kept coming to the radio station, asking about Irina.'

Morwenna couldn't help noticing his clothes. He was wearing jogging bottoms, a smart watch. Her mind raced.

'So, what happened to Irina?'

'She asked too many questions – she wanted to know too much, just like you.' Tom sniffed, as if it were nothing. 'I told her to leave it alone. I took her on as a DJ, a pretty face that the dumb locals would warm to. But no, she wanted to investigate. She found out about the Woodpecker site, she went up to Scatterbee Farm and some blabbing van driver was ready to tell her all about the new intake of workers, half of whom didn't speak English. We were on to a winner up there before she found out. She was going to tell the police.'

'But I don't get it.' Morwenna glanced at her mother with what she hoped was a reassuring look. 'You were engaged. You must have loved her.'

Lamorna shook her head slightly as if she was afraid the questions might anger Tom. But he gave a sarcastic laugh.

'It was a good front, wasn't it? A nice radio station, a beautiful fiancée. I had everything set up nicely, a great little business. If she'd shut her mouth, we'd have been fine.'

'But she found out,' Morwenna said.

'The stupid bitch couldn't keep quiet. She'd done a degree in journalism and she thought she was something special. She had to be stopped.' He inspected the gun for a moment and then pointed it back towards Morwenna. 'Nosey women with big mouths annoy me.'

Lamorna put a ringed hand against her lips, terrified. Morwenna wasn't exactly calm. Her heart was banging in her chest. She took a deep breath in an attempt to steady her voice. She needed to keep him talking.

'So what did you do to Irina, Tom? Did you kill her?'

'You tell me – you're so clever.' He was gloating.

Morwenna spoke slowly, deliberately. 'Well, I think she was drowned in water first. Someone held her under for a long time. I think she couldn't breathe – she must have struggled.'

'She did.' Tom waved the gun, enjoying himself. 'Go on.'

'Then she was thrown in the sea to make it look like accidental drowning.'

'Exactly. Full marks.'

Morwenna felt as if her heart might burst, it was thumping so hard. 'Did you kill her yourself or did one of those men who were pretending to be MCIT do it?'

'You mean am I The Cream Tea Killer?' Tom thought this was hilarious. 'What do you think, Morwenna? Am I capable of killing a beautiful young reporter with a great career in front of her?' His tone was suddenly nasty. 'And while we're on the subject, am I capable of killing two interfering old women who just happened to be in the wrong place at the wrong time when a burglar came in?'

'Burglar? What burglar?' Lamorna didn't understand.

'I've been waiting for you to come home, Morwenna, so I can get rid of you both. Two pathetic old biddies.' Tom's voice was sing-song now, as if he was telling a story. 'Oh, what a shame it was. The house was broken into, everything smashed up, and the poor old dears must have disturbed a burglar, who shot them both and ran away into the night, never to be seen again.' He laughed. 'Of course I killed Irina. She came to the office to talk about the *Elsa Kerr*. She knew it was me, that I was trafficking. She just had to say it to my face. Do you know, she even tried to give me the engagement ring back?'

Morwenna took another deep breath, wishing help would come. Tom was bragging now; she focused her eyes on his, hoping he'd continue. 'So I put gloves on, wrapped my fingers round her neck and dragged her to the sink. It was easier than you'd think.' His eyes gleamed, frenzied. 'It didn't take long.'

'You dumped her body in the sea,' Morwenna said.

'With her bag and her phone.' Tom's face contorted. 'She was no use.'

'Then you came back to the office and tidied up,' Morwenna told him. 'And took her laptop away.'

'How do you know that?' He looked at her sharply.

Morwenna wasn't about to admit that she had watched him. 'Someone must have done it.'

'And now there's something else I have to do.' Tom pointed the gun meaningfully.

'Hang on.' Morwenna made her voice as gentle as she could. 'There's one thing I don't get.'

'Oh?' Tom raised an eyebrow. 'Have I been too clever for you?'

'I think so.' Morwenna was desperate to continue the conversation. Jane had to be on her way. 'Where does Debra Rice fit in?'

'Debra? She was useful. Rich. Good connections. And not bad in bed either.' He gave another laugh. 'Better than Irina. And much better than Trudi. Debra passed the time of day. And she organised work for the boatloads of foreign kids hoping to make lots of money for their poor parents. When they arrived, they were put to work and the money came straight to me. It was easy.'

Morwenna was running out of time, clutching at straws. She had to think of a way of delaying him. 'So how does it feel to be called The Cream Tea Killer?'

'Mike Sheridan's name for me. Funny, isn't it?' Tom said. 'Stupid Mike, a lonely man with no talent, lying in a hospital bed, fighting for his life.'

'Did you beat him up?'

'No, I had those two idiots to keep the kids in order so I paid them a grand each to do a number on him.' A new thought made him sneer. 'I only offered them half that for you and the old fisherman. As it was, they messed up and I didn't pay them a penny.' He shrugged. 'I expect they're banged up now. But I'm out of here. I have a plane waiting in Newquay. No one will see me again. But I need to get rid of you.' He pointed the gun. 'Which one first – the snoopy old bag or her crone of a mother?'

Tom looked from Morwenna to Lamorna and back to Morwenna. She heard her mother gasp and she took a deep breath, trying to calm the pulse that pounded in her ears. Her voice came weakly.

'So – was it you who threw me overboard?'

'If it had been me, I'd have stuck a knife in your back first to make sure the job was done properly.' Tom said. Morwenna saw the cold look in his eyes and she knew he meant it. 'Those two men I employ are amateurs.'

Morwenna tried to speak calmly. 'Tom – I think you should put the gun down. It's not too late to just walk away.'

'But I'm The Cream Tea Killer.' He laughed. 'It's expected of me – I don't want to disappoint.'

Morwenna felt cold sweat trickle down her spine. 'Let Mum go, then.'

'She can be first, while you watch. That's why I didn't kill her before you came back,' Tom said. 'You can be second – you'll never blab again.'

'Wait.' Morwenna tried again.

'I'm running out of time,' Tom glanced at the steel watch. He stood up slowly, deliberately, raising the gun, pointing it at Lamorna. Then he slumped to the ground, the weapon falling from his hand as he writhed on the carpet. Blood seeped from his arm.

Morwenna wasn't sure what had happened, but there had been a double cracking noise, a window had been broken. The sound in her head was her own blood pounding. She dropped to the ground, dragging Lamorna with her. She wasn't sure if either of them were alive or dead.

She eased herself up and saw Tom reaching out a hand towards the gun. He was wounded, his shoulder bloody. She had just enough energy left to push out a foot and kick it away. She turned to Lamorna, who was sitting up, trembling, and they both burst into tears.

The room was full of people wearing black clothes, protective vests. Tom was on the floor screaming in pain. Two of the officers grabbed him, shouting words Morwenna couldn't hear because of the ringing in her ears. He was hauled away. Blessed was next to Morwenna, an arm around her, and Jane was comforting Lamorna.

'You're going to be fine,' Blessed said. 'We brought in the AFOs.'

'AFOs?' Morwenna was completely confused.

'Authorised Firearms Officers.'

'What happened?'

'Tadas found Ruan, he called us and we sent in the AFOs. They were watching everything from the garden,' Blessed explained gently. 'When Tom Fox stood up, they had a clear shot. He's wounded, but he'll live.'

'Where's Ruan? Where's Tadas?'

'They're outside by the gate,' Jane explained. 'And I'm afraid you'll have to leave too. This is a crime scene now. You can't touch anything.'

Morwenna gazed around. Men and women in uniform, some in protective vests, were everywhere. She needed to get outside into the fresh air. She wrapped her arms around Lamorna, who was still shaking. 'We'll go back to your house, Mum.'

'I'll drive you there, stay with you for a while,' Jane said. 'Tomorrow afternoon, I'll need you to come in for a debrief and make a statement.'

Blessed appeared, Brenda in her arms. 'You'll want to take this little sweetheart with you – she's been asleep on your bed the whole time.'

Lamorna put out her hands to cradle the cat. She needed every hug she could get.

Jane wrapped both arms around Morwenna. 'You came up with the goods again. You're incredible.'

Morwenna didn't feel incredible. She felt dizzy, shaken, dead on her feet. She turned to Lamorna. 'Are you all right?'

Lamorna forced a smile, although her lip was quivering. 'Nothing that a good night's sleep and a cuppa won't cure. You can't keep a good Cornish woman down.'

Then she burst into tears again.

31

Morwenna's sleep was filled with ragged dreams. She woke, Brenda at her feet, at midday. She could hear Lamorna moving around downstairs, the radio jangling. She assumed it wasn't Bay Radio – they wouldn't be on air this morning. She sat up in bed and realised she was wearing an old nightie that had belonged to her mother. Her leggings and cardigan, the ones she'd worn last night, were at the bottom of the bed, and all the terrible emotions suddenly flooded back. She shuddered a sob and felt her body tremble.

Her phone was on the bedside table and she read the messages. There was a dozen of them, maybe more.

Louise had sent several: Morwenna was not to come in to the library today. Donald was there already; he'd stay all day, and tomorrow. Pawly had arrived for a meeting about Lady Elizabeth. They'd all cover for her. She should consider taking a holiday – Louise could easily postpone hers. It would do her good. She was amazing.

Tamsin messaged that she was so proud of her. Ruan had brought Tadas to the tearoom at nine o'clock, told her everything that had happened and offered to work Morwenna's shift. Tamsin had called Imogen, who was delighted to take on extra work for as long as was necessary. In fact, Tamsin wanted to talk to Morwenna about offering Imogen more hours, to give her a break. Morwenna closed her eyes – some down time would be nice. She read on. Tamsin said Elowen sent her love and wanted to see her after school, so could she come to the tearoom for her dinner and bring Lamorna?

Ruan had sent one message. He hoped she was fine; he was getting a hire car for the week; he'd taken the day off because his rib was still sore. Besides, they had to go to the police station later and did she need a lift? Tadas was staying with him until his future was resolved. Ruan was practical as ever.

Jane texted that she'd pick Morwenna and Lamorna up at two and that Tom Fox, Debra Rice and the two henchmen had been charged. Everyone at the nick was toasting Morwenna. She glanced at the clock – she'd better put yesterday's smelly clothes on and get up. Tonight, hopefully, she'd be back in Harbour Cottages, in her own shower, her own bed – could there be anything better at the moment? She reached out an arm and stroked Brenda, who rolled over on her back and stuck out her paws. She'd sleep anywhere, that cat, as long as there was food available.

The mobile buzzed with an incoming call. It was Barnaby. Morwenna felt a rush of anxiety, wondering if he had heard about what happened.

'Hi, Morwenna – how are you?' he asked, his voice light and cheery. Clearly, the news of last night's debacle hadn't reached London yet.

'Fine.' She was relieved not to have to go through the whole story again. 'How are you?'

'I'm busy – appointments all day. I've had to move a few of them around.'

'Oh?' Morwenna assumed he was trying to fit all his clients in so that he could travel to Seal Bay in time for the weekend. The idea of spending several days on the *Pammy*, sailing in the bay, suddenly sounded wonderful. She'd do nothing but relax on deck in shorts, drinking wine. Or she'd swim in the sea, blue sky above her, seals frolicking. It would be heaven.

'The thing is,' Barnaby said, and Morwenna knew something was coming to change her plans. 'You know Pam is going to Barbados for a month?'

'And you're house-sitting at Mirador?'

'I was – but Pam's thinking of buying property out there, for her and Simon. She's asked me to go with her, to help her choose something.'

'To Barbados.'

'Exactly.'

'Oh.' Morwenna felt a twinge of disappointment. 'Well, I hope you have a great time.'

'So, I thought...' Barnaby began enigmatically.

'What did you think?' Morwenna asked.

'Come with me. I'll get tickets today. We can fly next week. What do you say?'

Morwenna said exactly what was in her mind. 'I need a holiday, that's for sure.'

'Let's go, me and you. We can help Pam find a place, drink at Simon's beach bar in the evenings. The rest of the time, it'll be just the two of us.'

'Mmm.' Morwenna was already imagining walking on the beach, hand in hand with Barnaby, crystal sea frothing around her ankles.

'It would be so good. I'll find us the perfect hotel.' Barnaby's voice was husky. 'We'd relax by day, have dinner together. There's buzzing nightlife. You could swim with sea turtles, drink rum with welcoming Barbadians, go shopping in Bridgetown.'

Morwenna thought he sounded like a tourist brochure. He continued. 'Stunning beaches, shimmering ocean, breathtaking views. We'd go snorkelling, scuba diving...'

Morwenna was smiling. 'It sounds lovely.'

'Will you come?'

Morwenna was tempted to say yes straight away. Instead she said, 'Can I think about it and ring you this evening? I have a bit of a busy day today.'

'Have they caught The Cream Tea Killer?' Barnaby had remembered.

'Yes, it all kicked off and I'm helping the police. I'll explain later, if you don't mind – it's a long story.'

'Are you all right?' Barnaby's voice was suddenly filled with concern.

'I'm fine,' Morwenna said as cheerily as she could, stroking Brenda, who was luxuriating in the warmth of a sunbeam that filtered through the window.

'And what about Barbados? Say you'll come.'

'It would be wonderful.' Morwenna had already decided she'd go, almost. She'd have to talk to Tamsin and see if Imogen would cover her shifts, ask her mother to look after Brenda. Donald would be only too happy to cover at the library. 'Let me just line up a few ducks and we can finalise it this evening.'

'Perfect,' Barnaby said. 'Call me then. I have to say, I'm really looking forward to it.'

'Me too,' Morwenna agreed. She'd be mad to turn the opportunity down. Her body needed the rest, the sunshine, some fun. And Barnaby was good company. He was a nice man. He was fond of her.

Morwenna sprang from bed, already feeling more energetic. She was ready to run downstairs in her mother's old winceyette nightie and ask if there was enough hot water for a bath; they'd grab a bite to eat, go down the police station, give statements, then they'd have dinner with Tamsin.

And after all that, she'd ring Barnaby and arrange a holiday in Barbados.

* * *

The afternoon statements at the police station had been hard going, but not half as bad as Morwenna had feared. Rick Tremayne had been the perfect gentleman. He and Blessed had framed their questions kindly, taking time being empathic. Morwenna thought wonders would never cease.

Everyone had congratulated her; they'd said it had been a good night's work and she was the heroine of the hour. Even Lamorna had perked up. She'd struck up a conversation with a senior police officer whom she'd found drinking coffee in a corridor and he'd bought her a treacle-strong tea and a chocolate bar from a machine. They'd spent an hour talking about how Cornwall had changed over the last twenty years and not always for the better, how you couldn't get cheap fish like you used to, how there weren't enough buses and the roads were full of potholes. He'd kissed her cheek and said she didn't look old enough to be a great-grandmother. In fact, she looked sixty, and not a day older. Suddenly, Lamorna was on cloud nine.

At half past five, the Mutton and Pascoe family sat around a table in the tearoom, six pair of hands diving into takeaway fish and chips, mushy peas, glasses of lemonade, wine for the adults. Elowen was delighted to sit next to Tadas, explaining everything Cornish to him as if she were an expert.

'You never had proper Cornish fish and chips before, Tadas?'

'No, but I like them a lot.' Tadas crammed another three chips into his mouth.

'And did you ever eat a Cornish pasty before you came here?'

'No, but Morwenna brings me food – I think the pasty is very nice...'

Elowen was on a roll, explaining everything she'd learned at school. 'Pasties are proper Cornish. When mining boomed in Cornwall, pasties were the all-in-one meal that could be taken down the mines and the miners didn't need knives and forks. Their proper name is Oggy. The wives of Cornish miners would make them for the men but nowadays they can bleddy well cook their own – isn't that right, Great-Grandma?'

Lamorna met Tamsin's eyes and said, 'Sorry – my bad,' before refilling her wine glass.

Tamsin said, 'It was a great idea to buy fish and chips to share, Dad. This is what we all need. Family time.'

Ruan pushed a hand through his hair. 'It's been a long day. But it's all done now. We can put it behind us. Before the end of the week, things will get back to normal.'

Morwenna closed her eyes, thinking of the end of the week. She was looking forward to something better than normal: sunshine and the stunning scenery in Barbados were just what she needed, with nothing to do but eat, drink, laze around, swim. She hadn't mentioned it to anyone yet – she wondered if now was the time, or if she ought to wait until she'd phoned Barnaby.

Ruan said, 'How about we all go for a walk on the beach?'

'And can I have an ice cream, Grandad?' Elowen asked.

'Chocolate chip.' Tadas smiled, remembering. 'I like it very much – it is my favourite.'

Tamsin stood up. 'A walk would be great. Come on, let's go out.

There'll be loads going on – it's still lovely and warm. There's an ice-cream van down at the seafront too.'

They crossed the road and made their way towards the sand. The beach was crowded with families playing ball games, couples lying on mats snoozing, dogs chasing sticks. Elowen looked hopefully at Tamsin. 'Mummy, can I have a—?'

'Not now – we'll talk about it when it's the right time,' Tamsin said firmly.

'But I know the way of peace now,' Elowen protested. Ruan met Morwenna's eyes and he winked.

'I'm puffed out and my hip is giving me trouble. And my heart...' Lamorna put a hand to her chest.

'What's wrong with your heart?' Morwenna asked, anxiously.

'Oh, after what happened last night, how can you even ask? What I went through, with that gun pointed straight at me. I thought my time had come.'

Morwenna had thought the same thing. She stared across the sand to where a young man in a magician's suit was surrounded by a group of children. He produced an apple from his top hat and the children clapped. Sheppy was doing great business.

Lamorna said, 'There's Susan Grundy. And she's with Barb. They are over there knitting. I'll just go and tell them about what happened – they'll want to know all the gory details.'

Morwenna watched her mother scurry away to where the Grundy sisters were waving knitting needles, calling her over. She watched Lamorna sit down precariously on a deckchair, leaning forward, talking nineteen to the dozen. Tamsin had stopped to chat to a group of surfers; she was laughing with a young woman with brightly coloured cropped hair and lots of beads on her wrist, who she assumed was Imogen. Morwenna recognised others in the group: Becca, Tristan Pengellen and a tall man, who must be Seb from London.

Elowen, with Oggy Two and Three clutched beneath her arms, skipped in front with Tadas. She called over her shoulder. 'I can see Billy Crocker. I want to show him my new friend Tadas. Can I tell him Tadas is my brother? I'd like him to be my brother.'

'Just go and say hello,' Morwenna called as she watched Elowen tug Tadas towards Billy and his parents, who were busy playing football on the sand.

She gazed up at Ruan. 'And then there were two.'

'There have always been two,' he said with a smile. The flesh around his cheekbone was still swollen, but he was handsome as ever.

Morwenna asked, 'How's the sore rib?'

'On the mend. I was thinking of going back on the trawler before the end of the week. But...'

'But?'

'I might take a break.'

'You need one all right,' Morwenna agreed, her eyes on Elowen as she tackled Billy Crocker, stealing the ball from him easily. 'Your idea about taking Elowen to football practice once a week is a goodie.'

'I'm full of great ideas,' Ruan said.

Morwenna inhaled, a little nervous. Now was the time to tell him she was going to Barbados. She wondered how he'd react. She was sure he'd understand.

'The thing is, Ruan, I need a break too. I was thinking—'

'I know – you're exhausted.' Ruan met her eyes. 'When you were in the house and Tom Fox was there with a gun, I was outside with Jane. I was shaking with fear. She told me the firearms officers had surrounded the place and I thought, what if things go wrong? What if I lost you? I promised myself that, if you came through it, I'd tell you what has always been in my heart.'

'So, Barnaby's asked me to go to—' Morwenna stopped. 'What *is* in your heart?'

'You must know,' Ruan said gently. He took her hand.

Morwenna frowned. 'Not if you don't tell me.'

'I can do better than that. I've never been good with words.'

'That's been our prob—' Morwenna attempted to say more, but Ruan wrapped his arms around her and was kissing her lips. She closed her eyes.

For a moment it was lovely, heavenly. More heavenly than Barbados.

She opened them.

'Ruan?'

'I can't help what I feel.'

'No.'

'And you still feel it – I hope you do.'

'Oh, Ruan.' Morwenna shook her head. 'I do. But I'm terrified of things coming unstuck again. One minute I want it to be just us again. The next it all changes – and I can't take a risk of it going wrong.'

'And Barnaby?'

'He's kind. I like him. But I don't know...'

Ruan said, 'It was simple when it was just us.'

'It was.'

'Do you think we could get it back again, that special thing we had?'

'Maybe we could. I don't know.' Morwenna sighed. 'I just don't know.'

'Grandma, Grandad.' Elowen was running towards them, Tadas behind her, grinning. 'Can we have ice creams now? I want an ice cream. You promised I could have one and Tadas wants one too.' Elowen stopped level with Morwenna and Ruan. 'Can we? Please?'

Morwenna watched Ruan take Elowen's hand; he wrapped the other one around Tadas. She said, 'Of course, you can, my bewty. We'll all have ice cream. Chocolate chip cones all around.'

She met Ruan's gaze for a moment, and his eyes were full of affection. Then he hurried ahead, shepherding the children towards the ice cream van.

She called after him, 'Get me one, Ruan. I'll catch up with you dreckly.'

Morwenna smiled. It was her way of telling him that she was happy. And that the future would take care of itself.

ACKNOWLEDGEMENTS

Thanks to Kiran Kataria and Sarah Ritherdon, whose professionalism and kindness I value each day.

Thanks to Boldwood Books; to designers, editors, technicians, voice actors. You are magicians.

Thanks to Rachel Gilbey, to so many wonderful bloggers and fellow writers. The support you give goes beyond words.

Thanks to Jan, Rog, Jan M, Helen, Pat, Ken, Trish, Lexy, Rachel, John, Shaz, Gracie, Mya, Frank, Martin, Cath, Avril, Rob, Erika, Rich, Susie, Ian, Chrissie, Kathy N, Julie, Martin, Steve, Rose, Steve's mum, Nik R, Pete O', Chris A, Chris's mum, Dawn, Beau CC, Slawka, Katie H, Tom, Emily, Tom's mum, Fiona J and Jonno.

Thanks to Peter and the Solitary Writers, my writing buddies.

Also, my neighbours and the local community, especially Jenny, Laura, Claire, Paul and Sophie, Naranjan and all at Turmeric Kitchen. Special thanks to James and Nina, whose knowledge of police procedures is invaluable, and Kitty, who knows more about wild swimming than I ever will.

Much thanks to Ivor Abiks at Deep Studios. To Darren and Lyndsay at PPL. And to BBC Radio Somerset and Simon Parkin.

Thanks and love go to Ellen, Hugh, Jo, Jan, Lou, Harry, Chris, Norman, Angela, Robin, Edward, Zach, Daniel, Catalina.

So much love to my mum and dad, Irene and Tosh.

Love always to our Tony and Kim, to Liam, Maddie, Kayak, Joey.

And to my soulmate, Big G.

Warmest thanks always to you, my readers, wherever you are. You make this journey special.

ABOUT THE AUTHOR

Judy Leigh is the bestselling author of *A Grand Old Time* and *Five French Hens* and the doyenne of the 'it's never too late' genre of women's fiction. She has lived all over the UK from Liverpool to Cornwall, but currently resides in Somerset.

Sign up to Judy Leigh's mailing list here for news, competitions and updates on future books.

Visit Judy's website: https://judyleigh.com

Follow Judy on social media:

facebook.com/judyleighuk
x.com/judyleighwriter
instagram.com/judyrleigh
bookbub.com/authors/judy-leigh

ALSO BY JUDY LEIGH

Five French Hens

The Old Girls' Network

Heading Over the Hill

Chasing the Sun

Lil's Bus Trip

The Golden Girls' Getaway

A Year of Mr Maybes

The Highland Hens

The Golden Oldies' Book Club

The Silver Ladies Do Lunch

The Vintage Village Bake Off

The Morwenna Mutton Mysteries Series

Foul Play at Seal Bay

Bloodshed on the Boards

The Cream Tea Killer

Poison
& Pens

POISON & PENS IS THE HOME OF
COZY MYSTERIES SO POUR YOURSELF
A CUP OF TEA & GET SLEUTHING!

DISCOVER PAGE-TURNING NOVELS FROM
YOUR FAVOURITE AUTHORS &
MEET NEW FRIENDS

JOIN OUR
FACEBOOK GROUP

BIT.LYPOISONANDPENSFB

SIGN UP TO OUR
NEWSLETTER

BIT.LY/POISONANDPENSNEWS

Boldwood

Boldwood Books is an award-winning fiction publishing company seeking out the best stories from around the world.

Find out more at www.boldwoodbooks.com

Join our reader community for brilliant books, competitions and offers!

Follow us
@BoldwoodBooks
@TheBoldBookClub

Sign up to our weekly deals newsletter

https://bit.ly/BoldwoodBNewsletter